ANNA DEAN lives in the Lake District with a husband and a cat. She sometimes works as a Creative Writing tutor and as a guide showing visitors around William Wordsworth's home, Dove Cottage. Her interests include walking, old houses, Jane Austen, cream teas, *Star Trek* and canoeing on very flat water.

www.annadean.co.uk

By Anna Dean

THE DIDO KENT SERIES

A Moment of Silence
A Gentleman of Fortune
A Woman of Consequence
A Place of Confinement

A Gentleman of Fortune

ANNA DEAN

Allison & Busby Limited
12 Fitzroy Mews
London W1T 6DW
www.allisonandbusby.com

First published in Great Britain by Allison & Busby in 2009.
This paperback edition published by Allison & Busby in 2012.

A CIP catalogue record for this book is available from
the British Library.

10 9 8 7 6 5 4 3

ISBN 978-0-7490-0709-6

Typeset in 13/16 pt Adobe Garamond Pro by
Allison & Busby Ltd.

The paper used for this Allison & Busby publication
has been produced from trees that have been legally sourced
from well-managed and credibly certified forests.

Printed and bound by
CPI Group (UK) Ltd, Croydon, CR0 4YY

For Mum, with love

Chapter One

Richmond, Wednesday 27ᵗʰ May 1806

My Dear Eliza

The great Mrs Lansdale is no more.

She was carried off on Tuesday night by a sudden seizure. It is a very heavy loss, for now the neighbourhood can no longer discuss the alarming symptoms of her nervous complaints, nor can it exclaim over every rumoured disagreement between the lady and her nephew.

However, it seems we are not done with Mrs Lansdale; she may yet provide a subject of conversation – for there is already an <u>alarming rumour</u> begun about her death.

Besides that half-pleasurable sorrow which is always felt at the death of a fine lady one hardly knows, there is a great distrust of the nephew. For it has not passed without notice that he has lost a remarkably tyrannical relation and gained a <u>very</u> fine inheritance.

Miss Dido Kent lifted her pen from the page and gazed beyond the little pool of light thrown by her candle, to the open window and the warm darkness beyond. She knew that she should not continue. What she was about to write was hardly proper. A letter should contain news but never gossip, and the great rule was to mention no person or event which could not be written about with charity.

But then, Dido mused with a smile, if the rule were adhered to *too* faithfully, letters would become so exceedingly dull that they would not be worth getting. They would scarcely justify their cost to the receiver.

And, besides, she had a very good reason for communicating this particular piece of gossip to her sister.

It is the odious Mrs Midgely who has begun this rumour. She has 'the gravest doubts' about Mrs Lansdale's death. Mrs Midgely considers it as being altogether 'too convenient' for the nephew. In short, she believes that he took steps to hurry his poor aunt out of this world...

There! It was said. And very shocking it seemed now that it was written down.

Please do not blame me for repeating this slander, Eliza. If you will only keep from throwing my letter aside in disgust – and will but continue reading to the end – I hope you will understand why I must write to you upon this subject.

You see, it all came out yesterday during Flora's exploring party to the river.

And a very pleasant party it would have been, but for Mrs Midgely and her venomous conversation. Everyone was punctual, the sun shone upon us and there was an abundance of walking about, sitting down, fine views, pigeon pie and cold lamb.

Sir Joshua Carrisbrook was returned from town in time to join us – which pleased Flora greatly. And, by the by, it seems that what we had heard of Sir Joshua is true — he is to be married again, and very soon. And you may tell all his friends at Belsfield that he seems vastly contented — and in a great hurry to get to church! For, by his own account, the lady only gave her consent a week ago, but he is determined to be married before the end of another week and has got himself a special licence for that purpose. I suppose he does not wish to wear out what youth he may suppose remains to him in waiting a full three weeks for the banns to be called.

It is extraordinary to see a man of his advanced years so very much in love! And I could not but pity him; for he was so wanting to tell us all of how he was soon to become 'the very happiest of men' and to enumerate the many virtues and talents of his lady; and he had scarcely begun to describe her musical genius and had not spoken one word about whose music she chiefly plays, when his happiness was quite hurried out of the way by Mrs Midgely who was wanting to be talking herself.

So I confess that I remain in ignorance upon the important issue of whether the future Lady Carrisbrook delights most in concertos or in folk airs — and I cannot even tell you what her maiden name may be…

But, to return to Mrs Midgely and her suspicions. By her account, Mr Vane, the apothecary, is uneasy about Mrs Lansdale's death. He says that, 'there was nothing in Mrs Lansdale's general condition to make him expect such a seizure as carried her off! Which,' says Mrs Midgely, looking about at us all, with a very red face and a satisfied manner, 'which, I think you will all agree, seems very odd indeed, does it not?'

'Oh, but I do not know that it is so very odd!'

This mild protest came from little Miss Prentice — Mrs Midgely's boarder — who seems to rent from Mrs Midgely not only her back parlour but also a share in her right to spy upon all the grand people of the neighbourhood.

'If I must give my opinion,' says Miss Prentice – though no one there had asked for her opinion – 'I do not think it is so very odd at all. It does sometimes happen that a person can be taken with a sudden attack such as they have never had before. For it happened to poor Lord...'

But Mrs Midgely had no patience to let her go on. For once Miss Prentice is begun upon lords and sirs there is no end of it.

'Mr Vane,' says Mrs Midgely, speaking very loud, 'is very much puzzled by the lady's death. And, in my opinion, he ought to take the appropriate steps.' And she lowered her voice to a suitably portentous whisper. 'I have told him that he must _speak to the magistrates._'

And then we had all to listen to a great many accounts of what I had heard many times since coming to Richmond: of how Mrs Lansdale had demanded a great deal of attention from her nephew – on account of her many illnesses – that he had often wanted to 'pursue his own pleasures' in town, but had been restrained by her poor health and nervous disposition which would not permit her to be left alone. Mrs M was very eloquent upon these subjects – and no less so upon the subject of how 'young men these days' do not like to have their pleasures curtailed.

Well, Eliza, what I have not told you of yet, is how _very_ distressed poor Flora was looking all the while that this was carrying on. For, you see, Mr Henry Lansdale, the nephew – this very gentleman that Mrs M was slandering – is a great favourite with our cousin. She and her husband met the Lansdales at Ramsgate last autumn and, though I have not *yet been introduced to the young man, I have observed that she always speaks very highly of him.*

I do not think Mrs Midgely knows of Flora's connection with the Lansdales and believes them to be strangers to her, as they are to everyone else here in Richmond. At least I sincerely hope that she knows nothing of the friendship – or else she was being unpardonably rude to be talking so of her hostess's acquaintances! (Though, in truth, I do not put anything beyond the licence that woman allows her tongue!)

However, I think that, maybe, Mrs Midgely's ward, young Mary Bevan, was quick-witted enough to suspect the truth, from her gentle efforts to smooth things over. She pointed out, in her quiet precise way, that, 'Mr Vane had been attending upon Mrs Lansdale for little more than a month,' and suggested that, 'he might not have a very accurate knowledge of all the poor lady's disorders and symptoms.'

This did little to stop the abuse; but one must admire the real elegance of mind which prompted it; and one cannot help but wonder how such a pleasant, sensible girl can have been brought up by the dreadful Mrs M.

But, to return to Flora. She was close to tears by the time the carriages came, and she broke down completely in our journey home.

'I cannot understand,' she said again and again, 'why Mrs Midgely should say such things! Why should she wish to malign poor Mr Lansdale? And why should she wish to persuade the apothecary to cause trouble for him? I have never known her be so <u>very</u> unkind before.'

And, in all honesty, neither can I understand it, Eliza. It is a level of interference and trouble-making <u>far</u> beyond the usual malice of gossip.

11

Poor Flora! She keeps to her room today with the headache which, I make no doubt, was brought on by yesterday's distress. Her sufferings are, I believe, all the worse for being unfixed and uncertain; for neither she nor I can judge the exact degree of danger in which Mr Lansdale might stand – I mean if Mr Vane should yield to the tiresome woman's advice and refer the matter to the magistrate. And, since Flora's husband is still absent upon business in Ireland, we have no gentleman here to whom we can turn for advice upon such a delicate matter.

And this, my dear sister, is the reason for my troubling you with this most unpleasant business. It occurs to me that, since you are staying at Belsfield Hall, you might seek advice on our behalf. Would you be so kind as to ask Mr William Lomax…

Dido was forced, by the shaking in her hand, to stop writing.

There was already a blot spreading through her neat black words. And her cheeks were burning too. She laid down her pen and turned her face into the night air which was blowing in through the open window of her bedchamber, bringing with it the scents of roses and cut-grass and dew – and the high, shivering call of an owl from somewhere down beside the river.

She had thought that she had long outlived the age at which the mere writing of a gentleman's name could bring a blush to her cheeks. Yet she could not help but wonder what Mr Lomax would think – how he would look – what he would say – when Eliza mentioned her name and her request.

Dido's situation with regard to this gentleman was a particularly delicate one.

Mr William Lomax was the man of business who overlooked the running of her niece's husband's estate at Belsfield Hall. Last autumn, when she had been at Belsfield, Dido had come to esteem him very highly indeed and, before she was called away, she had been certain – almost certain – as certain as a lady can ever allow herself to be – that he returned her regard: that he was, in fact, only prevented from making a declaration by a want of wealth and independence.

Then she had been full of hope; sure that they could not be separated for ever; sure that the particular circumstances which kept him poor just then, could be removed. But now, after six months of hearing almost nothing of him, it was all but impossible not to be desponding: not to believe that her influence over him was weakening; not to calculate very exactly her five and thirty years, or to disregard the opinion of all her friends who had long reckoned her a settled old maid.

As she had once overheard her sister-in-law, Margaret, remarking: 'An heiress may fairly look for a husband at any age. But a portionless woman had better give up all such thoughts when she is thirty, and spare her family the expense of going much into company. For it will all be wasted. Nothing will come of it.'

Until she had come to know Mr Lomax, Dido had been, if not quite content to be a spinster, then at least reconciled to it because she had never found in the usual round of dinners and balls and visits much temptation to change her state. But a remarkable set of circumstances had brought her together with Mr Lomax and authorised a kind of communication far beyond the usual littleness of social intercourse. She had learnt the pleasure of sharing ideas and confiding in a way which she had never known before. And now...

And now, as she sat beside the window of her bedchamber in Flora's pleasant summer villa, she was beginning to suspect her own motives.

For, oddly enough, it had been a murder and the mystery associated with it which had first brought her together with Mr Lomax. So, was she now only taking an interest in this affair of Mrs Lansdale's death because it was a means of bringing herself once more to the gentleman's attention?

She smiled. Hers must be a very singular affection if it could only thrive upon infamy and mystery! But she would not allow one half of her to suspect the other. There could be nothing wrong in only asking a gentleman's advice and, besides, she really did wish to discover the exact degree of danger in which Mr Lansdale stood.

Would you be so kind as to ask Mr William Lomax – for I know that he has a very thorough understanding of the law – whether, in his opinion, Mr Lansdale is in any danger? Might Mr Vane's information lead the magistrates to bring a prosecution? And, if it should go so far, how heavily would the testimony of such a man as this apothecary tell against him? It cannot be denied that the young man has gained a great deal from his aunt's death: if there was a suspicion of murder, would not that suspicion fall immediately upon him?

Flora is most anxious that we should somehow find a way

of putting an end to these dreadful rumours, before they have any serious consequences.

I agree that it ought to be attempted; but I cannot conceive how such a woman as Mrs Midgely is to be worked upon. I doubt she has ever, in the whole course of her life, held her tongue at someone else's request. And she seemed to take such an inordinate pleasure in spreading her poison that I could not help but wonder whether she has some grudge or cause against the young man. Something which might make her particularly venomous in this case.

And I do not think we can silence her without first discovering her motive.

Chapter Two

Richmond, mused Dido as she walked to the post office with her letter next day, was a remarkably *proper* place. There was something particularly elegant and refined about the pretty little villas clustering around the river and up onto the hill, with their verandas and their French windows and their shady gardens. Maybe, she thought, it was this air of prosperity and tranquillity; the scent of syringa and lime trees; the sight of comfortable barouches and fashionable little landaulets driving by, which made the rumours Mrs Midgely was spreading so very shocking.

It certainly was a very strange, distressing business. This morning poor Flora was still suffering from nervousness and headache, and Dido's resolve to silence Mrs Midgely and save Mr Lansdale from a dangerous slander was compounded as much of compassion as a strong desire for justice.

But, as she walked, she had to confess to herself that there might be another, secondary motive which was rather less virtuous. She could not help but feel it would be very pleasant indeed to have something to *think* about! For the unaccustomed leisure of the past week had left her mind quite remarkably empty.

It was, she acknowledged, extremely kind of her cousin to invite her to Richmond. For, although Flora had been considerate enough to solicit her company as a favour and to represent herself as in need of a companion while her husband was absent on business, Dido knew that the visit was intended to be a holiday. And never had she been more in need of a holiday; for the past winter had been spent attending upon a very young, very nervous sister-in-law and her new and sickly child.

However, Dido was beginning to suspect that unmarried women who were past their youth were not constitutionally suited to holidays and that the usual system of employing them to their families' advantage as temporary, unsalaried nurses, governesses and nursery maids had more kindness in it than she had previously supposed.

While she had been in Hampshire, though Henrietta had been a no more rational companion than Flora, Dido had had little time to spare from the demands of colic and red-gum and the leaking of melting snow into the pantry, to notice the deficiency.

Here, in the luxury of Flora's summer villa, she was nearer to suffering from ennui than she had ever been in her life before – and had, furthermore, too much time in which to remember the many perfections of Mr Lomax.

She stopped. She was come now to the substantial, red-brick bulk of the Lansdale's house, and its closed shutters, its weedless gravel sweep and its sombre cedar tree seemed to throw an air of mourning across the hot afternoon. The gateposts were topped with imposing urns of stone and, on the left-hand post, there was a very fine, very new sign with the name of *Knaresborough House* carved in thick black letters. It looked remarkably respectable, and to imagine a murder taking place in such a house was all but impossible.

She stepped away, and, as she did so, she noticed that upon the opposite side of the road was Mrs Midgely's villa – with little Miss Prentice watching from the back parlour window.

Dido paused, looking thoughtfully from one house to the other – and at the three or four yards of dusty road which was all that divided them. And she wondered… Perhaps the very proximity in which Mrs Midgely and Mr Lansdale lived had some bearing upon the case…

The post office was crowded: so very full of ladies and bonnets and gossip and little yelping lap-dogs that there was no one free to attend to Dido at the counter and she was obliged to wait. The room was confined and stuffy. Its small, dusty window and its dark panelled walls made it so very gloomy after the brilliance outside that at first she could recognise no one in the little crowd.

Then, after a moment or two, when her eyes had grown accustomed to the poor light, she saw that the young woman standing before her at the high counter was Mrs Midgely's ward, Mary Bevan, enquiring after letters. A narrow ray of dusty sunlight falling through the office's single high window was just catching the side of her fresh, delicate cheek, displaying the lovely long dark eyelashes to great advantage. And, as Mary turned away from the counter, putting a letter into her pocket, Dido could not help but wonder anew that so very elegant a creature should be the ward of such a vulgar woman as Mrs Midgely.

Miss Bevan smiled and began upon a gentle greeting, but her words were immediately lost in the loud throwing open of the door behind them and the bustling entrance of her guardian. Nearly everyone in the room turned to see who it was.

'There you are Mary! I wondered where you were got to! And Miss Kent too, I believe,' peering through the gloom. 'Very pleased to see you, I'm sure Miss Kent.'

Mrs Midgely was a large woman of about fifty years old, dressed in yellow patterned muslin with a great many curls on her head and a great deal of colour in her broad cheeks. 'Such a delightful exploring party yesterday,' she continued. 'I am sure we are all very much obliged to dear Mrs Beaumont for inviting us. You may tell her that she will soon receive a letter of particular thanks from me.'

Dido began upon a civil reply, but was not suffered to continue long. Mrs Midgely was just come from the haberdasher's and so was full of news and delighted to have chanced so soon upon someone to whom she could tell it.

'Well, Miss Kent,' she burst out, 'it seems it was the Black Drop that did the damage. Mrs Pickthorne says that Mr Vane says it was the Black Drop for sure.'

'The Black Drop?' repeated Dido.

Mrs Midgely smiled broadly and comfortably: sure of having her attention. 'It was,' she said loudly, 'the Black Drop which killed Mrs Lansdale.'

There seemed to be a little quietness around them in the post office: a sense of listening. Dido noticed that poor

Mary Bevan's eyes were turned upon the floor and a blush of shame was creeping up her cheek. It seemed that years of experience had not inured the girl to the behaviour of her guardian.

'And what,' asked Dido, as quietly as she might, 'what is the Black Drop?'

'It is,' announced Mrs Midgely, 'a barbarous medicine, made in the north country, which Mrs Lansdale had got into the habit of using. The *Kendal* Black Drop it is called.'

'Kendal?'

'Kendal,' said Miss Bevan quickly, 'is a town in Westmorland – near Mrs Lansdale's home – quite near to the Lake Country I believe. I wonder, Miss Kent, if you ever happened to read Mr West's delightful *Guide to the Lakes*?'

It was a valiant attempt to turn the conversation but the poor girl might as well have held up her hand to halt a raging bull. There was no stopping her guardian from telling her news.

'The Kendal Black Drop,' she reiterated with great weight – and cast a withering look at poor Mary. 'It is a stuff four times stronger than laudanum and it seems that poor Mrs Lansdale was quite addicted to its use.'

'I see.'

'And dear Mr Vane is sure that if she had but taken his advice and given it up, he could, in the end, have cured her of all her illnesses. For, you know, Miss Kent, he is a very clever man…'

'And so, Mr Vane believes that it was her use of this medicine which brought on Mrs Lansdale's seizure?' said

Dido more loudly. 'What a very unfortunate *accident.*'

She attempted to step away to deal with her business at the counter, where there was now a vacancy. But so eager was Mrs Midgely to finish her tale that she laid a hand upon her arm.

'Well,' she continued in the same inconveniently loud voice. 'It was the Black Drop killed her for sure. *But a great deal of it.* He is quite sure that she had drunk *four times* as much of the stuff as she should have done.'

'Four times?' echoed Dido. Internally she could not but admit it was a very large amount. But she only said, 'how...regrettable.'

'Well, what Mr Vane cannot understand is this: how did she come to drink so much all at once?'

'I am sure,' said Miss Bevan firmly, 'that with so powerful and dangerous a medicine, an *accident*, though very sad, is hardly to be wondered at.'

'Quite so,' said Dido, hastily putting aside her own doubts.

'Accident indeed!' cried Mrs Midgely. But she had said all she wished to say and seemed well satisfied with the looks of interest she was receiving from the people around her. She allowed Dido to escape to the counter. 'And did you get any letters?' she asked Mary.

'No, Ma'am, none at all.'

Dido turned back at the sound of the lie – and saw that it had brought another, brighter, blush to Mary's cheeks.

Chapter Three

Next morning Dido accompanied Flora upon a visit of condolence to Henry Lansdale. She was very eager to meet him; reasoning that a man who could earn such affection from his friends and such malice from his neighbours, could not fail to be interesting.

It was another exceedingly hot day with not a cloud to be seen in the sky. Down beyond the river the hay was being cut and the scent of it carried right into the town. The two women walked slowly along the tree-shaded street.

'I do not doubt,' said Dido after walking for some time in silence, 'from everything I have observed, that Mrs Midgely is a very malicious woman. But what I cannot yet quite determine is why her malice should be particularly directed against Mr Lansdale. Do you know of any reason why she should be his enemy?'

'No, I do not!' Flora Beaumont frowned prettily in the deep shade of her bonnet, her soft white nose wrinkling in a way which always put Dido in mind of a rabbit. 'He is such a *very* delightful man. Why, I cannot conceive that he could have an enemy in the whole world! And besides, Mrs Midgely does not *know* him.' Her lips puckered in a childish pout. 'The Lansdales have been here but a month and Mrs Midgely is not even upon visiting terms with them, you know.'

'Then perhaps she had *heard* something ill of him.'

'But I have told you, there is nothing ill to hear! Nothing at all!'

'There were, I understand, quarrels between aunt and nephew.'

'Oh, but they were nothing! It was just her way.' Flora paused in the shade of a tree, twisting one finger daintily in the long ribbon of her bonnet. 'I rather fancy she liked to quarrel sometimes, you know. There was always a great making up afterwards.'

'Perhaps,' Dido suggested, trying her best not to injure her cousin's sensitive feelings, 'perhaps it is jealousy which turns Mrs M against him. He is after all so very fortunate – a poor young man taken in by his aunt, and now inheriting a great estate in Westmorland…'

'Dido! Do not talk so! I cannot *bear* it. You sound so *horribly* suspicious.'

'No, no,' Dido assured her hastily. 'I am not at all suspicious. I am only trying to understand why other people might be suspicious.'

'Well!' cried Flora, clapping her hands together. 'I can tell you why such a woman as Mrs Midgely is suspicious. It is because she is spiteful and cruel…and horrid. And we *must* find a way to silence her. *You* must find a way, Dido. You are the clever one. The whole world is forever saying how very clever you are.'

'I am sure I am very much obliged to the world for its good opinion. And I certainly intend to silence Mrs Midgely if I can. But…'

She stopped suddenly because they had come now through the gates of Knaresborough House and, as they started up the sweep, she had caught sight of something rather strange.

A young boy in a gardener's smock was digging a hole beneath the great boughs of the cedar tree which stood close by the gate. As Dido and Flora watched, he thrust his spade into the pile of excavated earth, picked up a bundle wrapped in sacking and dropped it into the hole.

'Oh dear!' cried Dido, almost without thinking, 'is that a grave you are making?' Impelled by overwhelming curiosity, she hurried towards him, leaving Flora frowning upon the gravel.

The boy looked up, pushing damp hair out of his eyes. He was about twelve years old with fair, almost white hair and a drift of freckles across his cheeks and nose. 'It is Sam, is it not?' said Dido. 'We met when you came to dig the new flower-bed in Mrs Beaumont's garden. Do you remember?'

'Oh yes, miss,' he said with a smile. 'I remember. You was very kind about that wasp sting.'

'And today you are working for Mr Lansdale?' Dido looked inquiringly towards the hole.

'Yes miss,' he said. 'I'm burying Mrs Lansdale's little dog.'

'Oh? Indeed!' said Dido with great interest.

'Been dead nearly a week, miss. I'd not come any closer if I were you.'

She took a step back, for there was indeed a very unpleasant odour mixing with the scent of lilac and the dark smell of the cedar. 'Nearly a week?' She glanced anxiously back at Flora and calculated rapidly. 'Then the dog died about the same time as Mrs Lansdale?'

Sam nodded. 'They say he went missing the very night the old lady died. But they only found him this morning – dead and hidden in among the laurel bushes.'

'I see. How strange.' How *very* strange. She gazed thoughtfully at the gaping hole in the ground. Why should the dog die at the same time as his mistress? It seemed a remarkable coincidence – indeed it seemed a great deal more than a coincidence... 'But,' she said carefully, 'they do say, do they not, that a dog will sometimes pine away when the person to whom he has been devoted dies?'

'I don't know about that, miss,' said Sam. He too looked down at the open grave and rubbed the side of his nose, smearing dirt into the freckles. 'It may be a dog'd pine away,' he said slowly. 'But I can't see how any dog would be so heart-broke it'd crawl away into a bush and cut its own throat.'

'Oh no, no indeed,' said Dido as she turned away, 'you are quite right. Quite right.'

'I do not see,' said Flora irritably, 'why you should be so concerned about the death of a dog.'

'But my dear cousin, it is of the greatest importance. For it would seem the dog died at the hand of man, and that must mean...' She stopped herself. There was something so remarkably innocent about Flora's childlike face – the wide blue eyes gazing at her in such a puzzled, unsuspecting way...

Dido shrugged up her shoulders and merely said, 'Well it is very strange, is it not?'

But her thoughts were working rapidly. The dog had

26

been killed. Why? Why should the animal meet its death at the very same time as its mistress…? Unless there had been dark forces at work here at Knaresborough House.

The great question must be: had the death of the lady been as unnatural as her pet's? Dido found herself remembering the apothecary's account of the large amount of opium mixture Mrs Lansdale had drunk. She could not help it; she was beginning to wonder whether there could be some truth in the rumours. Perhaps there was some agency at work here worse than the malice of gossip.

She approached the respectable red-brick front of Knaresborough House with increased interest – and more than a little suspicion.

A remarkably young and inexperienced maid opened the door to them. She was very unsure of herself. She was unsure of how many curtsies she should make; unsure of whether Flora was to be addressed as 'Miss' or 'Madam'; unsure whether her master was at home. And then, having ascertained that he *was* at home, and that he would be 'down directly', she was very unsure indeed about which room the visitors should be shown into.

She stood for several moments in the spacious, white-painted entrance hall, looking anxiously from one closed door to another, her hands twisting clumsily in her apron. No superior servant appeared to advise her and Dido observed the scene with great interest, wondering how it came about that such a fine house should be so ill-served. She had expected a manservant to open the door – a fellow with a bit of dignity about him: and a footman perhaps in attendance too.

'It had better be the drawing room, I think,' said the girl at last, throwing open a door, 'though it's not been used or put to rights since the day before the mistress died and I hope you'll excuse it not being aired.'

They walked into the room and Dido looked about her with great interest.

It was very gloomy from the blinds still being half-drawn, and the furnishings were as impersonal as those of any house that is offered to be let by the month – though very rich and substantial, as befitted one advertised as *a spacious residence suitable to a gentleman of fortune.* There was a wealth of solid mahogany furniture and silver candlesticks, a magnificent, steadily ticking wall clock, and sumptuous, over-long curtains of cream brocade which lay in folds upon the Axminster carpet; but there was little that spoke the character of the present occupants – except, perhaps, some pretty red shades which had been fitted over the candles by the hearth.

'I believe,' said Dido, turning to her cousin, 'that, in general, it is possible to learn a great deal about our acquaintances from looking at their drawing rooms.'

'Is it?' Flora looked startled. It was not an idea that had ever come into her head before.

'Though,' Dido admitted as she began to walk about the room, 'on the present occasion, I do not know that I can deduce much beyond the fact that Mrs Lansdale was a rather vain woman.'

'Why do you say so?'

'What other purpose is there in a red light but to flatter a woman's face? And,' she said, turning to the open pianoforte, 'I see that she was a musical lady. And on the evening that she died she had been playing – or listening to…' She took the sheet of music from the stand, '…*Robin Adair*.'

'Oh no! You are quite wrong, you know,' said Flora, following her across the room. 'I have never in my whole life known such a *very* unmusical woman. She *never* played herself, and she quite hated to hear anyone else play.'

'Did she? That is strange. But perhaps that is why there is no other music here. And yet,' Dido added thoughtfully, 'it seems *someone* has been playing: for here is the instrument open and the music set ready upon the stand…'

She picked up the sheet of music and studied it more closely. It was the usual kind of thing – to be found on music stands everywhere: paper bought from the stationers with the lines already ruled, but with notes and words filled in afterwards by hand. In this case certainly by a woman's hand… Yes, most certainly a woman's hand. The notes were drawn very neat and black and clear and the words were written in a pretty, flowing hand which put a great many twists and turns upon the letters – particularly upon the Ss and the Ws.

She put it down and crossed to the hearth, where her eye was caught by a mark upon the back of a chair. She touched it and found it to be sticky. She put her fingers to her nose and smelt pomade and powder.

'Well,' she said, 'I would guess one thing about *Mr* Lansdale. I would guess that he puts powder in his hair.'

'Indeed he does not!' cried Flora, shocked at the suggestion. 'Such a nasty, old-fashioned habit! My dear cousin, no gentleman under forty puts powder in his hair now!'

'Well then, if you are quite sure, I think we may say that, on the evening of his aunt's death, Mr Lansdale was visited by an ageing and unfashionable man...Or rather,' she said, looking across at the chair on the opposite side of the hearth, and seeing a similar stain, 'by *two* ageing and unfashionable men – one of whom was considerably taller than the other.'

'Dido, now I am sure that you are making things up! How can you possibly know how tall the gentlemen were?'

'By the places at which their heads rested upon the chairs. Look. Do you not see that one of the powder stains is much higher than the other?'

'Oh yes! Why it is true, you *are* clever!'

'Thank you.' Dido turned aside knowing that she ought not to take so very much pleasure in the compliment.

As she turned, her eye fell upon the mantel shelf. There was a white and gold china shepherdess, thinly coated in dust, and a very fine pair of branching silver candlesticks – and, propped behind one of the candlesticks, there was a little bit of pasteboard. With a quick glance at the door to be sure they were not overlooked, she picked it up and read what was written on it...

She stared. Read it again. And then again a third time as if she could not quite believe what she had seen.

'Flora,' she said. 'Mrs Midgely claims that she is unacquainted with the Lansdales – is that not so?'

'Yes.'

'She says she does not know them at all?'

'Yes.'

'Then she is lying.' She held out the piece of pasteboard. 'Look, here is her calling card.'

Flora's little mouth dropped open in surprise. But before she could speak, there was a sound of heavy footsteps behind them.

'I beg your pardon,' said a very deep voice. The two women turned rather guiltily and saw, standing in the doorway, precisely the kind of manservant Dido had expected to find in this house: a very tall man – not many inches short of six feet in height – with a high-domed, bald head, an air of extreme dignity and a voice so low that it seemed to echo somewhere deep inside her.

'I am sorry,' he said, 'there has been a mistake. Young Sarah should not have brought you into this room.'

'Oh!' cried Dido cheerfully. 'Do not worry about us. We are quite comfortable here.'

'I am very glad to hear it, miss.' The man regarded her with solemn disapproval. 'But it is not Mr Lansdale's wish that this room should be used. If you will just step across into the breakfast room…' he said.

And there was nothing for it but to put aside all thoughts and suspicions of Mrs Midgely for the moment and follow the manservant across the entrance hall into a smaller, sunnier apartment where they were soon joined by Mr Lansdale – and Miss Neville, the lady who had been Mrs Lansdale's companion.

Henry Lansdale, she discovered, was a very handsome young man indeed. And as charming as Flora had made him out to be. He had lively blue eyes, a fine bearing, and a pleasant, unreserved manner. During the first ten minutes of the visit he behaved exactly as he ought upon receiving a visit of condolence. He ran through an account of his aunt's death; explaining that she had retired to bed early on her last evening. She had been tired, he said, but they had had no reason to think she was at all in danger – until the housemaid discovered her dead in her bed next morning.

He expressed all the proper sentiments as he told this melancholy tale and spoke with very becoming simplicity – and great feeling. But Dido noted that he was not easy; he paced from the hearth to the window and was anxious and restless to a degree for which grief alone could not account.

As he talked, Miss Neville sewed and smiled.

Flora had explained to Dido that Clara Neville was a cousin of the Lansdales who had been living with her mother in Richmond in 'very reduced circumstances' before her grand relations came to Knaresborough House and she was invited to join them as a companion. She was a tall, bony woman of perhaps five or six and forty who could not, even in her youth, have been thought pretty – having rather more forehead and less chin than is usually considered desirable.

The smile which occupied her mouth was at odds with the deep lines of discontent and ill-humour on her brow. And, since her mouth was small and her brow wide, the discontent and ill-humour rather got the better of it.

Her speeches too were a mixture of perfunctory pleasantry and irrepressible discontent. She lamented the death of her cousin loudly, but Dido could not help but suppose that the loss of her own comfortable position was the saddest part of the business, from her, 'I suppose I shall have to return to mother soon,' following on almost immediately.

After a while there was a pause in the conversation and Dido took the opportunity to politely regret the death of the dog – watching Mr Lansdale closely for any sign of consciousness or guilt, as she spoke.

But he only seemed as puzzled as she was herself. 'That,' he said turning from the window at which he was standing, 'is a very strange business indeed. I cannot account for it at all.' He began to pace about the room once more.

'Oh dear!' cried Flora. 'I am very sorry! We have raised a subject which distresses you.'

'No,' he said in a softened tone, 'my dear Mrs Beaumont, please do not be uneasy on that score.' He sat down beside her. 'The subject does not distress me,' he said very gently. 'It merely puzzles me. I cannot get it out of my head. You see, I know the creature was alive at seven on the evening that my aunt died.'

'Are you sure of that?' asked Dido, rather more abruptly than she intended.

'Oh yes,' he said, 'because I took it down to the kitchen at that time and fed it as I always did. Then I let it out to run about in the garden. It was still in the garden when I left at about half after seven to keep my evening engagement in town.'

'You were from home that evening?' asked Dido keenly.

'Yes,' he said looking at her in some surprise.

She blushed. 'I am sorry. I only meant to say that I

suppose you were not able to search for the dog.'

'No, I was not. But Miss Neville was here all evening and she says that the butler, Fraser, searched the lawns and called for it. Did he not, Miss Neville?'

'Oh!' Miss Neville dropped her work and put her finger to her mouth. 'I beg your pardon?'

'I was telling Mrs Beaumont and Miss Kent about the little dog. He was searched for during the evening, was he not?'

'Oh yes. Yes. Several times.'

'I see,' said Dido, with her eyes fixed upon a little spot of fresh blood on the white linen lying in Miss Neville's lap.

'And I suppose,' she said, carefully, 'I suppose you have asked everyone who visited that evening whether they saw the dog?'

'There were no visitors that day,' said Mr Lansdale unhesitatingly. 'Nor had there been for some days past.'

'Were there not?' said Dido with some surprise, remembering the signs of company which they had found in the drawing room.

'Oh no,' said Mr Lansdale, 'we kept hardly any company.'

Dido could not let the opportunity pass her by. 'Did you not?' she said, her mind upon Mrs Midgely's calling card. 'Your aunt was not upon visiting terms with any of her neighbours?'

'Oh no. They were not such people...' He stopped himself and smiled. 'My aunt, you see, was very particular about the company she kept. It is an invalid's privilege, is it not?'

'And of course,' added Miss Neville in her whining voice, '*we* were not allowed visitors on account of her nerves... Though I am sure,' she added hastily, bending over her work once more, 'for my own part I did not mind it one bit. It is much pleasanter to be private, is it not?'

There was another short silence which was broken by Mr Lansdale's sighing. 'I am grateful,' he said feelingly, 'that my poor dear aunt never knew what had happened to the pug. She was extremely fond of the animal.'

'Oh dear yes! I am sure you all were,' cried Flora politely.

He made a strange noise and covered his face with his hand. It almost seemed that he might be smothering a laugh.

At the same time Miss Neville's grating voice burst out with: 'Yes, to be sure it is a very great pity. My poor cousin would have been quite heart-broke... Though it was not a nice little dog – barking away every time there was a knock on the house door. And it bit me once. I only picked up and returned a length of sewing cotton which Mrs Lansdale had dropped, and it bit me! And I am sure the servants disliked it too. I doubt there is one of them who has not been bitten by it.'

'Do you think perhaps one of them...?' began Dido.

'No,' said Mr Lansdale quickly. 'Its death would have upset my aunt to such a degree...put her into such a passion. She would...' He recollected himself again and stopped. 'I am sure you understand, Miss Kent, that the state of the mistress's temper must be of the first importance to her servants.'

'Yes, of course,' said Dido, noticing once more his

determination to always speak of his aunt with respect – and the effort which it sometimes cost him. She did not doubt that the lady had been just as difficult to defer to when she was alive.

Mr Lansdale drummed his fingers on the side of his chair for a moment. Miss Neville continued to sew and smile. But there was something uncomfortable about her smile which Dido could not understand.

Nor could she quite form an opinion of Mr Lansdale. He *seemed* all handsome appearance and proper feeling; but how deep this manly beauty went – whether it was a matter of person and manner only, or whether it was rooted in his character, she could not yet tell.

He was certainly unreserved. He had, while talking about his aunt's death, already alluded to the unkind gossip concerning him and now, after sitting thoughtfully for a few moments, he gave a wry smile. It seemed his youth and high spirits could not long be held in check even by death and danger. 'What I cannot quite determine,' he said, 'is whether the death of the dog will exonerate me in the eyes of my neighbours, or whether it will confirm me a murderer.'

'A murderer!' cried Flora. 'How perfectly horrid! I beg you will not say such things.'

But Dido held his gaze and said quietly. 'Yes, Mr Lansdale, I am finding that point difficult to settle myself.'

The remark served to fix his attention upon her. Until that moment she had been only the lovely Mrs Beaumont's poor cousin; but now, all at once, she had an existence of her own.

'Miss Kent!' he cried, smiling, 'I do believe that you suspect me!'

Flora hastened to assure him that her cousin had no such doubts, that it was just too horrid for words to even suggest it.

But Dido waited until she had finished speaking and then, finding that the young man was still regarding her with slightly raised brows and shining eyes full of questions, she said, very seriously, 'No, Mr Lansdale. Upon consideration I do not think that I suspect you. From what you have told me, the evidence seems to be in your favour.'

He shook his head and became suddenly solemn. 'I am very glad to find that I have your good opinion, Miss Kent – and,' turning with a softened voice, 'yours too Mrs Beaumont.' He sighed deeply. 'And you are quite right. Those who can suspect me of lacking affection for my aunt quite mistake the matter.' He paused again. 'If I am guilty of anything,' he said with great feeling, 'it is certainly not a *lack* of affection.'

It was said very quietly, very properly and Dido did not doubt he meant to convey regard and respect for his dead relation. But, all the same, she could not quite like the way in which his gaze fell upon Flora as he spoke.

It started a new – and entirely unwelcome – suspicion in her head.

Chapter Four

'"Something",' said Dido thoughtfully as the door of Knaresborough House closed behind them, '"something is rotten in the state of Denmark".'

'Is it?' said Flora anxiously. 'I am very sorry to hear it... But what has Denmark to do with us?'

'It is a quotation from Shakespeare,' Dido explained. 'It is said by...one of his characters, in...one of his plays.'

'Oh, that is all right then.'

'I meant that, in the present case, for "Denmark" we should substitute "Richmond".'

'Oh yes! "Something is rotten in the state of Richmond",' Flora mused. She looked about her at the smooth lawns and the raked gravel of Knaresborough House, and, beyond the sweep gates, the new-built villas which lined the hill, sloping down to the slow, wide river with its willows and hayfields. A heat haze shimmered over everything and all was still but for one fashionable gig driving past at a smart pace, its high yellow wheels a blur of dust and speed. It all appeared very ordinary and proper. The warm air was full of the scents of hay and lilac – and still, just a hint of that other, less pleasant smell. Flora looked towards the cedar tree and the raw grave beneath it. 'Yes! Of course!' she cried. '"Something is rotten". Yes, I quite see what you mean. Something is very rotten.'

'No, no,' said Dido, 'I did not mean that. I meant to say that something strange is carrying on here. Something is wrong. Very wrong indeed.'

'Oh. Is it?' Flora considered a moment. 'It certainly is strange that Mrs Midgely's card should be in the drawing room.'

'Yes, it would seem that there is, after all, an acquaintance of some kind between the two families. Is it, I wonder, the cause of Mrs M's vehemence against Mr Lansdale? And, besides the card, there are the other evidences of visitors – of powdered gentlemen and a lady who played upon the pianoforte – on the very evening before Mrs Lansdale died. Altogether it would seem that Mrs Lansdale was much better acquainted with her neighbours than we have been led to suppose.'

'But Mr Lansdale said that she did not receive calls – that there had been no visitors for many days.'

'Yes. Precisely so,' said Dido, pacing along the gravel. 'And the great question must be – was he lying when he said…?'

'No!' cried Flora, hurrying after her, in a flutter of muslin and anxiety. 'No, no, you must not say such things! You have seen him, Dido. How can you suppose such a man capable of a falsehood? There is truth in all his looks!'

'Well, well,' said Dido, unconvinced by this powerful argument, but reluctant to press the point. 'Maybe he knew nothing about the visitors. After all he was absent on the fateful evening. And it may be that his aunt was quite in the habit of receiving secret calls.'

'Yes,' said Flora firmly, 'it may.'

Dido judged it best to say no more of Mr Lansdale. 'However,' she pointed out, 'one thing is certain: Miss Neville *must* have known about the visitors. She was at home all evening.'

'Miss Neville may be lying,' suggested Flora.

'She may indeed, for *she* has not a handsome face to prevent her telling falsehoods.' Dido threw her cousin a sidelong look as she spoke.

But Flora was thinking and twisting her finger in her bonnet's ribbon. The result of her musing was: 'I do not like Clara Neville. She has a nasty, unhappy look.'

'You are quite right; the woman is certainly guilty of unhappiness – and a very grave crime it is. But I think there may be something else besides. A greater guilt. Did you see how she started and ran her needle into her finger when that last evening was spoken of?'

'No, I did not. Do you suppose...' Flora stopped. They were come now to the cedar tree at the end of the sweep and she was disconcerted to find that her cousin was once more staring thoughtfully at the grave. 'You are thinking about the dog again?'

'Yes, I am.'

'Why are you so very interested in it? It was only a dog – and rather a horrid dog too.'

Dido's mind was full to overflowing upon this subject. She was thinking of the mystery of the creature being killed at the very same time that its mistress died. She was thinking of the character it had been given by Miss Neville

– a noisy little thing which had bitten anyone who came near it. She was thinking that it would have sounded the alarm if anyone had tried to harm Mrs Lansdale: thinking that it was just the kind of animal which a murderer might wish to destroy.

She looked at Flora's little white face tipped questioningly to one side: blue eyes wide as a child's, one shining curl slipping prettily across her smooth cheek.

'The death of the dog,' said Dido cautiously, 'does rather suggest that there was something…strange…suspicious about the lady's death…'

'Dido!' Tears sprang immediately to the wide blue eyes, hung upon the lashes. 'You are not saying…?'

'No, no. I am not accusing Mr Lansdale. Did you not hear me tell him that I believe the evidence to be in his favour? For, if someone did kill the dog in order to harm its mistress undetected, I do not think it was Mr Lansdale.'

'Oh…' Flora hesitated, looked puzzled. 'Why do you say so?'

'Because he told us that he regularly fed the dog. And I think you will agree that, however ill-tempered a dog may be in general, it will usually tolerate the presence of the person from whom it receives food. I cannot see that *he* would have had any cause to kill the dog – even if he intended harm to his aunt.'

'Yes. Quite. I see.' Flora blinked away her tears. 'Then that is all right then?' she said uncertainly.

'Well, perhaps not. For, if a murder should come to light, then I fear Mr Lansdale will *certainly* be the one accused. He has, after all, gained a great deal from his aunt's death. And the rumour which Mrs Midgely is spreading...' She stopped, shivering a little in spite of the warmth of the day. 'Flora,' she said firmly, 'we *must* put a stop to these rumours.'

'Of course we must. That is just what I have been telling you.'

'And we must find out exactly what has been carrying on here.'

Flora looked less certain about that. But Dido was now walking on, deep in thought. At the end of the sweep she stopped.

From here they could clearly see the windows of the houses opposite and in one of them was visible a white cap which Dido recognised as belonging to Miss Prentice – Mrs Midgely's little boarder. She paused for a moment, looking at the window, then turned and looked back up the sweep to the sombre lawns and the red-brick front of Knaresborough House.

'Flora,' she said suddenly. 'What do you say to paying Miss Prentice a morning call?'

'Well,' came the puzzled reply, 'I daresay I owe her the attention. I have not set foot in that house once since our coming down from town. But, why should you wish to call upon *her*? She is such a very dull woman!'

'On the contrary,' said Dido cheerfully, taking Flora's arm and steering her towards the house, 'I think she may prove very interesting indeed. For she has a remarkably interesting view from her window – and she spends a great deal of time looking at it. In fact, I do believe that if anyone can tell us who has been visiting Mrs Lansdale, it is Miss Prentice.'

They crossed the road and followed the path which led

along the side of the house. The front parlour window was open and there was music drifting out among the severely clipped hedges of box and yew. Mary Bevan was playing upon the pianoforte and singing so beautifully that both women could not help but stop for a moment to listen...

'What's this dull town to me
Robin's not near
What was't I wish'd to see
What wish'd to hear
Where all the joy and mirth
Made this town heaven on earth
Oh, they're all fled with thee
Robin Adair...'

Flora merely smiled appreciatively; but Dido raised an interested eyebrow as they walked on to the front door.

The visit did not begin well.

Miss Prentice was not alone when they were shown into the back parlour; Mrs Midgely was sitting with her and, at first, Dido despaired of being able to ask any of the questions which were filling her head. There was no breaking in upon the torrent of Mrs Midgely's tedious prosing. At first there was nothing to be done but to take their seats upon hard, narrow chairs and to listen.

Attending with only half an ear, Dido looked about her. The room certainly had an excellent view of Knaresborough House; but that was the only thing to be said in its praise. It was not a pleasant room. It was very small and, facing backwards, it received no sunlight even now in the middle of a day in June. And into it there seemed to be gathered all the oldest and shabbiest articles of furniture that might be found in any moderately sized house. The only handsome piece was a gentleman's broad mahogany desk – very fine, but with its drawers badly scratched and scarred – pushed into one corner, occupying a great deal of space and offering in return little convenience for the room's present mistress. And there was also an air of incongruous masculinity in the stains upon the wallpaper which had, almost certainly, been made by tobacco smoke...

The name of Lansdale caught her ear and she returned all her attention to Mrs Midgely.

'...I believe the business *must* come soon to the attention of the magistrates,' she was declaring happily as Flora turned pale. 'It is a very shocking business, and much to be regretted for the sake of the whole neighbourhood.'

'Though I can hardly understand how the neighbourhood has been injured by it,' said Dido sharply, 'since it has only gained a subject about which it may talk at a time when news from town is rather thin.'

Colour mounted in Mrs Midgely's broad, rouged cheeks. But, luckily, she was prevented from replying by the arrival of a note which sent her hurrying off in high spirits to 'consult with Mary directly.'

As the door closed behind her a silence fell upon the room which was very welcome to all three remaining ladies. But poor Miss Prentice was looking anxious. She sat for several moments, her little hands fidgeting in her lap. 'Oh dear,' she said at last, 'I rather fancy that her note is about poor Mary going away.'

Flora looked concerned. 'Is it true, then,' she asked Miss Prentice quietly, 'that Miss Bevan is to go out as a governess?'

Miss Prentice nodded sadly.

'I had heard it spoken of,' cried Flora, 'but, you know, I hardly gave the rumour credit. For I am sure Mrs Midgely has as pretty a fortune as any woman in the world! And she has not another creature to leave it to. I do not at all see why she cannot provide for poor Mary.'

'Well, if I must give my opinion, neither can I,' said Miss Prentice. 'I never heard this plan of making her a governess until just a few months ago. And I am sure it was always the intention of Colonel Midgely to provide for the girl when he took her in. But he has been dead a year now and...' She checked herself and gave a smile, turning her little face to one side as she did so. 'Well, well, it is no business of mine to have an opinion on the matter, is it Mrs Beaumont?' She sighed deeply. 'But the poor, dear girl is being so very brave about it. She has set her mind to it, I know, and has had her gowns packed and her travelling dress ready this last week.'

Flora politely hoped that Miss Bevan would find a situation with a pleasant family and then introduced more general topics to take the poor lady's mind from the distressing subject.

Dido was quite struck by this new view of Mrs Midgely's character. It certainly showed a hardness of heart and, perhaps, a love of money. But how these qualities might bear upon her determination to harm Mr Lansdale, she could not quite determine...

She turned her attention back to little Miss Prentice, who was now chatting quite merrily. Sitting with her little pink hands folded in the lap of her plain brown dress, a neat grey curl hanging on either side of her cap, she was a pleasant sight – delightfully eager and animated. She was perhaps a year or two older than Mrs Midgely but there was about her something which suggested she had once been pretty in a small, unobtrusive way.

Dido could not help but think her cheerfulness out of place in the dark, confined little parlour. But, it seemed, the deficiencies of her present home were more than compensated, by its being in so fashionable a place as Richmond. Miss Prentice certainly shared her friend's interest in 'the neighbourhood'. Only, while Mrs Midgely valued fashionable people for the reflected grandeur she believed they threw upon herself, Miss Prentice's regard for them was perfectly disinterested: she delighted innocently in wealth and titles as a naturalist delights in the birds and beasts that he watches.

'And I hear that Sir Hugo Wyat is to take the red house near the top of the hill.' she was saying now. 'And Sir Hugo's is a very old title. I do so love the old titles. There is such solidity about them, is there not? Such Englishness! And so, when Sir Hugo comes, that will be three Baronets residing here in this street. Which is so very… For last summer, I understand, there was but one.'

'You do have some very – interesting – neighbours,' said Dido, looking thoughtfully out into the bright sunshine beyond the window, at the dusty road and Knaresborough House. From here it was possible to see the whole of the sweep and the house-front, with the smooth green lawns sloping upward to the dark mass of laurel bushes that shut out the offices at the back of the house.

'Ah!' cried Miss Prentice, following her gaze. 'You are thinking of the Lansdales, I don't doubt. It is a sad business,' she continued in a half-whisper, 'and, for myself, I do not care what Susan says. If I must give my opinion, I am all for the young man. He seems a very pleasant gentleman indeed and he always bows very prettily when he walks past and sees me at the window – which not many fine young men would think to do.'

Dido smiled and ventured to say, 'You have perhaps heard of the death of Mrs Lansdale's little dog?'

'Oh yes. I have indeed!'

'Mr Lansdale tells us that it went missing on the evening that its mistress died. And I wondered... You have such a remarkably clear view of the house and its grounds... I wondered whether you might have seen what became of it...'

'No.' Miss Prentice thought carefully. 'No, I do not believe that I did.'

'But I daresay you saw the butler searching the garden for it?'

Miss Prentice looked very thoughtful and pressed a bent finger to her lips: seemed pleased that, for once, she had indeed been asked to give her opinion. 'No, I cannot say that I remember that at all. But Mary came to sit with me for a little while after dinner, and Susan had company that evening. Mr Vane and Mrs Barlow came to play at whist – and I went in to join them. Dear Mary insisted that I join them. "You must come", says she, "for I am sure I cannot bear to think of you sitting all alone". Which was so very... So, you see, I do not think I was by the window for long.'

'I quite understand. But, I wonder, what exactly did you happen to see that evening?'

Miss Prentice considered very carefully, so gratified to

be consulted that she did not seem to wonder at Dido's motives. 'Well now, let me see,' she said, her cheeks flushed with pleasure. 'What can I remember? This is like that game we used to play when we were children. Did you play it too? With all the little objects – reels of thread and pennies and oranges and I know not what – all put upon a tray and then a cloth put over them and we must say all that we could remember.'

'Yes,' said Dido, 'it is just like the game, is it not?'

'Well...' She closed her eyes. 'I do not remember the dog. No, he was not there. Nor the butler. I saw Mr Lansdale: he drove away in his barouche... And I believe I saw the maids going away to their homes... And a beggar came and stood against the gate post... And then I saw Mr Henderson. I saw him walking across the lawn in his way to the front door.'

'Mr Henderson?'

'Yes,' said Miss Prentice, opening her eyes. 'Mr Henderson is the gentleman who used to live in Knaresborough House before the Lansdales came there. He left it but three days before they came.'

'And are you quite sure it was him?'

'Oh yes. I remember it very clearly, for I remarked upon it to Mary. "Why look!" I said, "here is Mr Henderson come to call upon Mr Lansdale". Because Mary was a little acquainted with him you see. At least she was a little acquainted with his daughters.'

'And at what time did you see him?'

'At about eight o'clock I think – for it was just before we went to cards.'

'I wonder,' said Dido after a pause. 'Do you know if

Mr Henderson wears powder in his hair?'

Miss Prentice looked all amazement. 'Why, how remarkable that you should guess that, Miss Kent! Yes, indeed he does. He is a well-looking, tall man. He has very fine black side-whiskers; and he always has his hair *very* nicely dressed. And I think it is such a becoming fashion, do not you? And so few gentlemen take the trouble these days to put on powder. Yes, so very becoming.' She smiled fondly – as if, perhaps, she was remembering a particular powdered gentleman from her distant youth.

Dido thought for a moment or two, then risked asking: 'You are quite sure, that Mrs Midgely had a card party that day – that she was at home all evening.'

'Oh yes. Quite sure.'

'I just wondered whether…whether, perhaps, Mrs Midgely went herself to visit Mrs Lansdale that day.'

Miss Prentice's little face twisted about in surprise. Her eyes widened. 'Susan?' she said, 'Susan, visit Mrs Lansdale? No indeed! Why ever should you think such a thing? She was not at all acquainted with her.'

'Oh but she was!' cried Flora before Dido could prevent her. 'She certainly had visited the house you know. We found her visiting card in Mrs Lansdale's drawing room!'

There was a gasp from Miss Prentice: something between surprise and pain. All the colour drained from her round cheeks. Her lips moved but no sound came from them.

'Miss Prentice? Are you unwell?' Dido stood up and went to her – and was but just in time to catch her as she slipped from the chair in a dead faint.

Chapter Five

Next morning Dido walked beside the river – alone. She had received such a letter from her sister as made liberty and solitude essential: such a letter as must turn her mind away from the mysteries surrounding her in Richmond: such a letter as must, for a while, even make her cease to wonder why Miss Prentice should faint upon hearing of her friend's visit to Mrs Lansdale.

Dearest Dido, wrote Eliza, quite unaware that she was about to inflict severe pain upon her sister, *I take up my pen to assure you that I put your questions to Mr Lomax at the earliest opportunity. However, I very much regret that I am not yet able to give any report of his opinion upon the matter of Mr Lansdale's danger under the law. For, although he listened very courteously to my request, (and, by the by, he is a very pleasant man, is he not? And I quite agree with you as to his profile which I remember you describing as particularly fine. And I agree too about his kindliness and consideration, which I think are quite remarkable.) But, what I mean to say is that, although he attended to the matter like the perfect gentleman which I make no doubt he is – and I am sure he did not mean to disappoint you – for I do not believe it is in his nature to disappoint anyone. But, the fact is that before he could properly consider the matter, he was called away from Belsfield upon business. And, since he was not able to give any idea of when he may return, I am afraid that I cannot give any idea of when I may be able to send an answer to your questions. Though I assure you that I will send an answer just as soon as I have one to send...*

Mr Lomax's going away from Belsfield just now, and leaving her questions unanswered, was a severe blow. It spoke such an indifference to her and her concerns, as must make her doubt that he retained any affection for her at all...

How was it to be understood? Did he mean to convey to her some message? To let her know that she must think no more of him? Or had he merely forgotten the understanding which had seemed to exist – which *had* existed – between them? Was she become just another acquaintance whose requests could be brushed aside as convenience demanded?

These were the questions which had sprung up to torment her in the morning room as soon as she had read the letter. These were the questions which had followed her as she walked out. Now, seated upon an old log on the river-bank, concealed from the world by a willow which hung low over the water, she took the letter from her pocket, unfolded it and read it again.

The sunlight sparkled upon the slow running river. The air smelt of cool water and mud and wild garlic. Waterfowl slid lazily along upon the current and the turquoise wings of a dragon-fly flashed in and out of the tall rushes as

Dido reread the hurtful words. But they had not changed. They conveyed the same message as they had back in the morning room.

He was indifferent. If he had ever cared, he cared no longer... Unless... Unless it was only a show of indifference designed to release her from an attachment which he felt could never be fulfilled. There were, after all, such obstacles to their ever coming together, that he might well feel the kindest thing to do was to put an end to all hope.

She let her letter fall into her lap, turned her eyes upon the shining water, the long strands of weed swaying in the current and the brown velvet heads of the rushes, and considered this idea.

It was true that, at present, it was impossible for an engagement to be formed between them. Prudent, clever and hard-working though Mr Lomax was, his financial affairs were in disarray. There was a son by his first marriage – a hateful, dissolute boy. And this son had gaming debts: debts which would have put him into prison, had his father not pledged himself to pay them.

Dido had no notion of how long the paying of these debts would take – how long it might be before Mr Lomax could, with a clear conscience, make her an offer. Perhaps he had decided, after long and painful consideration (her heart insisted that the consideration should be painful – she loved him too well to excuse him from suffering) that he should give her up.

She smiled. This was a great deal better than supposing him to be indifferent... But... The smile slipped away from her lips. But it was, in fact, just as hopeless. For if he had decided they were not to be together, what was to be done about it? She must accept his decision. She must not pursue him – no gentleman could bear such forwardness...

The dazzling water beyond the curtain of willow leaves shifted and blurred as tears forced themselves into her eyes. And she sat for some time lost in misery and loneliness, hardly aware of anything around her.

It was a slight, unexpected movement which first roused her from wretchedness.

Something small was drifting and spinning upon the water. She blinked away her tears and peered through the overhanging leaves; it was the inevitable reaction of strong native curiosity. An irregular fragment of...something, was drifting in the current, a point of dullness on the gleaming stream. Another joined it, and another. They drifted slowly in amongst the bulrushes – more and more of them collecting among the thick green stems.

Dido wiped her eyes and, hardly knowing what she was doing – or why she was doing it – she leant over the river. There were torn fragments of paper slowly darkening in the water and beginning to sink.

Interested in spite of her misery, she pushed aside a twig of willow and looked upstream to learn whence the pieces of paper had come.

On a sandy bank a few yards away stood a woman – a small woman in a brown dress – urgently tearing at a bundle of papers and throwing the pieces down into the river. Now and again she would look quickly to left and right as if to ensure she was not observed, then she would return to her tearing and throwing.

As she finished her task and shook the last fragments from her hands she lifted her head in relief. The sun shone full upon her face... It was Miss Prentice.

Dido stared, wondered...and looked down at the pieces of paper drifting within her reach among the rushes. Some of them were already sunk down into the mud – but many others were still floating, the black words upon them still visible. She hesitated, struggled against temptation – and failed. In one swift movement, she stooped, plunged her hand into the cool water and snatched up some of the pieces.

Then she stood for a moment, allowing the water to drain away through her fingers and fighting off the last attacks of conscience. The papers were almost certainly letters which the lady wished to destroy. It was not honourable to look. But why had she been so intent upon disposing of them quietly? Was it in any way connected with the shock which had made her faint yesterday? Was it connected with Mrs Midgely's mysterious visit to the Lansdales – and the rumours which were circulating against Mr Lansdale?

She *must* look.

She held one dripping fragment up to the dappled sunshine that fell through the willow branches and was very much surprised to see, not handwriting but squarely printed words. It was not letters which Miss Prentice was throwing away, it was the pages of a book!

And a rather boring book too. The words upon her scraps were long and closely printed and rather smudged from the water, but here and there a phrase was discernible.

Phrases such as: *the inevitable progress of improvement* and *inalienable privileges of all mankind* and *justifiable opposition.*

Dido turned the pieces over in her hand, quite at a loss as to why they should merit such eager destruction. As she did so, something else caught her eye. On one fragment, there was a little bit of faded handwriting in slightly bluish ink. At first she thought it might be a note or comment that had been written in a margin, but, when she looked closely, she saw that it was the torn end-paper of the book – with *Richmond Circulating Library* written upon it.

Her surprise increased and she peered upstream through the curtain of branches. Miss Prentice had now regained the path and was hurrying away between willows and hawthorns and trailing pink dog-roses, her narrow brown back bent over in haste. Dido watched her go with a frown and a puzzled shake of the head.

What possible reason could there be for a respectable, middle-aged lady to take a book from a circulating library, tear it up in secret, and cast the pieces into the Thames?

Dido soon caught up with Miss Prentice. She was resting upon the step of a stile where the shade of willows gave way to more open ground and the long grass foamed white with cow-parsley and wild garlic. The path was busier here, with several gentlemen, ladies and parasols strolling by, and an anxious nursemaid urgently forbidding her charges to wander near the river. Beyond the stile a small herd of cows tore rhythmically at the rich June grass and, in another field close by, two men with gypsy tans were tossing hay onto a wagon.

'I am very glad to see that you are recovered from your illness of yesterday,' said Dido when the first greetings were over.

'Oh yes! Thank you. As to that... It was the heat you know,' replied Miss Prentice with some confusion. 'Nothing but the heat I assure you. I am quite well today. I am seldom ill – quite blessed with good health, which is so very...' Her voice trailed away. She stood up and proposed their walking back to the town together.

Dido gladly agreed, and fell into step beside her. Her curiosity was now once more in full play, acting like a kind of half-effective analgesic to blunt the edge of painful disappointment. She looked sidelong at her companion; there was a rapid blinking of the eyes which spoke of some agitation, but a very determined pretence at calm.

It was as fair an opportunity for conversation as she was likely to get, and there were a great many questions which she was longing to ask. But she judged it best not to reveal that she had witnessed the tearing of the book. That mystery would be more likely solved by strategy than questions. And, as for pursuing the business of Mrs Midgely's acquaintance with the Lansdales – *that,* she thought, had better not be attempted. A fainting fit in the heart of the countryside would be very inconvenient indeed!

So she settled upon what seemed a safe branch of the interesting subject and began cautiously with: 'Before you were overcome by the heat yesterday morning, Miss Prentice, you were telling us about Mr Henderson – the gentleman who used to live at Knaresborough House.'

'Oh yes! Mr Henderson – we were talking of him, were we?' She seemed relieved.

'You were telling us,' Dido continued, assured that she was upon safe ground, 'that he visited Mrs Lansdale – on the evening before she died. And, I wondered, if you have ever seen him visiting before?'

'Oh, no. No I do not believe that I have. The Lansdales had very few visitors as a rule. Very few. Which I always thought rather a shame – for such a fine house. It was *very* different when Mr Henderson lived there himself,' she continued eagerly. 'He kept a great deal of company – not dinner company...' She leant close and whispered – though there was no one to hear but a pair of swans sliding by upon the river. 'Between ourselves, I rather fancy that money was not very plentiful with Mr Henderson. However, though he gave no dinners, he kept a *great deal* of evening company... But the Lansdales, they were very quiet...'

There was no mistaking the note of regret in her voice. The Lansdales, it seemed, were unsatisfactory neighbours – they provided too little to watch.

They walked on a little. Dido's mind was busy with a new idea – the idea of a 'fine- looking', but impoverished man visiting in secret an ageing, wealthy widow, and visiting her, furthermore, in a room fitted up with red, flattering lights.

Had he perhaps come in the form of a lover? And had Miss Neville been sworn to secrecy lest the nephew find out?

Dido paused when they came to the next stile. 'What manner of man is Mr Henderson?' she asked. 'Is he a married man? Has he any family?'

'Oh! He is a widower, my dear. A widower with three

unmarried daughters – very pretty girls. At least, I suppose they are pretty. One did not see their faces – close bonnets they had on when they walked out. And very plain gowns... Which was another thing made me think the family were a little distressed for money.'

'I see.' Dido mused a moment. 'But he was a gentleman of some standing I imagine – to have rented such a house, I mean.'

'Oh yes! He was well connected for sure. The people who came to his evening parties! The Wyat's carriage was often there.' Miss Prentice began to check the illustrious names off upon her fingers. 'And Mr and Mrs Edward Connors – their chaise came very often. And that gentleman who was at Mrs Beaumont's delightful picnic, Sir Joshua Carrisbrook. Oh yes...' She considered a moment. 'Yes, all in all, I think Mr Henderson is of a good family, but that he has been obliged to retrench lately.'

'I see.' Dido's suspicions deepened. And, as they did so, she began to feel more and more uneasy about Mr Lansdale. All this did not bode well for him.

By the time she reached home she had worried herself into a little fever on this subject and she was very much looking forward to a little quiet reflection and an opportunity to write a reply to her sister's letter. She was not pleased to hear, as she paused in the welcome cool of the hall, the sound of voices coming from the drawing room. She sighed, laid aside her bonnet, and prepared herself unwillingly for company.

And then, upon opening the drawing room door, she saw Mr William Lomax sitting in quiet conversation with Flora...

Chapter Six

She stopped and stared, almost supposing that she had made a mistake. But it was indeed Mr Lomax sitting there in solid certainty beside the open french doors of Flora's pretty, flowered drawing room. It was the same lean figure she had been remembering; the same long legs stretched across the polished wooden floor; the same, rather grave face – certainly past its first youth, but with remarkably clear grey eyes and that kind of strong chin and profile which give a man distinction as he ages.

Her surprise was very great: so great as to leave – at first – no room even for pleasure: so great as to overcome her manners and make her demand, rather abruptly, how he came to be there.

He stood up to greet her, laughing at her amazement – and apologised for being its cause. 'But your cousin has invited me into her drawing room,' he assured her solemnly. 'I am no intruder.'

'I am sorry, Mr Lomax.' She recovered herself a little and held out her hand. 'But it is so strange, so very strange, to suddenly meet with a friend I had supposed to be a hundred miles away.'

'A hundred and fifty,' he said, as he took her hand.

'I believe it is nearer one hundred and fifty miles, from Belsfield into Surrey.'

'You are a very exact reckoner.'

He smiled and bowed over her hand. 'I would by no means wish you to underestimate the journey you have brought me on, Miss Kent,' he said.

'The journey *I* have brought you on?' Dido coloured with pleasure, but just then her gaze fell upon Flora. There was no mistaking her look.

Flora might not understand an allusion to Shakespeare, she might be entirely deaf to metaphors, but in matters of love she was *very* quick-witted indeed. She recognised an attachment when she saw it (and even, sometimes, when she did not). Before Dido had sat down, her cousin was delightedly planning a Michaelmas wedding and determining just where the happy couple should set up home.

Meanwhile, Mr Lomax was explaining his visit. 'I am staying eight miles away – at Brooke Manor, with Sir Joshua and Lady Carrisbrook. I believe he is a friend of yours, Mrs Beaumont?'

'Oh yes! Yes he is. A very good friend indeed.'

'Sir Joshua,' he said with a little lifting of his eyebrows, 'believes that my sole purpose in coming is to convey some papers concerning his property in Somersetshire – and I beg you will not disabuse him of that notion. But he has been so kind as to invite me to stay on for a few days – an invitation which I have been particularly pleased to accept.'

There was such meaning in these last words and they were accompanied by such an earnest look at Dido as made Flora wonder whether she had better not leave them alone together directly.

Dido herself hardly knew what she felt – so intent was she upon allaying Flora's suspicions. 'My sister told me that business had taken you from Belsfield, Mr Lomax,' she said as calmly as she could. 'But I had no idea of that business bringing you into Surrey.'

He leant forward, studied her face. 'I found,' he said eagerly, 'that I must try for an opportunity of seeing you. I could not be quite satisfied with answering your queries in a letter.' He stopped, seemed to recollect himself and turned slightly so as to include Flora. 'This rumour against your friend, Mrs Beaumont – it is such a very delicate business, I thought it would be better if we all three talked about it together.'

'You are so very kind Mr Lomax! I am sure we are both very much obliged to you. Are we not, Dido?'

'Oh yes, yes, of course.' Dido exerted herself against a great confusion of emotions – some of which were most unpleasant. An hour ago, when she had been sitting beside the river, she would have counted such a visit as this to be one of the greatest pleasures life could afford. But now that Mr Lomax was actually here in the room with her, she found that she could not be comfortable. She must reflect an hour or so in peace upon his looks and his words before she could hope to understand them; but for now, what mattered most was to seem calm – unconcerned.

'It is…' she began – and her own voice sounded as if it were a long way away – 'it is very kind of you, to make such a long journey for our sake.' She turned to Flora. 'Mr Lomax,' she said, 'has studied the law and I hope that he will be able to tell us how great the danger is – I mean as to Mr Lansdale and the rumours which are being spread about him.'

This was immediately effective in diverting Flora's mind from the discovery she had just made. She forgot to watch for signs of love and began instead to relate eagerly the whole business of the death, the picnic and all the details of the 'horrid, horrid, abominable' things which had been said by Mrs Midgely.

Mr Lomax listened to her very gravely with his fingertips pressed together and his chin resting upon them, his eyes only once or twice straying, rather anxiously, in Dido's direction.

Dido herself began to breathe more easily and by the time her cousin had finished her tale, she was tolerably calm. 'It is a strange business, is it not, Mr Lomax?' she said.

'It is certainly very unpleasant.'

'Can you tell us what might happen – I mean if Mrs Midgely prevails upon Mr Vane and persuades him to take some action?'

'Well,' he said very seriously, 'if the apothecary has a genuine suspicion of Mr Lansdale, then the law requires that he should bring a complaint against him.'

'And that complaint would have to be made to the magistrates?'

'Yes. And the magistrates would then put it to a Grand Jury – probably at the midsummer Quarter Sessions. And the men of the jury would either dismiss it, or else find it "a true bill" – which would mean that, in their opinion, there was a case to be made against the gentleman.'

'And what would happen then?' asked Flora eagerly.

'Then, I am afraid, he would be committed for trial at the Assizes.'

'But how dangerous is the accusation?' asked Dido. 'How heavily would Mr Vane's testimony tell against him if the matter were to be put to a jury?'

'That is a difficult question to answer,' he said thoughtfully. 'It would depend a great deal on just what he has to say of this "Kendal Black Drop".'

'But Mr Vane is an apothecary. The jury would believe what he told them about such things.'

'That is very true,' he acknowledged with a reluctant nod. 'It is so very difficult to determine the cause of any person's death that the opinion of a reputable medical man must always carry a great deal of weight.'

'Oh dear.' Flora began to wring her hands in great agitation. 'Oh dear, is there no hope for poor Mr Lansdale?'

He was dismayed to find that he had distressed her. He had, without knowing it, been addressing himself to Dido's vigorous mind and had quite overlooked the more delicate sensibilities of her cousin.

'Well, well,' he said with more gentleness, 'I would not say that there is no hope, Mrs Beaumont, by any means.' He turned kindly towards her. 'I rather think – I *hope* that the time which has elapsed since the poor lady's death must materially weaken Mr Vane's case. You see, if a case were brought, a jury would be sure to ask why, if his suspicions are strong and well founded, Mr Vane did not make his complaint as soon as he discovered his patient was dead.'

'Oh! And so they would not believe that he was telling the truth?' cried Flora.

'They would be a great deal less likely to believe him than they would if the matter had been raised at the time of the death. Yes,' he said firmly. 'Yes, upon reflection, I do believe that this must be Mr Lansdale's greatest security. In point of fact, I very much doubt that Mr Vane will take the matter any further now. If some fresh evidence were to come to light – something which Mr Vane could reasonably claim had heightened his suspicions – then it might be a different matter. But, as it stands, the case would be unlikely to convince any jury.' He paused and cast Dido a look of deep concern. 'I think you had better both put the matter out of your heads entirely,' he said.

'Oh thank you Mr Lomax!' said Flora with great feeling. 'You have quite set my mind at rest.' She was now smiling very happily. His kindly manner and quiet authority had been more than sufficient to bring conviction where conviction was so very welcome.

But Dido's mind was far from being at rest. She was thinking of fresh evidence: evidence which might increase suspicion against Mr Lansdale and send Mr Vane to the magistrates. She was thinking of Mr Henderson's secret visit; of red-shaded candles and a great many other things. But she said nothing – partly out of consideration of Flora's feelings and partly out of consideration of the very solemn look which Mr Lomax had turned upon her.

Chapter Seven

…It is very considerate of Mr Lomax to travel so far just to ease Flora's mind, is it not, Eliza? He is a remarkably humane man.

But I confess that I can take little comfort from the information which he gave us and I remain as anxious as ever about Mr Lansdale. For, you see, by Mr Lomax's account, the young man's security must rest upon there appearing no new evidence against him… And I am afraid, Eliza, I am <u>very much</u> afraid, that new evidence may appear.

Supposing Mrs Lansdale was…receiving attentions from Mr Henderson.(For, though her age must argue against it, her large fortune would certainly render it possible – if she was sufficiently vain and he was sufficiently flattering.) The anticipated marriage of his aunt would be a severe blow to Mr Lansdale's expectations – and if it should come to light – if Mrs Midgely should know of it and decide to spread it abroad – then is it not the very kind of evidence which would tell most heavily against him? The very circumstance which the jurymen might believe had driven him to desperate action?

And there is something else which I keep remembering and which troubles me greatly: Mr Lansdale's remark that he was not guilty of feeling _too little_ affection; did he mean to say that his fault is rather that he feels _too much_? And, if so, to whom is that affection directed? I _will not_ suppose, for the sake of our cousin's reputation, that she can be his object — in spite of the look which he gave her as he spoke. But there is no escaping the thought that an unsuitable attachment of his own — one which his aunt would disapprove; one which might have caused her to disown him — would also strengthen the case against him: provide, in the eyes of the jury, a reason for his wishing his aunt dead.

And, all in all, it seems to me that, if the justices are brought to believe that Mrs Lansdale was murdered, then they will certainly believe Henry Lansdale to be the murderer. The rumours against him _must_ be stopped. I must, somehow, find out the 'rottenness' in Richmond before it is too late.

No doubt, having read so far, Eliza, you are beginning to fear that I am in danger of setting up as a professional solver of mysteries as I once threatened to do. But do not worry: I have not yet leased consulting rooms in town, nor arranged with the brass engravers to announce my existence to the world. I will proceed very cautiously indeed.

There are, however, several questions to which I am most eager to find answers...

Dido stopped writing, for it had occurred to her as she completed the last words that the question foremost in her mind was one which she could not share with her sister — or with anyone else...

It was dusk now and she was once more writing beside the open window of her bed chamber, with a slight cool breeze blowing in upon the stored heat of the day and just lifting the pale curtains. The owl was calling again from the river, and the laughing voices of people returning on foot from a party drifted up from the road. A crane fly had found its way in and circled about the candle before dropping down to tiptoe daintily across her letter. She watched its progress through the black words and once more let her mind return to Mr Lomax's visit: recalling every speech, every look, every meaning – and every imagined meaning.

Why had he come? That was the question which kept recurring.

She wished most earnestly to believe that his motive was simple affection – a desire to be in her company. And his laughing insistence that she was the true cause of his journey had promised well... But afterwards there had been other remarks which were much less satisfactory – and his looks! Sometimes it had seemed there was more anxiety than affection in his looks. Sometimes she had even suspected disapproval...

And then he had been most decided in refusing Flora's invitation to stay to dinner. Of course his excuse that he was expected back at Brooke must be allowed – but he could have regretted that expectation a little more!

What did it all mean? Was she as dear to him as she had once been, or had he changed?

The uncertainty was very painful. Perhaps, she thought, a woman of five and thirty was not constitutionally suited to love. The agitations and heightened emotions which were delightful at one and twenty were now become tiresome...

Although, upon reflection, Dido recalled that she had

always been a little impatient in these matters… There had been the young man at her uncle Grainger's ball, many years ago… Mr Willet… No, *Captain* Willet. Everyone had said he would make her an offer that evening. And he had been half an hour stammering the most trivial nonsense to her on the terrace, after saying that he particularly wished to talk to her… Half an hour of the state of the roads and its being, 'a remarkably dry season, do you not think, Miss Kent?' In the end Dido had lost patience with him and returned to the dancing – and so had never known whether she might have aspired to the dignity of becoming Mrs Willet.

Ah well! She would certainly listen for more than half an hour to Mr Lomax, if he was ever got to the point of stammering upon a terrace, but, in the meantime, there was little she could do but wait for more opportunities of being in company with him, and watch his behaviour closely when they were together…

And, while she waited, she had more than enough to occupy her mind, for the danger in which Mr Lansdale stood seemed to be increasing. The need to solve the mysteries surrounding him was becoming urgent – and an exercise in strict reason was just what was needed, at the moment, to make her calm and rational.

She would set out a considered list of all the questions which troubled her.

…Firstly, I would like to know why Mrs Lansdale's little dog was killed – and by whom.

Second: what was the exact nature of Mrs Midgely's connection with the dead woman? They cannot have met regularly or Miss Prentice would surely have known about it. But there was one visit for sure. What was the purpose of that visit?

Third: why was Miss Prentice so shocked to hear of the visit that she fainted?

Fourth: who else, besides Mr Henderson, came to Knaresborough House on the evening before Mrs Lansdale died? There was certainly another gentleman, and, very probably, a lady too.

Fifth: why did Miss Prentice borrow a book from a library and tear it up?

Sixth: why should Mary Bevan wish to conceal from her guardian the fact that she had received a letter? I know that this does not seem to be at all connected with Mrs Lansdale's death, but nonetheless it troubles me. It is so out of character for her to tell a lie – and, from the colour in her face, I would judge that it caused her a great deal of pain to do so.

And lastly, the question which I feel is of the utmost significance, why does Miss Neville not acknowledge that Mr Henderson – or anyone else – visited her cousin on that fateful evening?

For, you see, Eliza, she continues to deny it – and in the strangest manner!

She and Mr Lansdale called here today, soon after Mr Lomax left us. And, since Mr Lansdale was very happy to monopolise Flora in conversation, I was able to have a quarter of an hour's uninterrupted talk with Miss Neville.

It was a useful quarter of an hour – though hardly a cheerful one. For behind her habitual smile, Miss Neville has a great many grievances and discontents which want only a sympathetic listener to bring them forward. Or perhaps I should rather say, an insignificant listener, for I do not doubt that, with people of rank and fortune, Miss Neville knows well enough how to make herself agreeable – or she would not have continued long with Mrs Lansdale.

She was much concerned with her own future and told me that Mr Lansdale has invited her to stay on with him until the house is given up in a week's time. Which is, of course, quite remarkably civil of him. Though she does not suppose for one moment that she will be idle, in that week, for there is a great deal to be done as to settling what is to become of her cousin's gowns and a great many other little matters which a gentleman has no idea of. And she does not doubt that all this will fall upon her shoulders…though, of course, she does not mean to complain…

And, all in all, she presents a very amusing mixture of gratitude and resentment.

As to Mr Henderson's visit: well, Eliza, I am becoming an adept at the business of discovering secrets and so I came at that by strategy. I wondered, I said, towards the end of her visit, since I understood that she had lived in Richmond all her life, whether she was at all acquainted with a gentleman that my brother knew – a Mr Henderson.

She shook her head. 'No,' she said, 'I do not believe that I am.'

And, Eliza, there was not the least trace of consciousness in her voice or in her manner. I will almost swear that she had never heard the name before in her life – unless of course she is such a consummate actress that she ought to be making her fortune in Drury Lane rather than playing the part of a poor relation here in Richmond.

So I said no more of Mr Henderson. But then, almost as they were leaving, I contrived to turn the conversation back to her recent loss. 'It is a great comfort to you, I am sure,' I said, 'to know that the poor lady died quietly and peacefully; but you must also regret that it was not possible for you to bid her farewell, for I understand that you had no reason to believe her unwell when she retired for the night.'

'Oh no, no reason at all. And you are quite right Miss Kent,' – with an expression of great feeling – 'quite right. It grieves me terribly that I did not go to her all that evening. If I had heard the slightest sound from her chamber, I would have gone.'

'Or,' said I, 'if you had only had a message to take. If, say, there had been a visitor called.'

'Oh,' said she, 'but there were no visitors. There never were – I believe Mr Lansdale explained as much before. All her acquaintance knew that she went very early to bed and, in general, she slept so lightly that even a knocking on the house door was enough to wake her. Evening visitors were quite forbidden.'

'I see,' I said. 'Then my friend Miss Prentice must have been mistaken.'

'Miss Prentice?' she asked.

'Oh it is nothing,' I said. 'But Miss Prentice thought that she saw a gentleman call at the house that evening.'

And then, Eliza, she looked very conscious indeed! The colour flooded to her cheeks. And, though she continued to deny that there had been any visitor, her voice was shaking dreadfully as she did so!

So what can all this mean? The name of Henderson meant nothing to her, and yet the news that his visit to

73

Knaresborough House had been observed threw her almost into a panic.

Why? Could it be that she saw the gentleman that night, but did not know his name? Was she disconcerted to hear that the house was watched? Or could it be that for some reason she did not know of the gentleman's having called and was shocked to find that she had been so deceived? Yet it is scarcely possible that she could have known nothing of his visit, for the drawing room at Knaresborough House is at the front and hard by the house door.

Well, I shall soon have further opportunity for talking to her for Flora and I have been invited to eat a family dinner with them. And, in the meantime, there are other enquiries which I wish to make. I think I shall pay a visit to the circulating library...

Chapter Eight

For anyone at all addicted to overhearing conversation and gossip, there is nowhere quite like a fashionable circulating library, for, among its shelves, rumours circulate quite as freely as novels and poems – and a great deal more freely than serious histories.

And it was, in part, this consideration which took Dido to the library at Richmond, while Flora completed some errands at the linen draper's shop. She wished most particularly to know whether Mrs Midgely's poison was spreading among the general population and, also, if she could discover it, whether the apothecary had been persuaded into pursuing his accusations.

The library was situated in a spacious, light room, well furnished with shelves of books, drawers of trinkets, and loitering readers. Sunlight fell in through the large windows, to make great squares of brightness on the wooden floor and raise a pleasant smell of warm leather from the bindings of the books. A cluster of smart officers was gathered by the door, more intent upon looking at young ladies than novels. And most of the young ladies in the place had been drawn away from the novels, the rings and the brooches, to gather in tight knots, pretend indifference, and whisper about officers.

Meanwhile, those women who had attained an age at which it is possible to remain unmoved by a red coat were occupied with the more serious business of the place: books – and gossip.

Dido wandered in among this last group, provided herself with a volume of *Moss Cliff Abbey* and, while pretending to read, listened intently to the talk around her. In the course of ten minutes she learnt a great deal. She heard: that there was a new preacher from Northamptonshire visiting Saint Mary's – who was expected to preach a very interesting sermon on Sunday, which would be 'all about the French and their terrible way of carrying on'; that 'Mr Vane, the apothecary, believes that Mr Lansdale killed his aunt'; that there was thieving carrying on in the shops of Richmond, with two bottles of eye tincture stolen from the apothecary and a whole ten yards of 'good yellow ribbon' from the haberdasher; that Sir Joshua Carrisbrook's new wife was 'Quite lovely! but just a bit of a girl, not half his age,' and, finally, that 'Mr Vane is gone to the magistrate today to tell him that Mr Lansdale poisoned his aunt…'

As this last piece of news burst upon her, Dido was just reaching the head of the room. There was a broad table here and a chair beside it, into which she sank as she watched the speaker – an elderly woman in a black gown – hurrying off to spread her tidings elsewhere.

It was just exactly what she had most dreaded hearing!

Her first thought was for Flora. She would be most dreadfully distressed. It was to be hoped that she had not heard it in the shops; that it could be kept from her for a little while at least. And her second thought was for justice. There was, when one looked into the case, so much to make Mr Lansdale appear guilty, that he was in grave danger of hanging even if – as she was more than half-inclined to believe – he was innocent. She must do everything in her power to prevent such a terrible mistake.

'It is altogether too shocking for words, the things people are saying about poor Mrs Lansdale!' said a voice from the other side of the table. 'Do you not agree, Miss Kent?'

Dido looked up to see Miss Merryweather, the lady who presided over the library. She was a remarkably refined woman. Her features were so refined that they seemed incapable of smiling and were fixed in an expression of strong sensibility. Her tightly curled hair was so refined that it did not stir when she moved her head, but rather clung about her face as if pasted in place. And as for her voice…it was positively tortured with refinement.

'I myself,' she whispered confidingly as she took her seat beside the table, 'I myself am *deeply* affected by the poor lady's death!'

'Oh!' said Dido, in some surprise. 'Were you acquainted with Mrs Lansdale, Miss Merryweather?'

'Oh yes! Vastly well acquainted!'

'Indeed! Then I suppose she visited the library rather often?'

'Oh no! Not at all. What I mean to say is, I had not actually *met* her – for she was quite an invalid, I understand – but, aside from that, I knew her very well indeed.'

'Did you?' said Dido, becoming more interested. 'I am not sure that I quite understand you.'

Miss Merryweather shook her head – without disturbing the clinging curls one iota. She pressed both hands to her breast. 'I knew her *heart*,' she declared in a refined whisper. 'I knew her heart.'

Dido was exceedingly diverted, but more at a loss than ever. 'And how,' she asked, 'did you gain such an intimate knowledge of the lady?'

'Why! From books of course!' cried Miss Merryweather, casting out her arms to indicate her shelves. 'From the books which she read. There is no surer way of knowing a person. The books which we choose, Miss Kent, are a veritable window upon our souls! A window upon our souls!'

'Are they?' cried Dido – aghast at how her own soul might appear when viewed through such a window.

'Oh yes!' Miss Merryweather folded her hands demurely upon the table and sighed feelingly.

Dido pondered upon this idea for a moment or two. 'And what do you know of Mrs Lansdale's soul?' she ventured to ask at last.

'Ah! She was full of tender feelings. For all they say of her being ill-tempered and illiberal, I know otherwise, Miss Kent, I know otherwise.'

'Do you?'

'Yes, I know that hers was a very sensitive soul. A large, sensitive soul. Love poems and romances! As soon as they were settled here, her nephew began to borrow books for her, and it was *always* love poems and romances. And the very last book which he took to her – not two days before the unfortunate lady died – was that greatest of all love stories: *Romeo and Juliet*.'

'Indeed!' Dido considered this. It was rather disturbing. In the weeks before she died, Mrs Lansdale had had romance on her mind. Had she been thinking only of fictional love…? Or did her view stretch further…? To Mr Henderson, perhaps…?

Meanwhile, Miss Merryweather was becoming confiding. She leant across her table. 'I, myself, do not spread gossip, Miss Kent,' she said, 'but I cannot help saying this – Mrs Lansdale had a larger, more sensitive soul than some of those persons that are now circulating rumours about her death.'

'Indeed?' Dido hesitated a moment – but decided that this was no time for excessive delicacy. 'You are referring perhaps to Mrs Midgely?' she said.

Miss Merryweather nodded significantly.

Dido was delighted. She too leant a little across the table. 'And what,' she asked very quietly, 'do you know about Mrs Midgely's soul?'

Miss Merryweather glanced around her domain at the dozen or so ladies standing and sitting about. Satisfied that they were all busy either with books or gossip, or officers, she lowered her voice. 'Mrs Midgely,' she said, 'no longer has a soul.'

'Has she not? How very…unusual. And how do you deduce it?'

'I deduce it from the fact, the palpable fact, that she no longer reads any books at all,' whispered Miss Merryweather. 'You see it used to be romances with her too. Not so many as Mrs Lansdale, but at least one a month. And then – after last November – nothing at all!' Miss Merryweather threw her hands into the air and then brought them together in a decisive clap. 'Nothing at all!' she repeated.

'That is very strange.'

'I, myself, have never known anything like it, Miss Kent. Never! To give up books!' She looked tenderly around her shelves, as if their occupants were innocent children, unaccountably spurned. 'I *cannot* think well of a woman who could do such a thing.'

'No,' said Dido soothingly, 'no, of course you cannot.'

For a moment or two poor Miss Merryweather was so overcome by her feelings she could say no more. She took a very large reticule from under the table, produced from it a very small handkerchief and applied it dramatically to her eyes. Meanwhile, Dido was considering her second motive for coming into the library – the torn book and the name of the library which she had found upon it.

'I wonder,' she ventured, when the handkerchief had been returned to the reticule and Miss Merryweather seemed to have recovered some measure of composure, 'what you would say about the other two ladies who live in Mrs Midgely's house: her ward, Miss Bevan – and her boarder, Miss Prentice?'

'Ah now!' cried Miss Merryweather with a softened expression. 'Miss Bevan is a *nice* girl. Very clever I think. We have not many books in French, but she has read every one of them. Every one! Apart from that, she is what I would, myself, call…straightforward. A very matter-of-fact young lady. No novels. She reads no novels at all. All very serious books.' She put her thumb and forefinger to her

80

brow as she considered. 'Doctor Johnson's essays...books on household management...travellers' accounts of the lake country. That sort of thing.'

'I see! How very interesting! And what,' asked Dido eagerly, 'what of Miss Prentice? What books does she read?'

'Ah yes! Miss Prentice...Dugdale's *Baronage*... Debrett's *Correct Peerage*... And...' Miss Merryweather frowned and put her finger and thumb to her brow once more. 'Something else which she took just the day before yesterday. I remember being a little surprised by it... Now, what was it?'

Dido waited, her mind full of those floating fragments with their long dull words. 'Was it perhaps a book of essays?' she prompted. 'History?'

'No, no. I do not think it was history. It was something that I do not remember any lady ever reading before. An old, thin book. A very *odd* thing. I do not know even how it came to be upon our shelves...' She pinched at her brow, screwed up her eyes in a great effort of remembering. 'I will have it in just a moment.' She pinched harder, closed her eyes entirely, and at last produced the title. '*A Treatise upon the Rights of Citizens*. That is it!' she said triumphantly. 'I can always recollect the name of a book if I only think a little while.'

'Indeed! That seems a very strange choice for a lady.'

'Very strange indeed, Miss Kent. And, for myself, I am convinced that poor Miss Prentice did not know what the book was. For, I thought when she came in that she was not looking quite herself – not at all well. And the book, you must understand, was not quite...' She leant confidingly across the table again and sunk her voice. 'I just looked into the thing myself... Just looked, you understand. I did not read far, for I saw straight away that it was not quite proper. It was written almost thirty years ago and was rather...' she leant closer and her lips formed the dreadful word *'revolutionary,'* almost in silence. 'I think,' she finished in a more natural tone, 'that the dear lady was a little distracted – and in a hurry too perhaps, for it was rather late in the afternoon. I am sure, myself, that she picked up the book quite inadvertently.'

Aloud Dido admitted that that was entirely possible. But, in private, she could not countenance it at all. There had been nothing inadvertent about the tearing up and throwing away of the pieces!

'And now, Miss Kent,' said Miss Merryweather, 'what kind of literature can we furnish you with today?'

'Oh!' Dido hesitated, remembered that window upon the soul, and quietly put aside *Moss Cliff Abbey*. 'I was wondering,' she said, 'whether you might have a volume of Doctor Fordyce's sermons.'

Chapter Nine

A revolutionary book! Why should little Miss Prentice concern herself with a revolutionary book? What possible difference could it make to her whether the volume rested quietly upon Miss Merryweather's shelves or sunk down into the mud of the Thames? This was so very great a puzzle that one could not possibly rest until an answer was found. It was entirely against human nature to be uncurious when so provoked! And, besides, Miss Prentice had taken the book late in the afternoon on the day before yesterday – when she was distracted and unwell – in short, immediately *after* she had heard of Mrs Midgely's visit to Knaresborough House! And, since that must argue for the destruction of the book bearing some relation to poor Mr Lansdale's extremely dangerous situation, it was a moral duty to solve the mystery, was it not?

All this ran so smoothly and rapidly through Dido's head as she walked down the steps from the library, that, by the time she gained the street, curiosity and virtue were very comfortably reconciled.

She stepped aside to avoid a pony carriage whose approach she had not noticed in her distraction, and stood a moment on the edge of the road, with people jostling past her and dusty heat breathing up from the pavement.

Now that Mr Vane had reported his misgivings to the magistrate everything was changed, she thought. Now the damage was done, the processes of justice had been set in motion and it would not suffice only to silence Mrs Midgely. Now it was absolutely *essential* to find out the whole truth.

And first she *must* find out what it was that connected Mrs Midgely, Mr Lansdale, Miss Prentice – and an improper book.

'Dido! I declare, there is the strangest look upon your face! Whatever are you thinking about?'

Flora was hurrying down from the linen draper's shop looking very concerned indeed.

'I am thinking about Miss Prentice.'

'Indeed? But I am sure I do not understand why you should be so concerned about *her* you would walk under the wheels of a chariot!'

'Do you not? Well, I shall tell you,' said Dido, 'but first of all I must call upon the bookseller.'

Dido took her cousin's arm and guided her across the street to the dark little shop of *Lister and Son, Stationers and Booksellers,* and would not say another word upon the matter until she had placed, with a rather shocked Mr Lister, an order for a copy of *A Treatise upon the Rights of Citizens.*

'Now,' she said as they emerged from the low shop door. 'Do not look so very worried, Flora. I am in no danger of becoming a Jacobin! I only wish to know what it is that Miss Prentice has been reading.'

'Miss Prentice has been reading a *treatise* about *citizens*?'

'It would seem she has.' Dido linked arms again and, as they threaded their way along the busy street, she told Flora all about the book and the river and Miss Merryweather's system of detecting souls – though she kept to herself the information which the lady in black had supplied.

Flora was all amazement. 'I would not have thought,' she said, wrinkling her nose, 'that two such women as Mrs Midgely and Miss Prentice could afford so much to puzzle over. I have known them for ever and I have always found them so very…ordinary.'

'And how long is "for ever" in this case?'

'Let me see…' Flora considered. They had left the shops behind them now and were come to the inn where the London coach was just drawing up with all its usual bustle. There was a green here and three broadly spreading horse-chestnuts, and they were both very glad to rest for a moment in the shade of these trees while all the busyness of Richmond flowed about them.

'I believe I have known Mrs Midgely for more than three years,' said Flora thoughtfully, 'but I have not known Miss Prentice so long. She came to Richmond this January last, you know; but James and I were not down from town until March.'

'I see.' Dido was disappointed to find that, in this case, Flora's eternity was so short, for she was anxious to learn as much as she might about the two ladies. 'Do you know,' she asked, 'how long Miss Prentice and Mrs Midgely have been acquainted with one another?'

'Oh yes. A great while. They were girls together you know – somewhere in Northamptonshire, I believe.'

'Hmm, I see.' Dido considered – the long acquaintance provided opportunity for a great many secrets between them… And yet they were so ill-matched one could not but wonder at their choosing to live under the same roof. 'Why do you suppose Mrs M decided to take her friend as a boarder?' she asked. 'Do you suppose that she has found herself a little short of money since the death of her husband?'

'No, I do not suppose any such thing!' cried Flora. 'I don't doubt Mrs Midgely has money enough – and to spare – but the dreadful woman takes a great deal more pleasure in saving money than she ever does in spending it, you know.'

'And so you believe it was her love of economy which made her let her back parlour?'

'I do indeed! Why I remember just how it was last autumn when she made up her mind to it. "That back room is wasted," she said again and again, "quite *wasted*. And it might be let very nicely if only all the old books and papers of the colonel's were cleared out of it. And there is a bedroom too," she said, "beyond the two that are needed for me and Mary. And I cannot abide *waste*!" I declare, it was all about avoiding waste!'

'I see. And do you suppose,' continued Dido thoughtfully as they left the inn and started to walk slowly up the hill, 'do you suppose that this sending out of Miss Bevan to be a governess is also a matter of economy?'

'Ah! Now that is a very strange business indeed. I cannot make it out at all.'

'Why not?'

'Well, it has all come about so very suddenly. There was

not a single word spoken about it until last November, you know. Not a word. But suddenly it was all, "she must make her own way in the world". And Mrs Midgely was looking out for a place for her. Everyone was surprised by it – and I am sure the dear colonel himself would *never* have countenanced such a measure. It is quite shocking that she should go against her husband's wishes – and so soon after his death too!'

'Ah!' said Dido, 'Miss Bevan, I presume, is a relation of the colonel – not of his wife?'

'Yes. At least she is a *connection* of the colonel's. No relation I think. Her father was an officer in his regiment and the colonel thought particularly well of the young man – there is some story about a camp fever – the colonel did not believe he would have survived without the attentions of Lieutenant Bevan. Something of that sort, you know. But I do not remember the details.'

'And so, when the little girl was orphaned, the colonel undertook her care? How very kind!'

'He was the kindest, most generous man in the world! And as unlike his wife as you can possibly imagine!'

Dido continued some way in silence, intrigued by this picture of the late Colonel Midgely – and surprised too. Somehow she had always imagined a husband as small-minded and illiberal as his wife.

And as for Mrs Midgely's character, she could not make that out at all. Cold-hearted and over-fond of money she certainly appeared, but there was nothing in all this to show why she should so dislike a rich and handsome young man such as Mr Lansdale. Indeed women of Mrs Midgely's stamp were usually but too inclined to seek the favour of the rich and powerful…

At last she stopped in the shade of an old pear tree which hung over a high garden wall. They were come now almost to Mrs Midgely's house and, looking at its shaded windows and dark, sunless garden, Dido sighed. 'There is only one thing I am able to conclude about Mrs Midgely,' she said. 'It would seem that Miss Merryweather is correct – the woman *did* lose her soul last November and it is that which is making her behave so very strangely.'

'Well,' said Flora comfortably, 'we need not worry about the tiresome woman any longer. Your charming Mr Lomax is quite sure that Mr Lansdale is in no danger.'

'Yes…' Dido was confused – partly from finding herself given possession of the gentleman, and partly from the memory of what she had lately heard in the library, which led her to suspect that Mr Lansdale was, in fact, in a great deal of danger. 'Yes,' she said, 'of course, we must hope that there will be no prosecution… But, I wish that I could understand Mrs Midgely a little better. How much does she know about events at Knaresborough House?'

Flora looked troubled and Dido's heart smote her. Hurting Flora seemed as wicked as hurting a child. 'There is, of course,' she added hastily, 'nothing to worry about. Nothing at all. But I think I may perhaps just call upon Mrs Midgely…since we are so close now to her house.'

'You will not find her at home,' said Flora frowning. 'For I saw her just now in the town.'

'Oh.' Dido was disappointed. But, in a moment, her mind had picked up one of the many other threads of the mystery. A new idea slipped into her head. 'Then perhaps I will take the opportunity of calling upon

Miss Bevan while she is alone,' she said.

In order to prevent any further questions, she began to walk quickly towards Mrs Midgely's grim little villa. But, as they passed the gates of Knaresborough House, something caught her eye. There was a movement by the bushes near the back of the house. Her curiosity was piqued. She stopped.

'What are you looking at?' asked Flora.

Dido waved a hand to silence her. 'Look,' she whispered, 'there on the path of Mr Lansdale's house. There are two women. Is not one of them Miss Neville?'

'Yes, I believe it is; but...'

'Who is the woman she is talking to?'

'I do not know, I am sure! Why...'

'Hush! they are coming towards us.'

The two women had emerged now from the shadow of the bushes into the bright sunshine. They walked slowly towards the front of the house. One of them was, indeed, Miss Clara Neville – looking as tall and bony and as discontent as ever – and the other was a stout woman in a grey gown and a shabby straw bonnet. They were too deep in earnest conversation to notice that they were being watched, and, when they came to the gravel of the sweep, they stopped. The stout woman thrust out her hand and Miss Neville put something into it. The woman frowned, said something – and walked away. Miss Neville turned back to the house.

'Now,' said Dido, drawing Flora further into the shadow of the gatepost, 'I wonder what they were talking about.'

They moved a few steps along the road as the woman approached the end of the sweep, but then, as she turned into the road, they stopped and looked back at her. She had a plump face, red and shining with the heat, and blemished with a great many broken veins. She was now smiling as she looked down at what she held in her hand. But it was not a pleasant smile.

'Why! What an ugly, trollopy-looking creature!' whispered Flora as the woman walked off. 'Do you suppose she was come to beg?'

'I do not know,' said Dido thoughtfully. 'But she had not the look nor the manner of a beggar.'

'No,' agreed Flora. 'And I am sure Clara Neville has nothing to spare for giving away to chance-comers.'

'Hmm,' said Dido as she watched the plump woman hurry along the shady road. 'Is Miss Neville so very poor?'

'Oh dear, yes! I have known her and her mother for ever. They have barely enough to live on, you know, and cannot even afford a proper servant. I believe Mrs Lansdale paid Miss Neville an allowance while she lived with her – but I think it was very small.'

'Indeed,' mused Dido. 'Then that is very strange indeed.'

'Why do you say so?'

'Because I am almost sure that it was a guinea which that woman was holding in her hand just now.' She paused and shook her head. 'Why would an impoverished lady like Miss Neville give so large a sum to such a very rough-looking woman?'

Chapter Ten

Dido found Miss Bevan sitting alone at the pianoforte in the dismal front parlour of Mrs Midgely's house, where the blinds were half-closed to prevent the sun injuring the furniture, every inch of carpet was covered with green baize, and a grim, hook-nosed old fellow in military dress stared down disapprovingly from his dark frame above the fireplace. It might be high summer beyond the walls, but here within Mrs Midgely's domain it was winter: a settled chill filled the room, together with the lingering smell of old coal fires.

Mary's greeting was pleasant and well-mannered and she fell into conversation easily enough; but there was something wary in her look – as if, perhaps, she suspected the motive of the visit. As they exchanged remarks about the weather, Dido studied her face. It was undoubtedly pretty, but the dark hair was dressed with unbecoming plainness, as if Mary had already chosen to adopt that self-effacing style which would be expected of her in her future life. And there was, besides, a pallor and thinness which spoke of sleepless nights and ill-health.

She was clearly anxious about something. Of course, with her future so unsettled, anxiety was quite natural;

but certain things she had noticed were beginning to make Dido suspect that Miss Bevan might have something else upon her mind...

'I am sorry,' began Dido after a short pause in the conversation, 'I am extremely sorry to find that we are soon to lose you from our society here in Richmond.'

'You are very kind.' As she spoke, Miss Bevan lowered her eyes with a sad smile.

'I hope that you will be settled with an agreeable family.'

'Thank you, Miss Kent.' There was a very serious little shake of the head. 'But, in truth, I cannot believe that the agreeableness of the family will be of much consequence, can you? At least it would be a very remarkable family in which the life of the governess herself could be described as agreeable.'

Startled by the young lady's honesty, Dido was forced to consider the governesses she had known, including her own, rather fearsome Miss Steerforth, who had not led a very easy life in their household.

'No,' she said, humbled by the memory of her own youthful transgressions, 'perhaps you are right.' They sat for a while in silence. 'I have heard you sing and play, Miss Bevan,' she said at last, 'and know how very accomplished you are. I am sure you will have no difficulty in securing a position.'

'Thank you.' Miss Bevan looked away, ran her fingers absently over the keys of the instrument.

'You are now searching for a place?'

'Yes.'

'Where have you made enquiries?'

'There are places...' Miss Bevan, paused, took her hand from the pianoforte and smiled wryly. 'There are places in town where enquiries can be made,' she said, 'offices that exist solely to deal in this...trade.' Colour mounted in her cheeks. She clasped her arms across her breast and stood up abruptly. 'We may hope, Miss Kent,' she said with great feeling, 'that our government will soon put an end to the barbarous trade in men and women which is carried on in the West Indies, but I doubt the abolitionists will ever set themselves against the governess trade. Here in England, even though women are not themselves for sale, I fear their *accomplishments* always will be.'

She stopped herself and stood in silence looking down at her feet. Then she drew a long breath and raised her eyes to Dido's. 'I am very sorry. I should not have spoken so violently. I hope you will forgive my outburst.'

'Of course,' said Dido gently. 'I am the one at fault. You are tired and anxious and I should not have asked so many questions. Besides, your feelings are entirely natural.' In order to give her companion time to collect herself, she rose, went to the instrument and began to turn over the music which lay upon it, making an inconsequential comment or two upon the pieces – and noticing, at the same time, that these songs were written in a neat, businesslike hand which put no loops at all upon its letters.

But Miss Bevan's little outburst had quickened her interest in the girl.

Once, a few days ago, Dido had made some passing remark to Flora, saying that Miss Bevan was a shy, quiet girl; but Flora had laughed. 'Oh no!' she had said, 'I declare it is only when she is at home with her guardian that she seems so. When we met her at Ramsgate, in the autumn, she was lively enough! She was staying with her friends the Hemmingways, you know – the pleasantest, merriest people in the world – and then she was very different: she played, she danced and she talked a great deal.'

At the time, this character had surprised Dido greatly; but now, as she looked at Miss Bevan, standing beside the pianoforte, just brushing the keys again with the tips of her fingers, it was brought more within her comprehension. Now she could not doubt that there was a great deal of feeling here – and the ability to express it. And there was, furthermore, something intriguing in the way in which the girl looked so directly as she spoke – and spoke with such startling honesty – and yet had such an air of reserve. Dido was convinced that, though she might avoid uttering falsehoods, Mary Bevan might yet have the knack of keeping a great many truths unspoken.

Meanwhile Miss Bevan herself was beginning to suspect her visitor's desultory interest in waltz tunes and Irish airs.

'Miss Kent,' she said gravely, looking up from the instrument, to gaze very directly at Dido. 'I would by no means wish you to think me ungrateful for your visit. I am very happy to see you. However,' the hint of a smile flashed across her pale face, 'I cannot help but feel there is some particular reason for your calling – some motive for your seeking me out alone.' She paused, her brows raised questioningly. 'If there is some such motive, I beg you will bring it forward immediately, for

I do not think we shall have this room to ourselves for very long.'

Dido stared, disconcerted. Here was a much more astute observer than little Miss Prentice, or any of the others she had so far questioned. Her mind raced in search of excuses…

And then, all at once, she decided to abandon pretence. She would state her case honestly – and see how her honesty was received…

She confessed her purpose – her desire of discovering the truth behind the rumours which were circulating about Mr Lansdale – watching her companion's face very closely as she did so. There was certainly a little start from Miss Bevan when the subject was introduced, a look of consciousness; but perhaps that arose only from shame at her connection with Mrs Midgely, for, although Dido took care not to mention that lady's name, Miss Bevan could not help but know her guardian was the culprit.

However, by the time the explanation was complete, Mary was smiling composedly. 'Well,' she said, 'I wish you success with your enquiries, Miss Kent. And I am very glad that you have told me of your purpose. For now, if I happen to see you going about this business, I shall not think you guilty of idle curiosity!'

'Thank you.' Dido laughed. 'For, though I know that I am frequently guilty of curiosity, I sincerely hope that it is *never* idle.'

'And now,' said Mary, sitting down in one of the straight-backed chairs and folding her hands neatly in her lap. 'I am entirely at your service. You may catechise me as you choose! How can I help you in this very serious undertaking?'

Dido considered for a moment and then began with: 'Miss Prentice is certain that Mr Henderson visited the Lansdales on the evening that Mrs Lansdale died. Do you know if she is remembering correctly?'

Miss Bevan frowned thoughtfully. 'I remember her calling out that she had seen him walking to the door,' she said very precisely.

'But you did not see him yourself?'

'No, he was gone when I came to the window.'

'I see. Did you know that Mr Henderson was acquainted with Mrs Lansdale?'

'No, I did not. But, my dear Miss Kent, I do not know anything about Mr Henderson.'

'Oh? But you were a little acquainted with his daughters, I believe?'

Mary looked uncomfortable. 'A very little,' she said with a slight blush. 'I should not have known them of course – there had been no introduction. But somehow, I hardly know how, we became a little acquainted.'

Dido looked at her in some surprise. 'I see,' she said. 'Did you visit the young ladies?'

'Oh no.' Mary looked down at her hands. 'I could not visit them because…Mrs Midgely would not have liked them. But I would meet them occasionally when they were walking in the park – and we would sometimes take a turn together.'

'I see.' Dido longed to know why Mrs Midgely should have disliked the girls, but it would be too impertinent to ask. 'And what kind of young ladies were they? Miss Prentice says that she thinks they were pretty.'

'Dear Miss Prentice! I doubt she ever saw their faces!

But I do not suppose that she would ever call anyone ill-looking.'

'Perhaps not,' agreed Dido with a smile.

'They were very accomplished girls,' Mary continued thoughtfully. 'Quite remarkably accomplished. They all three spoke very pretty French – and I think Miss Margaret had a grounding in Italian too. And Miss Henderson seemed to have a *very* sound understanding of music.'

'I am surprised that their father could have afforded them such an education. I understand that he was living in rather straitened circumstances while he was here in Richmond.'

Mary bit her lip. 'Is that the opinion of Miss Prentice?' she asked.

'Yes. The circumstance of his giving no dinners and keeping only evening company did not escape her observation.'

'No, I imagine it would not. And she is quite correct – there were a great many evening parties.' As she spoke these last words a strange look came over Miss Bevan's face. It was difficult to make it out clearly in the gloomy parlour, but it seemed almost to be...distaste. She clasped her arms about her as if she was cold. 'At these parties I do not doubt Mr Henderson was well able to display the girls' *accomplishments*.'

'You think he was very anxious to get his daughters married?'

'What would you suppose to be the motive of a man who has three unmarried women on his hands?'

'I would indeed suppose it to be matrimony. But...' Dido studied her companion rather anxiously. She was sitting with her arms clasped across her breast, her eyes troubled and downcast. 'But the idea does not disgust me as it seems to disgust you.'

'I am sorry,' replied Mary, unclasping her arms and trying to smile. 'In such matters anything contrived or mercenary...'

'You suspect that Mr Henderson was mercenary and worldly in his schemes?'

Mary coloured. 'Yes,' she said. 'I believe he was...But I am being foolish! No doubt, Miss Kent, I am merely reminded of my own situation. Like me the Henderson girls were poor and must rely upon their charms and their accomplishments to make their fortunes.'

Dido was concerned by her look of abhorrence. Such extreme delicacy did not promise well for the future happiness of a girl so ill-provided. 'Marriage,' she said gently, 'is generally considered to be the pleasantest preservative from want for women of small fortune.'

'Yes.' Mary unclasped her arms, seemed to resolve upon appearing unconcerned. 'And sometimes I am inclined to agree with the general opinion.'

'But sometimes you disagree with it?'

'Sometimes,' she said, 'sometimes I think that it is better to be a governess – better to be even a teacher in a school – than to...marry a man one does not care for.'

'I see.' Dido considered this carefully for several minutes – and remembered too what she had learnt of Miss Bevan's 'soul' in the library. 'But,' she said at last, 'what if one does care for the man? What if one cares for him very much indeed?'

Miss Bevan met her gaze, with an appearance, at least, of calm. 'To marry for love,' she said quietly, 'is a different matter entirely.'

Chapter Eleven

'Flora,' said Dido at they dawdled over the sunny breakfast table next morning, 'what do you know of the Henderson girls who used to live at Knaresborough House?'

'Nothing at all. I have told you before, the family was already gone from Richmond when we came down from town.'

'So I suppose you cannot tell me why Mrs Midgely might have disliked them.'

'Oh yes, I am sure I can tell you that!' replied Flora eagerly. She set down her teacup. 'They were, I daresay, pretty.'

'And you think that was the cause of her dislike?'

'Most certainly. She was a very jealous wife, you know. When the poor colonel was alive he was scarcely allowed to talk to a pretty girl. Mrs Midgely always avoided the acquaintance of pretty young women.'

'This argues a very great degree of jealousy. Was she really so very bad?'

'Oh yes! My dear Dido, you have to remember what a *very* fine man the colonel was – and he was several years younger than his wife, you know.'

'I cannot remember him at all. I never met the man.'

'Oh! But you have only to look at the portrait above the mantelpiece in Mrs Midgely's parlour to see…'

'To see what?'

'Well, to see that he was a great deal more handsome than his wife ever was! It was the most ill-matched marriage in the world!'

'Mrs Midgely was not pretty when she was young?'

Flora hesitated. 'Her fortune was too good for her ever to be considered positively *plain*,' she said.

'I see.'

Dido lapsed into thoughtful silence over her egg-shells. And Flora watched her a little uneasily. 'I am sure I do not understand why you should still be asking so many questions, Dido. Dear Mr Lomax is *quite sure* that Mrs Midgely can do Mr Lansdale no harm. He does not think that Mr Vane will go to the magistrate – and even if he does…'

'Well, if, by any ill-chance he does, it might perhaps be a good thing if we were…a little prepared.'

'Oh well!' cried Flora, 'I suppose it can do no harm. Though I declare it is a great shame that you should have so much trouble for nothing.' She shrugged up her shoulders and began to open the letters which had been left beside her plate.

The room was quiet for a while except for Flora reading out the occasional snatch of news or invitation from her letters – none of which was of much interest to Dido, until the last item. And this was a letter from Sir Joshua Carrisbrook – a letter of supplication.

It seemed that the poor knight and his lady were so plagued with a superfluity of strawberries that they must implore a party of their friends to come to their assistance. If only they would have the goodness to come, gather and eat as much of the troublesome fruit as they could, then they would be rewarded with spruce beer and a cold collation in the dining room of Brooke Manor.

'So you see,' smiled Flora, laying down the letter, 'on Tuesday you will be able to see your delightful Mr Lomax again – and spend a whole day in his company!'

Dido, who had already thought as much herself, endeavoured to look as if the invitation was of no great importance to her. 'It will be very pleasant to go to Brooke, I am sure,' she said demurely. 'I have a great desire to see the new Lady Carrisbrook and to discover whether she is so excessively young and beautiful as she is reported… And of course I shall be glad to see Mr Lomax too.'

Flora laughed and was about to say more, but fortunately for Dido, they were interrupted. The maid announced a visitor and, a moment later, Mrs Midgely hurried into the breakfast room – full of self-importance, and news.

'My dear Mrs Beaumont, Miss Kent, have you heard? Have you heard what has happened?'

Dido and Flora stared blankly at their visitor. This morning she was dressed in pink, spotted muslin and there were also two spots of pink upon each cheek – one the product of art and one beside it which was the result of emotion.

'Knaresborough House has been burgled,' she announced, before they could even gratify her by admitting their ignorance.

'Burgled!' they both echoed.

It had occurred to Dido that the news might be connected with that house – though she could not have foreseen burglary. For a moment she was too lost in surprise to say more.

But, in a crisis, Flora could be relied upon to make a well-mannered reply. 'Oh dear! Oh, how very distressing,' she cried. 'I do hope that Mr Lansdale has not lost anything of value.'

'As to that,' said Mrs Midgely reluctantly, 'no, I do not believe that he has. For he was roused by a noise and found the man, Fraser, already in pursuit of the thieves.' She frowned; two ill-natured little lines appeared above her nose. The spots of natural colour deepened. 'I do not believe they took anything at all,' she admitted.

But, thought Dido, she would dearly love to report that Mr Lansdale's losses were heavy. 'How did the thieves gain entrance to the house?' she asked.

'Through a window in the drawing room,' said Mrs Midgely eagerly. 'The window beside the front door. They broke open the catch upon it. And they left in the same way. When Mr Lansdale came into the room the window was wide open and, it seems, Fraser saw them escaping through it. Two big, rough-looking fellows, he says. And a great mess they had left behind them in the drawing room,' she added brightly. 'Drawers torn open and things thrown everywhere.'

'Indeed?' cried Dido. 'And are you quite sure that they took nothing at all? What of the candlesticks? Were they not stolen?'

'No, I do not think so.'

'But they are of good, solid silver! Very valuable.

102

Why would any thieves disregard such things and begin searching elsewhere? Unless…' she stopped, frowning thoughtfully.

Neither of her companions took much notice of her question. They were both too occupied in either lamenting or rejoicing over the business. But, later that morning, when Mrs Midgely had hurried away to spread the glad tidings and Flora was shut up with her mantua-maker, Dido had the breakfast room to herself, and she was able to sit down quietly to consider it all.

She sat in the sun which was flooding through the french doors, fixed her eyes upon a robin bobbing about upon the veranda, and gave herself up to very serious thought.

First she considered Mrs Midgely's glee over the burglary. It had been so very marked! She had positively delighted in it. What was one to make of this fresh evidence of the woman's dislike of Henry Lansdale?

And the burglary itself was a very strange business! Why, Dido wondered, had such valuable goods as the candlesticks been left untouched? Was it possible that the two 'big rough-looking fellows' had come not simply to plunder but to search for something particular – something which they did not seem to have found?

Well, she thought with a little shake of her head, perhaps it would all prove to be no more than a thing of chance, unconnected with Mrs Lansdale's death. After all, the very appearance of Knaresborough House spoke wealth loudly enough to tempt a thief. But somehow she could not quite think that it would prove to be a matter of chance. She could not quite forget Mrs Midgley's description of the drawing room – the evidence that a search had been made.

She was becoming restless now. She must *do* something... Perhaps she would just walk out to look at Knaresborough House – call upon Miss Prentice, perhaps. There must be more discoveries to be made about this burglary.

She jumped up and fetched her bonnet from her bedchamber – then hesitated upon the stairs. Mr Lomax might call on them again today – call while she was out. She half-turned – nearly took the bonnet back.

But, with so many important questions filling her head she did not think she could bear to sit quietly at home – even for Mr Lomax... She would not be away long... If he called, Flora would be sure to detain him until she returned.

She put on the bonnet and set off.

Chapter Twelve

Miss Prentice was delighted to receive another visit from Miss Kent: it was so remarkably kind of her to call; she did not know how to thank her enough; it was so very…

As Dido entered the gloomy little parlour, half-blinded after the brilliance of the sunshine, Miss Prentice was sitting at a corner of the large desk and very busy about settling her accounts; but she immediately swept her papers together, put them into the deep, scarred drawer of the desk and, after struggling a moment with its broken lock, succeeded in shutting them out of sight. Then she unhooked her spectacles from her ears and turned gratefully to her favourite seat beside the window.

Dido was particularly glad to follow her and to sit down there, for her chief motive in coming was that she might look at Knaresborough House unobserved. And it was very convenient indeed to sit in the dark room, listening with half an ear to Miss Prentice's chatter and looking out at the big house.

The sun was shining warmly upon the house-front, and gleaming upon its windows. There were, Dido noticed, three ground floor windows upon each side of the door. They were all casement windows and cut rather low down to the ground. And the one just to the left of the door – the one through which the burglars had broken – was particularly conveniently placed: close to the front steps. It could have been climbed through with the greatest of ease.

As she watched – and Miss Prentice talked about Sir Hugo Wyat's new curricle and Sir Joshua Carrisbrook's nuptials – a tall thin workman in a very long white apron appeared at the front of Knaresborough House and set to work upon mending the broken catch of the window. She watched him for several minutes and then took the next opportunity of a slight pause in her companion's talk to say, 'My cousin and I were extremely concerned to hear of Mr Lansdale's latest misfortune.'

'Ah!' said Miss Prentice with a little frown. 'I daresay Susan has told you all about it.'

'Yes, she has. She was with us before we had finished our breakfast this morning.'

'Oh dear,' fretted Miss Prentice, 'Susan has a thousand good qualities, I am sure, but I wish she was not quite so fond of spreading ill-tidings. It is so very...'

'It is only her way, I am sure,' said Dido, seizing upon the opening, 'but I cannot help but wonder... I wonder whether she may have a particular dislike of Mr Lansdale. She seemed almost pleased to convey this news of the burglary.'

Miss Prentice sighed deeply. 'I confess, I have thought as much myself, Miss Kent. But I know of no reason *why* she should dislike the young man. For he seems – from everything we hear about him – to be a remarkably *good* young gentleman. We hear nothing against him – his behaviour is unexceptionable and his opinions sound.' She paused, shook her head. 'If they were not, if it should appear that he had unsound opinions, or *progressive* ideas, then I should not wonder at her dislike. For she has quite a horror of progressive ideas – she always has. And, of course, I agree… But Mr Lansdale is a very proper young man.'

'Yes, I am sure he is.'

They sat in silence for a while, Dido watching the workman at the window and Miss Prentice watching a very smart carriage with a coat of arms upon its door.

'I wonder,' said Dido at last, 'whether you happened to notice any strangers approaching Knaresborough House yesterday evening – or anything which might be connected with the housebreaking?'

'Yesterday evening? No, I do not remember seeing anything at all. But Mary was with me again yesterday evening. She often sits with me after dinner now.'

Dido was about to ask her more, when she noticed that the man had finished repairing the window latch and was beginning to pack his tools away into his bag. She rose hastily, took her leave and was – by only loitering in the street a few minutes – just in time to accidentally fall in with him as he reached the gates of Knaresborough House.

'I am very glad to see that you have restored the catch of Mr Lansdale's window,' she remarked, 'for one cannot be too careful with such villains about in the neighbourhood.'

'Ah well now, miss, as to that,' said the man, shifting his canvas bag of tools from one shoulder to the other and looking exceedingly wise, 'as to that, I reckon you're right. Can't be too careful.'

'Do you suppose,' she asked, 'that it was very difficult to break into the house? Was the catch upon the window very strong?'

'Well…no… As to that, it'd only take one really good hard push of that window to break the catch.'

'So,' mused Dido, 'the burglar would not have needed any sort of tool to break it open?'

'No, Miss. There weren't no kind of tool or bar used to break that open. I'd have seen the mark of it on the window frame if there'd been anything like that.'

'I see. Thank you very much for explaining it to me.'

The man walked away, but Dido remained in the shadow of the gateposts a little while, contemplating the front of Knaresborough House.

Its shutters were open now that the first stage of mourning was over. In the thick creeper that covered one corner of the building, swallows were busy about their nests. It was a very pleasant, respectable prospect.

But there were secrets hidden here. She was sure of it… There was certainly something very odd indeed about this burglary…

She shook her head at the house. What did it have to hide? And how could one penetrate such respectability, to come at the truth? She dared not approach its door and question its master. Nor could she think of any reason to enter the kitchens and pursue her enquiries among the servants. And how else was she to discover anything? It seemed an impossibility.

However, as Dido's governess used frequently to remind her, we should 'despair of nothing we would attain' as 'unwearied diligence our point would gain'. And, though there might appear to be little diligence in only sighing over the view of a house-front – or at least none which the redoubtable Miss Steerforth would have valued – Dido almost immediately saw an answer to her question: a means of penetration and discovery.

Kneeling in the shadows by the corner of the house was young Sam, engaged in pulling weeds out of the sweep.

She walked over to him, bade him good morning and exchanged a few remarks upon the warmth of the day, the likelihood of there being thunder before long and the persistence with which groundsel grew in gravel.

'It makes a great deal of work for you, Sam. Are you employed here all the time now?'

'Oh no, miss, I only come to do jobs now and then – like burying the dog, and helping Pa fix that new name plate on the gate, and pulling up the weeds sometimes.'

'Is there no regular gardener employed about the place?'

'No miss,' he sat back on his heels and took a welcome rest. 'There's precious few servants here at all.'

'Yes,' said Dido, recalling the clumsy maid, 'I had observed as much. Why is the house so ill-served?'

'Well miss, I reckon the land-agent only keeps on Mr Fraser while the house is empty. And then, when the house is let out, Mr Fraser gets folk in by the day to do the work.'

'I see,' said Dido, making the best of her opening. 'That woman I have seen about here then: a large woman

109

in a grey dress and a straw bonnet. I have seen her here talking to Miss Neville. She comes to help in the kitchen I daresay.'

Sam shook his head so hard the damp hair fell down into his eyes. 'Oh no,' he said, 'that's Jenny White you mean, miss. Mr Fraser wouldn't have her sort working in the house.'

'Oh! Then what is her business here?'

'I don't know, miss, honest I don't. I wish I did.' He looked troubled. It was a fact which Dido had frequently observed that labouring people did not like to see their betters valuing anyone beyond their deserts. 'I reckon it's very odd the way Miss Neville lets her come around here and doesn't send her away. Because Miss Neville must know what Jenny White is as well as any one else.'

'And what is Miss White?' asked Dido with great interest.

'She's a bad lot, miss, that's what she is. She's been in prison. Been in prison a good long while. And my Pa says she was lucky the judge was a soft one or it would've been transporting for sure.'

'I see, and why was she sent to prison, Sam?'

'Well, you see, miss, Jenny White is a laundress...'

'And an excellent name she has for one of that profession!'

Sam gave her a puzzled look. 'But the point is, miss, every house Jenny worked in got burgled. And at the trial it all came out how she was working for a gang of housebreakers. Telling them all she could about locks and jewels and when the family were going to be away for the evening. That kind of thing you know, miss.'

'How very shocking!'

'It was, miss, and Pa says she'd have been transported for sure – or even hanged – but she made the judge believe she was frightened of the gang. Said she only did what she did because they made her. But Pa reckons…'

Unluckily, just at that moment, there came the sound of the house door opening. They looked up and there was Fraser standing on the step – watching them severely.

'I'm sorry miss,' said Sam, shuffling a little along the gravel and attacking a dandelion, 'I'd better be about my work.'

Reluctantly Dido walked away – and felt Fraser's disapproval staring at her back all the way to the sweep gates. She made her way home slowly, reflecting upon what a very remarkable thing it was, that she should have seen Miss Neville talking with – paying – a woman known to associate with criminals and that, the very next day, they should hear that Knaresborough House had been burgled.

Flora was still above stairs when Dido returned. And there was no sound of visitors. As she entered the hall she looked immediately to the table at the foot of the stairs – to see if any caller had left a card.

There was no card, but there were several letters just come from the post office. She picked them up – and found among them a letter addressed to herself in an unfamiliar hand.

She paused, her bonnet in her hand, its ribbons trailing on the floor, the heat of the morning cooling on her cheeks. She turned the letter over thoughtfully: studied its direction. It was not written in a flowing script, but in separated letters – as if it were the work of a child – or a person of little education.

Frowning to herself, she laid down her bonnet and carried the letter into the bright little breakfast room where everything was fresh and clean from the housemaid's hands and the french doors stood open upon the garden. She sat down and broke the seal.

There was but one sheet of paper and only a few lines written in the same clumsy letters.

Dear Miss Kent

You wish to discover what happened at Knaresborough House, but I think you had better not. There are some people of whom it may truly be said, 'The world is not their friend, nor the world's laws.' I beg you would remember it.

There was no name, no signature.

Chapter Thirteen

...As you may imagine, Eliza, we have puzzled over this letter a great deal. The writing is so remarkably ill-done that Flora believes it to be the work of a servant or someone of the sort. But I cannot agree with her. For, although it is written badly, the words are spelt very correctly and they are not such words, or expressions, as a person of no education would use. In short, I believe it to be the work of a man or woman who could write a fair hand if they wished, but did not choose to do so for fear of being recognised by it. Which suggests it is the work of someone well known to me.

It would seem that some acquaintance of mine knows the truth about Mrs Lansdale's death and is advising me not to enquire into it.

And then there is the quotation. Is the line at all familiar to you, Eliza? I am almost certain that it is from Shakespeare. But you know how I am about the great bard – I never can remember the names of his characters or plays. And I find that Flora has not a single volume of his work! Please tell me of any ideas that you have – and you might ask Catherine's opinion too, for she was more lately in a schoolroom than either of us.

I would dearly love to know just who it is that must

be supposed unfriended by the world and its laws. I have determined to ask everyone that I can about it – not only for the sake of discovering the meaning, but also so that I may watch for consciousness in the speaker.

Well, Eliza, I shall make no more apology for busying myself about this mystery. I consider that this strange letter, by seeking to prevent me, authorises me to proceed. For it proves beyond doubt, that there is _something_ to find out. And I very much fear that it might be something which will put Mr Lansdale in greater danger.

Though I regret that I still cannot determine even whether the greatest mystery lies in the cause of Mrs Lansdale's death – or the reason for Mr Lansdale having such an enemy as Mrs Midgely.

Why is she so vehement against him? I confess that I cannot make out her character at all; which is extremely vexing. For I had thought that my two weeks acquaintance was quite sufficient to see to the bottom of such a woman and it is just too provoking to discover that a fat woman who wears rouge and yellow muslin may have a deep and complicated character! There are so many things about her which I cannot understand. There is, besides this unkindness to Henry Lansdale, her sudden decision to send Miss Bevan away...

I say as little as I may about all this to Flora, for I do not wish to distress her. But I hope you will forgive me for troubling you about it all, for it is such a very great help to me to write down my ideas.

I must break off in a moment, for it is almost time for church – we are to go today to St Mary's to hear the Reverend Mr Hewit, who is, by all accounts, a very fine preacher and is to preach here for two Sundays only before travelling north *to take up a new parish. It seems the reverend gentleman has spent some years in France and everyone is in high hopes of a spirited tirade against the iniquities of that country.*

But, before I close, there is one more matter with which I wish, most particularly, to trouble you: the window at Knaresborough House.

I spoke with the man who mended it. And, Eliza, he was quite certain that no tool had been used to break the catch: that the damage had been done only by pushing – and do you see what this means?

I am almost sure that the windows in the drawing room at Knaresborough are like every other casement that I ever saw – I mean, they open <u>outwards</u>. In short, if the window was broken open by pushing, then I think it must have been broken open not from outside the house but <u>from within the room</u>.

So, this morning, in between puzzling over my letter and considering all the obscurities of Mrs Midgely's character, I must think about the burglary too. Do you see what a multitude of demands there are upon a woman's attention when once she sets herself to this business of solving mysteries?

I cannot cease to wonder about the window. Is it possible that someone within Knaresborough House admitted the burglars? And, if so, was that person Miss Clara Neville...

It being a Sunday, it was perhaps not quite right to be so busy about puzzles and secrets. Though, when she came to consider the matter, Dido could not *recall* any laws in the bible forbidding the solving of mysteries on the Sabbath. It seemed to be a point upon which holy writ was silent.

However, she was quite certain that she was straying

from the strict path of virtue by allowing her mind to range over broken window catches, corrupted laundresses and unsigned notes during divine service itself. And, as she sat beside Flora in their high-sided pew, she did strive most earnestly to rein in her thoughts to proper contemplation and devotion. But it was exceedingly difficult for just across the worn flags of the aisle, shut into another crowded pew, was Mr Vane himself – providing her with an opportunity for contemplation of a very unreligious kind.

Sunshine was flooding into the nave of the church through the old leaded windows, very bright against the plain white plaster of the ceiling and the colourful coats and gowns and bonnets of the congregation. And one ray of light was falling directly upon Mr Vane, lighting him up as if he were an actor upon a stage – though whether he should play a hero or a villain, Dido found hard to determine.

He was certainly not an ill-looking man. Indeed he had a rather handsome face – though it was too broad and habitually smiling to suit her taste. He had a kind of polished look, a gleam of self-satisfaction – and ingratiation.

He was a very ingratiating man.

She had first caught sight of him this morning in the churchyard. A black, bowing figure moving restlessly about among the bright colours of the gathering ladies, repeatedly baring his shining fair hair to the sun as he swept the hat from his head. He attended, she noticed, exclusively to wealthy widows – constantly smiling his care and concern at them.

Watching him, it had been impossible (even with all the virtuous intentions of a Sunday) not to wonder about his motives. They were mercenary. She did not doubt that from his slighting of all his poorer patients in the crowd. But she could not quite determine whether his ambitions reached only to substantial fees, or whether they might aspire to more. To legacies perhaps… Or even to marriage – for, after all, it was not unknown for rich widows to fall in love with their physicians…

It was just as her thoughts were got to this point that she noticed he was stopped in the shadow of the church porch – and talking very earnestly to Mrs Midgely. He seemed to be giving some very particular piece of information – and she was smiling at what she heard. Dido pressed forward eagerly through the crowd, certain in her own mind that he was telling of his visit to the magistrate and determined to hear what she could. But there were a great many twisting parasols and jealously guarded muslins between her and the porch and before she could come close enough to hear anything, the pair had been interrupted.

As Dido approached the porch, Mrs Midgely's broad yellow back was retreating and it was Miss Neville who was now standing beside the apothecary, her sallow face twitching nervously beneath a remarkably ugly grey bonnet as she whispered something urgently about 'my poor mother'.

The look of gentle concern was gone from Mr Vane's face. He seemed very far from sympathetic about Mrs Neville – although he seemed to think that she was very unwell, for he shook his head and said something about it being, 'A bad business. Very bad indeed.'

He began to walk away, but Miss Neville detained him with an anxious question. 'But, you will say nothing about...?'

Mr Vane bowed abruptly and walked off into the church before she could finish.

All of which was very strange and interesting; and now, as she sat in her pew, Dido could not help but dwell upon the memory of it – rather to the exclusion of Mr Hewit's earnest discourse. She could not like Mr Vane – it was weak of him to be influenced by Mrs Midgely – and why should he be so negligent of Miss Neville and her poor mother? But he looked so very much at ease with himself that she could not doubt his motives in going to the magistrate. He had all the appearance of a man who *believed* he was acting with integrity.

Her eye slowly moved away from Mr Vane, along the lines of dutifully attentive faces. There was Miss Neville, her hands plucking at her reticule, frowning at the preacher as if she resented his words; and, beside her, Mr Lansdale, one arm resting along the side of his pew, head thrown back, fine blue eyes fixed attentively upon the pulpit. And then, in the row behind, Miss Prentice and Mrs Midgely...

Dido's wandering eye was immediately halted. She stared – at least she stared as much as a person *can* stare while discreetly craning her neck in church.

The expressions upon both women's faces were arresting. Startling. Though they could not have been more different. Miss Prentice was enraptured; her eyes were wide and she was so moved that tears were running down her round

118

cheeks. But Mrs Midgely's face burnt red – the rouge all swallowed up in a flush of fury.

Hastily Dido turned her wandering attention in its proper direction – and began to listen to the sermon. What was Mr Hewit saying which could produce such widely differing effects in his audience?

'...Charity, my dear friends! St Paul teaches us that it is the greatest of all virtues. "Charity suffereth long and is kind," he tells us. Charity "thinketh no evil". It "rejoiceth not in iniquity, but rejoiceth in the truth". When we have charity in our hearts, my friends, we do not bear grudges, or resentments, we are able – we are willing – to forget the past mistakes and transgressions of others. We are willing to forgive what is past...'

He spoke gently and feelingly; but there was a great deal of power in his accents – and in the expression of his lined and careworn face. And, Dido noticed that, as he spoke, he was looking very directly at Mrs Midgely.

'That was a very moving sermon, Mr Hewit,' said Dido, pausing in the shady porch as she and Flora left the church.

Mr Hewit's sombre face broke immediately into a very kindly smile. 'Dear Lady! You are extremely generous to say so.' He bowed and lowered his voice. 'And may I say that your approval of my little discourse does you credit. In my experience it is the charitable who take most pleasure in hearing charity commended.'

'Thank you.'

The broad smile had somewhat eased the deep lines of the clergyman's face; but the sadness lingered in his eyes

– and there was something too in the stoop of his slight shoulders, his haggard face and, most particularly, in his rather shabby clothes and his unfashionably powdered hair, which was not like any other popular visiting preacher that Dido had ever met. He was now looking rather despondingly at the departing crowd. 'I do not think,' he continued, raising a thick white eyebrow in half-comical regret, 'that my discourse gave universal satisfaction.'

Dido found that the man was rather winning upon her. She smiled and stepped closer to him. 'I fear there may have been a little disappointment,' she whispered playfully.

'Disappointment?'

'Yes,' she confided, 'I believe you were expected to preach against the French.'

'Indeed?' He looked very thoughtful. 'But, my dear lady, why do you suppose that there should be disappointment? Did I not preach most eloquently against the French?'

'I beg your pardon? I do not quite understand you.'

'Was not every word which I spoke in praise of charity a rebuke to our neighbours across the channel? Are not a want of charity and compassion at the root of every violent scene lately enacted among them? Is it not the absence of charity which has turned the high ideals of their revolution into tyranny and outrage?'

'Oh!' said Dido, startled into seriousness. 'Yes…' She was quite struck by his words, and she could not help but wonder whether they might not have some bearing upon Richmond as well as France – and whether the lack of charity among her neighbours might not also end in a scene of violence…

She shivered – the old stone porch suddenly felt

remarkably damp and cold. And she was on the point of making him a more thoughtful reply, when his attention was drawn away.

'Ah!' he cried, 'Mrs Midgely, Miss Prentice! It is such a very great pleasure to meet with old friends!'

Dido turned just in time to see Mrs Midgely walking past with scarcely a nod, while Miss Prentice stopped and held out her hand smilingly. 'Such a beautiful sermon, Mr Hewit. It was so very...'

'Thank you! Thank you, dear lady!' He took her hand, folded it in both his own and seemed to study her face.

Dido watched with great interest.

But Flora suddenly seized her arm. 'Pray excuse us, Mr Hewit,' she cried. 'We must hurry away, you know.' And without more ado she pulled her cousin out of the cool porch into the sudden heat and glare of the churchyard.

'But I wished most particularly to hear what they said,' protested Dido as they came to a halt beside a gravestone, just a few yards from the porch.

'And they,' whispered Flora with a giggle, 'most certainly did not *wish* you to hear.'

'What do you mean?' Dido looked back through the ivy-hung doorway into the shadows where it was just possible to see the stooping clergyman leaning close to the neat little figure of Miss Prentice. Her eyes were cast down. He was still holding her hand as if he had forgotten to release it.

'Why, is it not obvious?' said Flora. 'I am sure it is plain for all the world to see! They are in love!'

'In love?' cried Dido. 'How can you know? You have never seen them together before.'

'Oh, but they are! Or at least they were when they were young. And now they have met again and they find they have not forgotten… Only look at how he is talking to her – and how she listens to him. Yes, they are in love for sure! I am *never* wrong about these things.'

'I do not know…' said Dido doubtingly. Miss Prentice was withdrawing her hand now, turning away. She walked out into the sunshine, her face pale and distressed. 'I do not know at all. *That* does not seem so very much like love. She seems in quite a hurry to get away from Mr Hewit.'

Flora laughed, linked her arm through Dido's and drew her away along the worn flagged path that led through roughly mown grass to the lych-gate. 'Oh!' she cried, 'but it is very like love. You see, I have noticed that some women are not at all comfortable about being in love.' She shook her curls and flashed a very meaning, sidelong glance at her companion. 'And I have observed,' she continued, 'that such women will go to quite extraordinary lengths to conceal their attachments – even from their most intimate friends. Why, I do not mean to shock you, but I believe that sometimes they will even try to hide their love from their *cousins!*'

Chapter Fourteen

...I am not at all sure whether to believe Flora – I mean as to Mr Hewit and Miss Prentice being in love. I do not at all share her belief that she is always right in these matters, though she can sometimes be quick-sighted enough... That is to say, I have known her guess correctly in another case...

And there did, <u>I suppose</u>, seem to be some evidences of affection – they were certainly very glad to meet. And he held her hand a great while longer than was necessary. And I think perhaps they were acquainted with one another when they were young, back in Northamptonshire... Maybe it is possible...

But if there is a real attachment, Eliza, why were they not married long ago? Flora, I should say, believes that they were parted by a lack or fortune on his side and a fiercely disapproving Papa on hers. She has made up quite an affecting little story about it.

But, whether or not there was ever a disapproving Papa, there is undoubtedly now a disapproving friend! For Mrs Midgely certainly does not like Mr Hewit. Dear me! I begin to think that that woman does not like anyone!

And I keep remembering Mrs M's visit to Knaresborough House – and how Miss Prentice fainted when she heard of it.

I wonder whether Mr Hewit might have played some part in that little mystery. In short I wonder whether…

But I had better not go on, or I fear I shall be in danger of telling a tale as rich in fancy and as poor in fact as Flora's. I shall instead wait and watch a little more – and hope that my book is soon delivered from the bookseller. And I think I shall also try to discover exactly where in the north-country Mr Hewit's new parish may be situated…

And, in the meantime, I shall tell you about our dinner last night at Knaresborough House.

I was, for a while, afraid that we should not be able to dine out. Unfortunately, while she was at the shops yesterday morning, the news of Mr Vane going to the magistrate was forced upon Flora's attention and she suffered afterwards with the headache. But she bore with the news much better than I had expected. She seems to rely entirely upon Mr Lomax's judgement and continues to believe that there is no great danger of a trial.

And so, since she was most anxious to prove to Mr Lansdale that he was not deserted by his friends, we kept our engagement. And very grateful I am that we did!

I wish most particularly to give you an account of this dinner, Eliza. You see it has produced what is perhaps the strangest mystery of all this unaccountable business.

First of all you must know that, although we had only been invited to a family dinner, when we arrived, we found that there was one other guest: a young man Mr Lansdale introduced as 'My great friend Jem Morgan.' And a great friend he was – both tall and broad!

I do not mean to suggest, however, that there was anything strange or mysterious about Mr Morgan himself. Indeed, he seemed a remarkably ordinary young man with a lot of unruly black hair which would not lie flat, and a rather ill-shaven chin with a cut upon it. He is one of those young men who, even when they are freshly dressed for dinner, have not quite the knack of looking tidy. He has chambers in the Temple, is studying law and suffers under the common delusion that a woman may be pleasantly entertained by the relating of endless anecdotes about his friends, his horses and his dogs. As you have no doubt understood from this complaint, I had all his attention throughout dinner. For Mr Lansdale, as usual, devoted himself to Flora – and by the by I rather wonder at our cousin. Does she allow the young man to engross her so when her husband is present? – well, I suppose that is no business of mine. All I meant to say was that I was Mr Morgan's sole object. And a heavy misfortune it was, because, besides his conversation, I had spilt wine and dropped knives to contend with, for he really is the clumsiest man I ever met.

And it is to his clumsiness that we are indebted for the great discovery of the evening.

Flora and I were not long alone with Miss Neville after dinner before the gentlemen joined us. Though I would not have you think that I wasted my time, for while Flora amused herself at the pianoforte, I talked again with Clara Neville about the evening on which Mrs Lansdale died. And I discovered two things which may be of interest.

Firstly, she said that Mr Vane visited the lady not long before she retired to her dressing room and administered to her 'her usual dose'. It seems that she complained then of disordered nerves and wished the apothecary to remain in the house with her. But Mr Vane was not overly worried and

125

said only that he would be at home all evening and she must send for him if her symptoms became worse.

And second, I found that she was served with chocolate in her dressing room before going to her bed. Now the chocolate I believe to be of some significance, for it seems to me that its strong, rather bitter taste would effectively disguise any physic put into it. If I was going to poison anyone, Eliza, I would certainly make use of a jug of chocolate if I could. With this in mind, I took some trouble to find out more about the chocolate and discovered that it had been prepared in the kitchen and that Miss Neville had carried it up to the dressing room. However when she arrived at the dressing room Mr Lansdale was there and, since his aunt particularly requested that they be left alone, Miss Neville handed the tray to him.

In short, both Miss Neville and Henry Lansdale had opportunity enough to introduce the opium mixture to the jug...if they wished to do so.

And another thing to consider is that we have only Mr Vane's word that it was no more than the 'usual dose' which he administered that evening.

By the by, I rather fancy Mr Vane for a murderer, though I confess that, try as I might, I have not yet been able to think of any reason why he should wish for the lady's demise. Nor why, having brought it about, he should wish to draw attention to his crime by starting the idea of an unnatural death.

But I do not quite despair of his being guilty. I must give the matter more thought.

For now I shall return to Mr Morgan and his clumsiness.

Well, he and Mr Lansdale soon followed us into the

drawing room, and once we were all gathered in that room it was only natural that conversation should turn to the burglars who had entered it. The subject, as you may imagine, had been discussed already in the dining room, but now the local interest of the window through which the ruffians had come and the drawers they had disturbed, soon led Mr Lansdale into a more detailed account of the events. We were all deeply interested and, when he stepped to a window saying, 'This was the one that had the broken catch,' we all naturally followed him and looked at it.

There was nothing to see – except that the window opens <u>outward</u>, just as I suspected. So, after a moment or two, we all turned back into the room. But, as we did so, Mr Morgan had the ill-luck to catch his foot in the long window curtain and fall headlong into a sofa.

And, as he fell, something bright caught my eye: something which had been lying hidden in the trailing hem of the curtain. I cried out 'Oh look!' or something foolish like that as one does on such occasions – and picked it up.

Eliza, it was an emerald necklace!

Well, you may imagine how we all gathered around and exclaimed over it. It was an extremely pretty thing: a slender gold chain with one stone hanging in the centre flanked by two pairs of smaller ones. Naturally Flora and I thought that it had been taken from elsewhere in the house and accidentally dropped by the thieves as they made their escape.

But – and this is the unaccountable part of the business – both Miss Neville and Henry Lansdale were sure that it had not. They both declared that they had never set eyes on the necklace before. And Mr Lansdale was quite certain that it had not belonged to his aunt. He said that he had carefully examined her jewel case when the intruders had first been discovered and he was certain that the case had not been broken into, nor was anything missing from it. Furthermore, he was sure that the emerald necklace could not have been his aunt's.

'For,' he said, 'I know she did not like emeralds at all. She fancied that they did not suit her complexion. Everything in her jewel case is diamonds or rubies and very different from this. This is very new,' he said. 'Fresh from the jewellers I should say. Everything that my aunt had was old-fashioned, heavy stuff. Believe me,' he said, 'she _never_ wore anything like this.'

My next suggestion was that it might have been dropped by the last tenants of the house and remained unobserved until now; but Mr Lansdale negatived that immediately. It seems that every inch of the house was cleaned before he and his aunt took possession. Every curtain had been removed, thoroughly cleansed and rehung. His aunt had insisted upon it.

So, Eliza, this is our mystery: thieves break into a house and take nothing from it – this might be explained by their being disturbed before they can find anything of value – however, they not only fail to remove any goods, but they leave behind them a valuable item which was not there before.

What kind of thieves are they who bring goods into a house and leave the householder a little wealthier than he was before they came?!!

Chapter Fifteen

Tuesday – the day of the party to Brooke Manor – dawned fair and still, and so very hot that even Flora – who did not like the countryside – thought that a drive out of town might be refreshing. But the air was heavy and Dido was inclined to agree with the coachman when he threatened them with thunder before the day was over.

She was very glad though that the storm was not yet come for she would not have liked their visit to be put off. She had high hopes of it – and not just in the enjoyment of strawberries either. For here was surely an opportunity of solving some at least of the many mysteries which surrounded her. Today there were to be, gathered around Sir Joshua's strawberry beds, all the people who interested her most. Mrs Midgely was to be there, with Miss Prentice and Miss Bevan. Mr Hewit, she had learnt from Flora, was invited, and Mr Lansdale was also expected, together with his friend Jem Morgan and Miss Neville.

'I confess,' she said to Flora, when they and their strawberry baskets were comfortably settled in the barouche-landau and they were rattling out of Richmond's streets, 'I am a little surprised that Mr Lansdale should consent to be of the party. To be in company with Mrs Midgely cannot be pleasant for him. He is very well aware of the unkind things she is saying about him.'

'Yes,' agreed Flora quietly. 'And he certainly knows she is to be of the party today, because her ladyship sent me a note asking me most particularly to acquaint him of the fact. Sir Joshua would invite him you see – for men are the last creatures in the world to notice gossip – but poor Lady Carrisbrook was most anxious that there should be no unpleasant scenes.'

'And you did as she requested and informed him?'

'Oh yes! But he was not to be put off, you know. He said... He said that while there was such pleasant company to be met with...' She blushed and lowered her eyes with a consciousness that was quite out of place in a married woman. 'Since there were such dear friends to be there, he would not, he said, be put off by the likes of Mrs Midgely.'

'Did he indeed!' said Dido and, while Flora endeavoured to regain her composure, she turned away disapprovingly and gave herself up to thought – for she had a great deal to consider this morning. As the carriage continued through bright hayfields and shady coppiced woodland, she drew a slim volume from her basket, turned over its pages and wondered...

'Is that your *Treatise upon Citizens?*' asked Flora when she had at last got the better of her blushes.

'Yes, it came from Mr Lister this morning.'

'Well then, I congratulate you upon its being so very short – for I think it will make remarkably dull reading.'

'Fortunately,' said Dido, 'I do not think I shall need to read beyond this title page. All the information I need is here.' And she held out the book to show Flora the name of its author – John Hewit Esquire.

'Oh!' cried Flora. 'A revolutionary! Mr Hewit is a revolutionary!'

'I think it would be more accurate to say that he was a revolutionary thirty years ago,' corrected Dido. 'From the things he said on Sunday I rather think that experience – and the late horrors enacted in France – have changed his views.'

'Well,' said Flora eagerly. 'Now, of course, we know why Miss Prentice had to give him up when she was young!'

'Yes,' said Dido rather doubtingly. 'Perhaps we do. But, unfortunately, we also know that Mr Hewit has a secret which he must hide. He is, I understand, shortly to take up a very good living in the north of England. I am quite certain that he does not wish anyone to know that he once held such very radical views.'

And she lapsed once more into very thoughtful silence.

Brooke Manor was a pleasant, respectable, old-fashioned country house, with the date of 1565 written up above its dark front door. Black beams and pale plasterwork comprised the greater part of its building and an arm of ancient forest curved around to embrace it at the back. In front, sunken lawns, moss-grown paths and old, old yew hedges led down to meadows and a stream shaded by willows.

The kitchen garden, very properly enclosed with warm, ivy-covered bricks, was, at present, so full of ripening strawberries that their scent reached Dido and Flora as they stepped down from the carriage.

Sir Joshua was on the front step to greet them as they arrived and very well did he suit his setting: a slight, grey-haired, healthy looking man of over fifty, dressed in the fashion of his youth. The young wife on his arm presented a very pretty contrast and, despite having been prepared by everything the Richmond gossips could say of the lady's youth and beauty, Dido found that she must look and look again at Maria Carrisbrook.

It was impossible not to do so. To say that she was beautiful fell far short of the truth. There was beauty certainly in the delicate features, the soft eyes and the pleasing, upright figure, but there was something more. In the expression of the eyes, the turn of the graceful head, the way of moving and speaking, there was a something which, at first, Dido must call 'charm', although, having watched Lady Carrisbrook a little longer, she wondered whether a man might not call it 'bewitchment'.

She certainly seemed to be a devoted wife, for, in between paying very proper attention to her guests, she worried that Sir Joshua's eyes were not properly shaded from the sun, sent a servant to fetch a hat and finally, being dissatisfied with the one which was brought, ran off to find exactly the right piece of headgear herself.

Her husband complained about, and enjoyed, her attentions. 'Now, now. Don't fuss, my dear. Don't fuss,' he muttered happily as he led them to the kitchen garden – where a large company was already gathered.

A glance around the garden soon told her that Mr Lomax was absent; but all her other acquaintance were here. It was a strange scene: ladies and gentlemen stooping and bending in a domain which is usually left

132

to gardeners. Elegant, well-modulated voices echoed about the old brick walls of the kitchen garden. Printed muslins brushed the earth between bright green and red rows of strawberry plants, and a pretty pink parasol had been set aside in a neighbouring bed of cabbages.

Everyone was intent upon strawberries – except perhaps Mr Hewit who was standing a little apart from the rest, wrapped in thought and only occasionally stooping down to dutifully pick at the fruit.

Dido and Flora set themselves to pick alongside Miss Bevan who had detached herself a little from her companions and who was looking decidedly ill and pale beneath her plain white bonnet. There was a little reddening of the eyes which could not but rouse a suspicion of tears against her.

She spoke very civilly to them, however, about the day and the garden and, after a while, seeing that Flora was very busy with her task, she said quietly to Dido, 'And how do your enquiries go on, Miss Kent? I hope you will soon be able to prove Mr Lansdale quite innocent.'

Dido sighed, set down her basket and straightened her already-aching back. 'They go on very badly indeed, I am afraid,' she said.

'I am sorry to hear it. I wish I could be of more use to you; but I regret that I know very little of the matter.'

'Perhaps you *can* help me, Miss Bevan,' she said looking very directly at her. 'There is a line of Shakespeare's – it has been brought to my attention in connection with this affair – I am not at liberty to say exactly how – but I believe it may be of some importance.'

'How very intriguing!' exclaimed Miss Bevan,

returning her gaze with fearless interest.

'You see, the difficulty is that, having no knowledge of its origin, there is no understanding its meaning.'

'I shall do my best to help, Miss Kent. But I hope you are not meaning to judge me by my answer.'

'Why should I mean to judge you?' asked Dido keenly.

But Mary laughed. 'I am only afraid,' said she, 'that I may reveal my ignorance and you will judge me unfit for my future task of educating children.'

'Oh no! No, I promise I am not testing. But can you tell me whether the line: "The world is not their friend, nor the world's laws," does indeed come from Shakespeare?'

Miss Bevan crossed her arms as she thought. 'I believe it does,' she said at last, 'though I am afraid I cannot think which play it occurs in. Why do you particularly wish to know?'

'Because,' said Dido, still watching her companion's face for any change of complexion or sign of consciousness, 'I would dearly love to know just who it is who must be considered unfriended by the laws of the world.'

Mary shook her head with a smile and bent once more over the strawberry bed. 'I am sorry I cannot help you, Miss Kent. I have heard the line certainly, but you know I may not even have heard it in its original setting. For Shakespeare is so much a part of our heritage as Englishwomen that we hear and read his lines quoted everywhere. We meet them every day, do we not? All the great writers of our own time describe with his phrases and adopt his beauties. His lines are to be found in almost every book – every periodical that we open.'

Dido acknowledged it and they talked very pleasantly

about the influence of the great poet upon the English language, until they were disturbed by Henry Lansdale's approach. He came, as usual, to devote himself to Flora, positioning himself carefully between her and Miss Bevan so that Dido found herself attending rather more than she should to his talk.

He was so pleased that they were come…he had been wanting their company very much…such a scheme as this was nothing without pleasant companions… He had been so afraid that the best of the fruit would be gone before they came…had in fact taken the liberty of saving some of the choicest berries…

Dido looked up as he proffered the basket in his hand. Perhaps he caught her eye – and her disapproval – for instead of holding it out to Flora he turned at the last moment and gave first pick of the fruit in it to Miss Bevan. Dido frowned at the little tableau and turned back very thoughtfully to the business of filling her own basket. There was something dangerous in Mr Lansdale's manner… Was he to be trusted entirely?

She was next roused from her thoughts by Miss Neville who drew along beside her and said plaintively, 'This is rather a singular occupation is it not, Miss Kent?

She turned. Miss Neville was peering suspiciously under a strawberry leaf and looking hot, tired and unhappy. 'In my opinion,' she continued, 'strawberries are all very well in a dish with a little sugar and cream – but I had never thought to have to gather them myself.'

'I believe it is generally considered the best – the most natural – way of enjoying the fruit. I am sure Sir Joshua means to give us pleasure.'

'Oh,' said Miss Neville. 'Oh well!' It was plain that her life had had rather too much necessary toil in it for her to regard as pleasure any exertion which might be avoided.

'You seem fatigued, Miss Neville,' said Dido solicitously. 'Why do you not sit down awhile in the shade?'

Miss Neville looked about her at the rest of the company who were happily picking and eating and praising. 'I do not like to go away,' she confessed in a whisper. 'It would look so very singular.'

Dido could not allow such an opportunity to pass her by.

'Then I shall accompany you,' she said with decision, popping one last strawberry into her mouth and standing up. 'Then it cannot look singular, you know.'

She led the way to a wooden seat in a rose arbour beyond the wall of the kitchen garden and Miss Neville sat down gratefully. 'Thank you, Miss Kent, this is very kind of you,' she said – which was the occasion of some guilt, for Dido's motives in suggesting the removal had not been ones of unadulterated humanity.

She smiled and allowed her companion to enjoy for a while the rest and comparative coolness. The arbour was deep and old and irregular, and composed of extremely pale pink roses of the kind which droop and fall almost as soon as they are opened. Little drifts of petals lay about their feet on the old brick path. Here they were hidden from both the house and the strawberry beds; their companions were no more than a buzz of voices beyond the wall – and an occasional ripple of laughter from Flora marking some more than usually outrageous remark from Mr Lansdale. In the alcove they were comfortably sheltered from the glare of the sun, but heat breathed up from the bricks at their feet. Three or four ornamental pheasants loitered about on the path.

Dido watched them for several minutes, and listened to a bee fumbling noisily in the heart of a rose, before she turned determinedly to her silent companion. 'Miss Neville,' she said, 'I am glad to have this opportunity of conversation with you. There is something which I wish most particularly to ask you about.'

'Yes?' The single word sounded wary. She looked worried.

It would be kindest to speak quickly and plainly. 'There seems,' said Dido, looking directly at her, 'to be a little confusion about the night on which Mrs Lansdale died. You see, Miss Prentice is quite certain that she saw a visitor approaching the house – and yet you assure me that you saw no such visitor. It is very strange, is it not?'

Miss Neville twisted her hands together and said nothing.

'In view of the events which followed – the lady's death – and the burglary too – I wonder whether more enquiries ought not to be made into this business. At the very least the man Fraser should be questioned, for he could tell us whether or not there was a visitor came to the door that day...'

'No! No, Miss Kent...I assure you...it will by no means be necessary... No such enquiries need be made. For I think I can explain to you everything that seems strange in the case.'

'Oh?'

'You see...' Miss Neville's hands writhed and twisted

harder than ever. 'You see when I told you…or rather, when Mr Lansdale told you that I was at home that evening…it was certainly not my intention to deceive you…or to deceive anyone.'

'So it was not true? You were not at home all evening?'

She stared down at her clenched fingers. 'No,' she said very quietly. 'The truth is, I left the house soon after Mr Lansdale.'

It changed everything. That was Dido's first thought. And for a little while the surprise of it was too great to allow her to think further.

The two ladies sat in silence for several minutes. The sun beat down upon the brick path and upon the roses – raising a sweet scent. One of the pheasants strutted past, turning its little bright head to eye them curiously.

It changed everything. It made a great deal possible that had before seemed only wild surmise. There *could* have been a secret tryst: a meeting between Mrs Lansdale and Mr Henderson… A meeting about which the nephew and companion knew nothing… Unless one of them, returning, should have discovered it…and the discovery had made him, or her, desperate…

Dido turned to Miss Neville and saw that her cheeks were very red and she was holding a plain little handkerchief to her eyes. 'And when did you return to Knaresborough House? Before Mr Lansdale, or after him?'

'Oh before him,' said Miss Neville eagerly, 'I was very careful of that – because, you see, he did not know that I had gone. And, Miss Kent, if you would be so very kind…I should be very grateful if you would not mention my going to him.'

'Why do you wish to hide it?'

'Because I should not have left his aunt. It was my duty to remain with her. I am quite well aware of that. But then you know,' she continued in a plaintive voice, 'it was also my duty to go… And, I ask you, how was I to decide?'

'What was it that took you out that evening?'

'I had to visit my mother.'

'Your mother?' repeated Dido disbelievingly. She could see no reason for concealing such a respectable errand.

'I always did visit mother on a Tuesday, you see. It was quite an agreed thing.'

'I see.'

'But, there was a problem. The truth is that there often was a problem,' she added irritably. 'It had become quite a habit with my cousin to complain on Tuesdays of feeling unwell – of feeling too unwell for me to leave her. And sometimes, as on this particular day, she would forbid me to go. You see, Mr Lansdale had told us that he was to spend the evening in town. It was not quite fair! But I thought there was nothing wrong with her, and after she had retired, I went out…to see mother. After all, she was expecting me…'

'I see. It must have been very difficult for you.'

'It was,' came the eager reply. 'The truth is, Miss Kent,' continued Miss Neville, who seemed to be as fond of enunciating truths as any clergyman in his pulpit, 'that I found myself in a *very* difficult situation. The role of companion, it is not an *easy* one, you know.' There was a little, self-pitying shake of the head. 'To be always at someone else's command. I do not mean to complain, for I know it was very kind of Mrs Lansdale to invite me to live with her. But I scarcely had a moment to myself. She would call me at any hour if she felt unwell.'

'I understand, of course. It must have been a very trying situation.'

'And you see, I was so very worried about mother.'

'Ah yes, your mother is unwell is she not?'

'Oh no, thank you, she is well – as well as a woman of her age can be. Why should you think she is ill?' she asked anxiously.

'No reason – it is just that you were consulting Mr Vane on Sunday – I thought you were perhaps worried about your mother's health.'

Miss Neville looked extremely uncomfortable. 'No, no,' she said, 'that was quite a different matter.'

'I see. But you say that you were worried about your mother on this particular day.'

'Yes, because she was going to be alone on that evening and…you know how it is with old people. They can become confused and forgetful. They cannot be left long unattended.'

'I see.'

'And she was expecting me to go,' said Miss Neville querulously. But then she recollected herself and added more calmly, 'Naturally now, I feel that I should have stayed. Poor Mrs Lansdale really was unwell, you see. Perhaps,' she said with great sentiment, 'perhaps, if I had stayed, I could have helped her.'

'It is only natural that you should feel so. Though I doubt your presence could have saved her. I am sure you have nothing with which to reproach yourself.'

Miss Neville seemed very grateful for this reassurance,

but, nevertheless, she soon afterwards stood up and proclaimed her determination of resuming the hard labour of strawberry picking.

'Before you go, Miss Neville, there is something else I was hoping to ask you,' said Dido. She was unwilling to lose this rather promising opportunity of putting a very important question. 'Can you tell me – was Mrs Lansdale at all acquainted with her neighbour, Mrs Midgely?'

Miss Neville stopped under the roses. A little cluster of petals spilt down onto the crown of her bonnet. She stared at Dido, rather perplexed. 'No, she was not,' she said. 'That is, Mrs Midgely had called at the house but once.'

'Ah!' cried Dido eagerly. 'And when was it that she called?'

'It was on the morning before my poor cousin died. But she was not admitted because Mrs Lansdale did not…feel equal to company that morning.'

'And so she left her card and went away?'

'Yes. And she left a message too – with Fraser – she asked to be allowed to call again. She had, she said, something she particularly wished to say to my cousin.'

'Did she indeed! And tell me,' Dido pursued, 'did Mr Lansdale know of her visit – and her message?'

'Why yes, I believe he did.'

Chapter Sixteen

Dido remained in the alcove. The heat became oppressive; the chatter and laughter from the strawberry beds became more languid as the pickers tired; bees droned in the pale roses. Hidden in her corner, she considered what she had learnt.

It would appear that when Mr Henderson called at the house, Mrs Lansdale was alone. That raised a multitude of possibilities.

And then there was Miss Neville herself to consider. There was a kind of dissatisfaction about the woman: a reined-in anger, which was most intriguing. And what was the 'bad business' she had been discussing with Mr Vane, if it was not her mother's health? Dido did not trust her at all. She had a great idea that anyone who was so very eager to point out that she was stating truths, must be concealing some other – perhaps more important – truths.

And finally, and perhaps most interesting of all, there was this visit of Mrs Midgely's. What had been its purpose…?

She was able to proceed no further in her musing. There was a heavy footstep on the path and she looked up to see

Mrs Midgely herself bearing down upon her, her cheeks very red and her cherry-coloured parasol aflutter.

'Miss Kent! Here you are! I hope that you are not unwell. Your cousin is becoming quite anxious about you.'

'No. Thank you, I am quite well – just a little heated.'

'Well then, I am very glad to have this opportunity of talking to you.'

As Mrs Midgely began to settle herself and her skirts upon the bench, Dido was busily considering a direct question about that visit to Mrs Lansdale. But, regretfully, she decided it had better not be attempted. To admit an interest in the matter would only put the lady on her guard and an honest answer was scarcely to be expected.

'I think,' she said, half rising, 'that I had better not stay – if Flora is worried about me.'

'There is something which I most particularly wish to say to you, Miss Kent,' said Mrs Midgely, lowering her voice to a very impressive undertone, 'something concerning Mr Lansdale and the late events at Knaresborough House.'

Dido decided that Flora might be allowed to worry a little longer.

'Dear Mrs Beaumont,' continued Mrs Midgely, 'has, I discover, a great regard for Mr Lansdale.'

'Yes,' said Dido carefully, 'I believe she has. She – *and her husband* – have been friends of the Lansdales this past year.'

'Yes, quite so. And I am sure it is very unpleasant for her to hear ill of him.'

'As to that...'

'My dear Miss Kent, as a friend I would wish to warn

144

her. I wish you would speak a word of warning to her in my behalf.'

Dido stared. 'What manner of warning, Mrs Midgely?'

'I would advise her to drop the acquaintance, for I believe there will soon come out such things! Things which will… Well, my dear, shall we say they are such things as will prove her confidence in him to be quite misplaced.'

'To what are you referring Mrs Midgely?'

She blushed so deeply that the colour of her cheeks was a fair match for her parasol. 'This business of his aunt's death – I fear that it will end in court you know.'

'I do not think,' said Dido, 'that that apprehension would turn my cousin against her friend.'

'Ah! But you see, she is not aware of all that may come out before the judge.'

Dido looked at her sharply: aware that there was something – something to the gentleman's disadvantage – which Mrs Midgely most particularly wished to tell her. Her interest was keen: but she took great care to keep that interest from her voice. 'And what is it that she is unaware of?'

Mrs Midgely looked sidelong at her. 'Are you – or Mrs Beaumont – aware that Mr Lansdale was heard to argue with his aunt on the day of her death?'

Dido was shocked; but it was absolutely necessary to exert herself. She would not, for the world, have Mrs Midgely suppose she had bettered her. 'And what… Or rather who… How is this known?'

Mrs Midgely shook her curls and whispered importantly. 'Mr Vane was in the house when it occurred. He heard it all.'

'And what was this "all" that he heard?'

'A great deal. You see Mrs Lansdale considered herself to be very unwell that evening and it seems that she quite forbade her nephew to leave her. But he said he had to see his friend Mr Morgan on very important business.'

'I see.'

'And that is not all. When he persisted in saying that he would go, she fell into a great passion. And she began to threaten him. Miss Kent, she threatened him with a new will which she said would leave him poor: "as poor as his foolish mother had made herself", that is what she said.'

'And Mr Vane heard all this?'

'Oh yes. For he could not help it, you know – it all being shouted so loud.'

'And now he has told it all to the magistrate?'

'Yes. He was very unwilling, of course. But as he said to me, on Sunday, Miss Kent, "Is it not the solemn and religious duty of every man to ensure that justice is done?"'

'He is, of course, correct,' said Dido thoughtfully. 'It is the duty of us all to bring justice about.' She sat considering for several minutes and, for once, Mrs Midgely was silent: as if content, now that her information was given, to wait for its effect.

Dido watched her companion. Her broad red face was complacent, her painted lips pursed up in a self-congratulating smile. Why, she wondered for the hundredth time, did the woman take such pleasure in spreading her poison?

Still watching closely, she said, 'Mrs Midgely, I wonder whether you might help me. I am trying to discover the source of a quotation.'

'A quotation, Miss Kent?' she asked with some surprise.

'Yes, it is something which has lately been brought to my attention and I find that I cannot understand its meaning because I do not know its origin. Do you know...? Have you ever heard the line, "The world is not their friend, nor the world's laws"?'

There was certainly a consciousness: a deepening of colour in the cheeks, a rapid movement of the eyelashes. Mrs Midgely twisted the parasol about in her hands. 'Why yes, Miss Kent, I know the line. It is by William Shakespeare.'

'And do you know which play – or poem – it occurs in?' cried Dido eagerly.

'Yes I do. It occurs in *Romeo and Juliet*.'

'Are you sure?'

'Oh yes, quite sure, for you see...' the parasol spun rapidly in her hands, a shy little smile curled her lips so that she looked, for a moment, like a rather ugly china doll. 'You see I once played the part of Juliet when I was a girl in school. The line is certainly from that play.'

After Mrs Midgely had gone, Dido yet remained in her alcove: reluctant to leave it as much for the sake of the information it had produced, as for the shade it afforded.

This latest intelligence was extremely troubling. Mr Vane's account of a quarrel appeared very bad for Mr Lansdale. And yet, Dido reasoned, if it had not been followed by a death, would it have been remembered? For might not it – and others like it – have been a part of Mrs Lansdale's usual intercourse with her nephew? One of those scenes which, according to Flora, Mrs Lansdale had delighted in. Wills were, all too often, the threat which the old and the rich held over their young people: the means by which they guarded themselves against neglect – real or imagined. And when they were in a passion, people frequently said things which they did not mean…

But in this case, murder – or death at least – had been the ensuing scene. And Dido found it impossible to determine either what was probable, or what was likely to be believed by a jury. And, all together, she could decide on very little, except that she should not – as Mrs Midgely wished – tell Flora of Mr Vane's over-hearings. There was nothing to be gained by increasing her distress and anxiety.

And, as for this discovery that *Romeo and Juliet* was the source of the quoted line: what was to be made of that? Was it to be connected with the copy of that play which Mr Lansdale had borrowed from the circulating library?

It was, in one light, unsurprising: for who was more likely to be considered excused from the judgement of the world than those star-crossed lovers?

But if it was lovers for whom the writer of that letter wished to plead, then who were the lovers? Mrs Lansdale and Mr Henderson? But that did not seem right; for, Dido reasoned, it is the youth and innocence of Romeo and Juliet which appeals to our sympathy as much as their love.

And where, in all this strange business, was there a couple of young lovers to be found? Dido hesitated upon that question… An answer suggested itself; but it was not such an answer as she was anxious to believe…

'Miss Kent,' said a quiet voice, close beside her, 'I declare you are looking very puzzled...again!'

She gave a start, turned – and saw Mr William Lomax smiling down at her.

'Hello,' she cried happily. 'I had begun to fear that you would not be able to join our party.'

'And so had I,' said he, sitting down beside her. 'I have but just escaped from the library and letters of business.'

'I am afraid you will find the best of the strawberries all gone.'

'It is no great matter.'

'You do not like strawberries?'

'I am very fond of them. But on the present occasion *they* were not my inducement to get away from business.'

Dido coloured and turned her eyes upon the path.

'I have been particularly anxious to talk to you.'

Dido fell to studying the pale rose petals that lay upon the path, noting how their edges were becoming dry and brown.

'I have,' he continued, 'been very concerned about you.'

'Concerned?' she cried, looking up. 'Why ever should you be concerned about me?'

'My dear Miss Kent,' he said with all the appearance of great seriousness, 'you must be aware that it is far from usual to find *two* young men of your acquaintance suspected of murder within a year.'

Dido raised her eyebrows. 'And what precisely is the nature of your concern, Mr Lomax? Do you suppose that I endanger young men by being acquainted with them?'

He smiled. 'I had considered that possibility,' he said.

'But, upon reflection, I have dismissed it as unlikely.'

'I am very glad to hear it! But why should you be concerned about me?'

'I fear that you are distressing yourself unnecessarily over this business of Mr Lansdale and his aunt's death.'

'Oh.'

'These accusations of Mrs Midgely's,' he continued gently, 'are probably no more than common gossip. As I had the pleasure of explaining to you and your cousin, it is unlikely that any harm will come of them.' He studied her face. 'I hope that you have now put them quite out of your mind.'

Dido hesitated – thought for a moment of putting off the subject and talking of something else, but found that she could not.

'I cannot put them out of my mind,' she said quietly. 'You see, I think there may be a great deal of harm to come. I think there will be new evidence against Mr Lansdale.'

'Why should there be?' he asked quickly.

'Because I believe that…that maybe Mr Vane is right to be suspicious of Mrs Lansdale's death…I think… In short, I think that she may indeed have been murdered…'

'My dear Miss Kent!'

'You think that I am being fanciful?'

'No,' he said hastily, 'no, not at all. I know that it is not in your nature to be fanciful. But…I think that perhaps your late, distressing experiences at Belsfield have – very understandably – biased your mind and made you a little too liable to see mystery and infamy. You are perhaps too inclined to suppose the worst because, last autumn – at

Belsfield – all your very worst suspicions were proved to be true.'

'I beg your pardon,' said Dido, rather vexed, 'but this sounds remarkably like fancy to me.'

'I am very sorry if I have offended you. I assure you that nothing but my very great interest in your welfare could make me speak so plainly.'

It was several minutes before she could answer him. Her feelings were in confusion. His concern for her well-being was very pleasing indeed. But his suggestion that she was behaving irrationally was intolerable.

She sat with her hands clasped in her lap, struggling for control, unwilling to speak until she could be sure that her voice would not betray her; and he watched her in silence, not wishing to say anything which might provoke her further.

The sun, almost at its highest, was beginning to find its way even into the alcove, warming her face. A cuckoo was calling in the wood. The housekeeper appeared a little way off and began scattering corn for the pheasants. Dido watched them as they ran jerkily to peck grain from the crevices of the old brick path.

She must remain calm, or how could she hope to convince him that she was speaking rationally?

'I am very grateful for your concern, Mr Lomax,' she said at last. 'And if I had been led astray in the way which you are suggesting, it would be very kind of you to set me right, I am sure. However...' She drew a long breath. 'However, I cannot by any means agree that I am biased, or that I am fancying intrigue where none exists. The evidences I have observed are too strong... In short, it would be dull and blind to see no mystery in this case.'

And then, before he had time to reply, she began to set forward, as calmly as she could, all the reasons for her suspicion; beginning with the unaccountable death of the lap-dog, through the mystery of the emerald necklace, and the extraordinary ill-will of Mrs Midgely towards Henry Lansdale; and winding it all up with an account of the strange letter which she had herself received.

As she talked, she was pleased to see, from his changing expressions, that he was very far from being unmoved by her story. Once or twice he interrupted her with a question.

Had the villains been apprehended? he wanted to know, when the burglary at Knaresborough House was mentioned. What steps had been taken to discover them?

And a little later: had anyone else any cause against Mr Lansdale? Was he an unpopular man in general?

But it was the letter which troubled him most. 'Have you no notion,' he cried when she described it, 'have you no suspicion at all as to who could have sent you such an extraordinary note?'

'None at all.'

'I do not like it.' He jumped to his feet and took a few restless steps along the path. 'It is very worrying.' He sat down beside her again with an agitated look. 'Miss Kent, has it not occurred to you that the letter might have been sent by the guilty party? That it might, in fact, be a threat.'

'A guilty party, Mr Lomax? I did not think that you believed there was guilt of any kind – except in my wild imaginings. Have I convinced you otherwise?'

He passed one hand across his face. 'I do not quite know what I think,' he confessed. 'But your account proves that there is something afoot. There is – at the very least – housebreaking. There is some villainy going on and you are known to be concerning yourself with it. I am very much afraid that you are putting yourself in danger.'

'Danger? I hardly think so. I have done nothing but ask some questions.'

He looked at her very earnestly. 'I have the pleasure of knowing your character too well,' he said, 'to suppose that you will easily abandon this mystery. And I do not have the right of a father or a brother to advise you. But,' he added feelingly, 'I do beg you, Miss Kent, to be careful. Very careful.'

Dido was silenced. She could only look into his anxious face. He was about to press the point further. For a moment it seemed as if he might take her hand – indeed she wondered afterwards whether she might not have half-offered it to him.

But just then they were disturbed by the sound of rapid steps on the gravel. They moved slightly apart.

Lady Carrisbrook was hurrying along a side path alone, in a state of such agitation that her bonnet was slipping off her head, exposing shining red-brown curls to the sun. Dido thought that she was coming to speak to Mr Lomax; but she did not seem to see them in their alcove. She ran instead to the housekeeper.

'Ah, Mrs Stephens!' she cried and then, lowering her voice, she began talking eagerly. It was not easy to make out her words, but the established habit of an over-curious mind prompted Dido to struggle for them. Mr Lomax gave an exasperated smile as he noticed her listening, but only shook his head and said nothing.

The lady seemed to be asking how something was to be done – and when. Her eyes were wide as she spoke, her gaze fixed upon the servant's face as if she were half-pleading with her.

The answer was clearer than the question. There was definitely nothing for her Ladyship to worry about. 'I will see to everything,' was spoken with assurance and an obvious desire to comfort.

It was not quite possible to see whether or not she was comforted by the answer; her face was turned a little away. Dido leant forward to see more clearly and at that very moment Lady Carrisbrook turned back – and saw them. There was a moment of confusion and then she came tripping along the path, holding out her hands and laughing.

'My dear Miss Kent! And Mr Lomax too! I pray you will not allow any other of my guests to know that I am so very anxious about the luncheon! You will not tell them, will you?' She sat down between them on the bench and prattled on about it being her first, her very first, party since she was married and how very, *very* particular Sir Joshua was that everything should be done properly.

It was all said very prettily and somehow managed to convey a flattering conviction that they might both be counted upon as close confederates and allies. But it failed to convince. There was no believing that any lady could be so very worried about a cold collation.

However, a little quiet reflection assured Dido that the intrusion had come at the right moment. For she had undoubtedly been enjoying Mr Lomax's anxiety for her safety rather too much.

Chapter Seventeen

Whether or not Her Ladyship had worried excessively over it, the luncheon was excellent, and plentiful enough to satisfy even the appetites of ladies and gentlemen who had toiled a full hour in the strawberry beds.

However there was among the guests an unease which was not surprising, if one knew the reasons that many of them had to feel awkward with one another, but which poor Lady Carrisbrook blamed herself for. She tried continually to introduce topics which might be of general interest and Flora did her best to assist. But the company seemed dull and heavy and too inclined to talk of whatever was uppermost in their own minds without reference to the interest or entertainment of their fellows.

Mr Morgan told interminable tales of his own cleverness; Mr Hewit remained silent and thoughtful; Miss Prentice talked nervously of titles; and Mrs Midgely triumphantly related to the company all the details of the delightful situation which she had secured for Miss Bevan as governess to the large family of a Mr Grimbould – a woollen manufacturer in Yorkshire.

This last Dido was very interested to hear about, since it explained to her the evidence of tears upon poor Mary's face. But no one else seemed to share her interest. Sir Joshua sighed deeply, Flora smothered a dainty yawn and Mr Lansdale was so disgusted by such tedious chatter that he settled into a grave silence and did not say another word throughout the whole time of their remaining in the dining room.

It was not a comfortable meal and, once it was over, a languor descended upon the party. The heat beyond the solid old walls of the house was excessive and the walk to the stream and hay meadows, which had been proposed in the morning, now seemed to be an exertion beyond the spirits of them all.

The drawing room was a pleasant place to linger. The leaded casement windows – open to catch what breeze there might be – and the low black beams gave at least a sense of coolness and a great mass of flowers that filled the wide hearth scented the air with roses and lilac.

There was a little chat, a little turning over of books – chiefly *Elegant Extracts* and Dr Johnson's *The Rambler*. No one seemed inclined to move.

Lady Carrisbrook began to look anxious – as if the enjoyment of her guests weighed heavily upon her mind. She again proposed walking, and then, when the company made no favourable response, she became very active in promoting their entertainment. Rather too active perhaps, for she began eagerly proposing games and conundrums – employments better suited to a winter evening than a summer luncheon party. She produced cards and counters and even a box of yellowing alphabets from Sir Joshua's long-abandoned nursery.

There was, Dido noticed, a moment of silent surprise

from the guests at the inelegance of the proposal. Mrs Midgely raised a thick eyebrow. 'Well I never,' she said in a powerful whisper, 'what a strange way of passing the time!'

Sir Joshua looked extremely displeased. There was an expression of confusion upon Maria Carrisbrook's pretty face: an awareness of having blundered; anxiety to put right the mistake; and uncertainty as to how this was to be achieved. She looked fearfully towards her husband.

And then those of the party with good manners and good nature prevailed.

Mr Hewit stirred himself from his thoughts and pronounced a conundrum in his strong pulpit voice:

'My first doth affliction denote
Which my second is destined to feel
And my whole is the best antidote
That affliction to soften and heal.'

It was not the most original of riddles and several voices had chimed the answer of 'woman' almost before he had finished the last line. But he succeeded in what Dido did not doubt was his chief aim of covering over her ladyship's embarrassment.

Others quickly followed his example. Mr Lomax produced another (fresher) conundrum and Henry Lansdale scattered the nursery letters across a table and began to make anagrams to puzzle his companions.

Meanwhile Flora's foot was pressing Dido's as she nodded in the direction of Mr Hewit. And there was certainly no denying that his own gallant conundrum had served to fix the gentleman's attention upon Miss Prentice.

In fact, the games answered rather well for people who were too hot to walk and too ill-assorted to have much to say to one another. Soon the drawing room seemed more at ease, more animated. Before very long even Sir Joshua was smiling and teasing his brain for puzzles and enigmas.

Dido watched with great interest the expression of relief upon her ladyship's face – noticed how she was becoming easy...

At the table beside her, Mr Lansdale was busy with his word games: mixing letters together and asking his companions to form them into words. 'Now this,' he said with a grave look, 'this is a great puzzle. I wonder if any of you can answer this for me?'

He pushed a jumbled collection of letters into the centre of the table and the others of his party bent over them. He was, perhaps, unfortunate in his companions, for it seemed that most of the sharper minds were busy with riddles at the other end of the room. Miss Neville and Miss Prentice applied themselves eagerly to the task of solving his puzzle, but could make nothing of it. It was Miss Bevan, who was seated opposite him, who found an answer. She studied the letters a little while, frowned at them as if, for some reason, they troubled her; hesitated a while, then leant forward:

'Pardon me, Miss Neville, Miss Prentice, may I try?'

'By all means my dear – it is much too hard for me,' said Miss Prentice cheerfully, 'I never am very clever at these sorts of things. It is so very... Ah! You have found it out!'

While she had been talking Mary Bevan had rearranged

the eight letters into a very neat little line.

'*Relative*! Of course, yes. How very clever of you!' cried Miss Prentice.

Mary kept her finger for a moment on the word and turned her fine dark eyes upon the gentleman's face. 'That I think is what you meant, is it not, Mr Lansdale?'

He smiled and gave a small bow. 'You are too clever for me, Miss Bevan,' he said gallantly.

'Then perhaps,' she said, 'you will allow me to answer you with a puzzle of my own.' She cleared the word away with a sweep of her hand, made another selection of letters and slid them into the centre of the table.

They all, including Dido – who was beginning to be intrigued by the game – leant forward to study them. She and Mr Lansdale seemed to discover the answer at the same moment, for just as she saw the word hidden in the letters, he reached forward his hand.

Dido smiled. This was indeed a very interesting game indeed – a much deeper game than it appeared to be.

Henry Lansdale's hand, instead of instantly rearranging the letters, hovered for several moments above them as he studied them thoughtfully. Then he smiled and formed the letters into a word, tapping them into a neat line in an exact imitation of Miss Bevan's actions.

License.

'That is the word you meant, is it not, Miss Bevan?'

Miss Bevan raised her brows and began to speak but unfortunately her words were lost in a much louder appeal from the other party.

'Margery,' called out Mrs Midgely, 'can you not remember that charming conundrum which used to amuse the colonel so well? It began "Kitty a fair but frozen maid…" but I cannot remember how it went on at all.'

Miss Prentice frowned thoughtfully, but was given little time to recall anything of fair Kitty, because just then the whole party began to be on the move.

The move originated with Lady Carrisbrook who seemed all of a sudden to be quite determined on walking out. She had noticed a little clouding of the sun and thought that, 'it must surely be a little cooler now'. And Sir Joshua remarked that if they did not take their walk soon, 'it would be dinner time before they knew it'. And Flora – always the most obliging of guests – was on her feet and declaring herself well rested and ready for exercise.

It would be rude to resist further.

Mary Bevan also rose, stepped to the window and noticed that there were quite a number of clouds gathering. Miss Prentice and Mrs Midgely began to move. However, Dido lingered a moment longer studying the letters before her. Then she picked out six more and pushed them across the table. 'Maybe,' she said very quietly, 'maybe you will apply yourself to that, Mr Lansdale.'

He looked from the letters to her. Very still in all the movement that surrounded him. There was recognition in his eyes, but he did not hurry to arrange the letters. 'Yes,' he said pleasantly, 'I see the word. And I don't doubt, Miss Kent, that it describes you very well.'

Dido coloured and looked confused for a moment.

Again the gentleman set the alphabets into a neat line. *Solver.*

He stood up and made a gallant bow. 'I am sure, madam, that you are a very fine solver of mysteries.'

Chapter Eighteen

Dido was rather pleased with herself as the party prepared to leave the house: sure that she now understood one part at least of the mystery. The word play had told her a great deal. She now knew the cause of Mr Lansdale's strange anxiety and agitation. She understood why he had expressed some doubt about retaining their good opinion.

To be sure she could not quite determine whether her new knowledge brought her nearer to thinking him a murderer, or whether it overturned that possibility altogether.

But she was more determined than ever to find out the whole truth and, if he was innocent, save him. And, just at the moment, she felt that she could accomplish almost anything. It was impossible not to have a rather good opinion of her own abilities just now; for not only had she discovered Mr Lansdale's secret, she had also succeeded in convincing Mr Lomax that her suspicions were well-founded – and overthrown his notion that she was fanciful. With so much achieved, she could not believe that the difficulties before her would prove insurmountable.

She was longing to tell Mr Lomax about her latest

discovery; but, in the confusion of the dark hall, she lost him. She was detained first by Miss Prentice who exclaimed over the elegance of the luncheon and was taken with a desire to tell over all the dishes, like a child reciting a lesson she is afraid she will forget. And then, when she had escaped from Miss Prentice, Lady Carrisbrook delayed her by pressing upon her the loan of a parasol. And finally, as everyone else trooped out into the sunshine, she found that the catch was stuck on the parasol and she must struggle with it several minutes before she could open it.

By the time she stepped out onto the terrace, the rest of the party were all dispersed about the gardens and she could not see Mr Lomax.

She hesitated for a moment and looked about her. In front of her, old uneven steps led down to a pretty flower garden edged with box and beyond that there were more steps and a wall through which a stone archway led to a bowling green and a wide lawn with a sundial set amid lavender bushes. From the terrace it was possible to look clear across the lawns, where the others were sauntering about, to the meandering stream and the meadow that bordered it – just ripe for cutting now and bright with buttercups and poppies.

The day had lost some of its brilliance, but none of its heat, and clouds of small black insects hung in the air with the warm scents of box and lavender. As Dido started down the steps she discerned, in the distance, the very faintest rumbling of thunder.

She had thought the whole company well ahead of her, but as she came to the bottom of the second flight she heard a voice talking just beyond the wall. She stopped.

There was something about its low, earnest tone which prevented her going on.

'Yes, of course.' It was Mr Lansdale's voice. 'Of course I have it safe. I am not a fool, Jem.'

'You had much better destroy it.'

'No. No I won't. I cannot do that.'

Dido stepped quickly into the shadow of the wall and was instantly ashamed of herself for doing so. But now it was too late to reveal her presence and, besides, Mr Morgan had begun to urge his friend in *very* interesting terms.

'Henry, do you not see that if that document was found – if it was known that you had procured it – and kept it hidden – it could hang you.'

'Hang me? My dear Jem, you make me laugh! You pay a great deal too much attention to gossiping old women.'

'I think you had better start paying them a little more attention,' began Mr Morgan. But they were interrupted. Gentlemen were too scarce in the party for them to be left long alone and now there were several voices calling out to them.

Dido waited a moment or two and then strolled slowly out onto the lawn, her mind very busy with all she had heard.

The party was dispersed about the garden.

Unfortunately, Mr Lomax was closely engaged in conversation with Sir Joshua. Mr Morgan was walking with Lady Carrisbrook, and regaling her with an account of the emeralds' discovery, in which it appeared that it was his own extreme dexterity and penetration which had brought the jewels to light; but the story was rather marred by his being so overwhelmed by the smiling attention of the lovely Maria that he could scarcely keep from falling over his own feet. His friend, meanwhile, was attending Miss Neville and Miss Prentice, his face open and laughing and looking very unlike a man who had, only moments before, been threatened with the gallows. And Mr Hewit was, Dido noticed with interest, speaking rather earnestly to a very sour-looking Mrs Midgely. Flora was talking to Mary Bevan beside the sundial and Dido moved in their direction meaning to join them. But as she drew near, she saw that Mary was too distressed and her companion too deep in commiserating conversation for either of them to welcome an interruption.

'I knew it was to happen,' Miss Bevan was saying in a low, wretched voice. 'I knew that I must be a governess. But I confess I have been trying not to think of it. And now I find it takes me quite by surprise.'

Dido only nodded and passed on to where a shaded walk led between yew hedges higher than her head, towards the stream. In its cool seclusion she allowed her mind to wander over all the strange possibilities which the overheard conversation presented to her.

What could the document be that was so dangerous to Mr Lansdale? And why was he unwilling to destroy it?

The idea which slipped most readily into her mind was that the document must be a will. A new will of his aunt's which disinherited him – as Mr Vane had heard her threaten.

The notion brought to mind the overblown dramas which her brothers had loved to perform on their makeshift stage in the barn when they were boys. Wills – destroyed by villains in black side-whiskers, or hidden by faithful family retainers, or miraculously recovered by heroes – had, as Dido remembered, played a large part in the plot of those plays.

But was it so fanciful an idea? After all, wills – and the arguments they occasioned – filled the pages of newspapers as well as fiction. They were a common part of the real, modern world…

And then there was the burglary. She recalled Mrs Midgely's description of the drawing room and the suspicion which had immediately started into her own mind of the intruders being intent on finding some particular object. Could it have been a will which they had been searching for – and failed to find because Mr Lansdale 'had it safe'?

But if he did indeed have in his possession a document which could deprive him of his fortune, why did he hesitate over throwing it into the fire – in the accepted style of literary usurpers?

She was seated on a stone bench in the yew walk, deeply immersed in these speculations, when she heard a faltering step behind her. She turned.

The stooping figure of Mr Hewit was just retreating into the shadow of the bushes. 'I am sorry, dear lady. Please accept my profound apologies.' He bowed deeply. 'I did not intend to intrude upon your solitary musings.'

Dido quickly reassured him. 'I shall be very glad if you will walk a little way with me,' she said, jumping up. He stepped forward politely and they started together down the walk which led between the high dark banks of yew to the sparkling stream and sunny meadows beyond, bright with the red, blue and yellow of wild flowers.

'I understand that we are to have the pleasure of hearing you preach only once more Mr Hewit?'

'Well, I will say nothing at all about the pleasure, Miss Kent, but it is true, I preach only once more at St Mary's.'

'And will you satisfy the congregation by railing against the French this time?'

He smiled and shook his head. 'No, I think not, dear lady. Though perhaps I may use their example to remind my congregation of the outrages that inevitably follow when we abandon our sense of duty and obligation, as the poor misguided French have done.'

'I think that will be very acceptable to your listeners,' said Dido, stealing a glance at his lined face, 'for it will prove you to be no Jacobin, which, you know, you must be a little suspected of since you have lived some time in France.'

He looked very solemn. 'No,' he said. 'I am no revolutionary, not now. I have seen too much...' He stopped, shook his head as if it were full of memories he would be rid of. 'At least,' he finished sadly, 'I advocate now only that revolution which our saviour preached – a revolution of the heart.'

He seemed oppressed by thoughts upon which Dido did not like to intrude and they walked in silence for a while. She found herself liking the man more and more: found herself hoping that Flora's guesses were correct and that – since his mind now seemed free of radical ideas – he and Miss Prentice might yet find happiness together.

They came to the end of the yew walk where the rest

of the party were now gathered at the side of the stream. Mr Hewit began to take leave of her – she suspected he was anxious to join Miss Prentice. But she delayed him a moment. There was one more question which she *must* ask.

'Where precisely is this living which you are to take, Mr Hewit?' she said.

'In Westmorland.'

'Westmorland!'

'Yes. Why should you be so surprised?'

'Oh, I am sorry, it is nothing,' she said hastily. 'It is just such a remarkable coincidence. For that is the county in which Mr Lansdale's estate is situated.'

But Mr Hewit shook his head. 'It is no great coincidence, dear lady,' he said calmly. 'For it was Mr Lansdale's aunt who gave the living to me. The business was settled just a few days before the poor lady died.' And then with a smile and a bow he left her, strolling out quite unconcernedly to join their companions in the sunshine.

But Dido was in no mood for company; she had a great deal too much upon her mind.

She walked past the company upon the river-bank and found her way to a little rustic summer house – a simple, open construction of stone walls and wooden benches that smelt very pleasantly of fresh timber and heather thatch. And here, as clouds gathered across the bright afternoon sky, she fell to thinking very carefully indeed about the reverend Mr John Hewit. She liked him; she could not help but warm to him; she certainly did not wish to suspect him. And yet...

And yet there was no escaping some very uncomfortable

facts about him. Firstly there was his person. He was a slight man who wore powder in his hair; just like the man who had sat in one of the chairs in Mrs Lansdale's drawing room on the final evening of her life.

And secondly there was his situation. He was dependent upon Mrs Lansdale for his living and he had a past which he wished to hide. His old acquaintance Mrs Midgely certainly knew his secret and she was known to have visited his benefactress intending to give her some information.

Miss Prentice certainly believed that Mrs Midgely had gone to Knaresborough House to reveal Mr Hewit's radical past – and so deprive him of his living. Hence the fainting and the tearing up of the book in an attempt to hide any evidence.

And perhaps Miss Prentice's guess had been correct.

It was, perhaps, very convenient indeed for Mr Hewit that death had intervened before Mrs Midgely could call again...

Another, louder crack of thunder shook the summer house and the afternoon seemed to darken more than ever. Sir Joshua stepped in under the thatch, looking anxiously at the sky.

'Oh dear! I fear the weather is turning, Miss Kent.'

Dido looked up from her musing. 'Well,' she said politely. 'It is too late to materially spoil our party. It has been a very enjoyable day. I am sure we are all very grateful to you and to Lady Carrisbrook for inviting us.'

'Thank you. I am glad so many of my friends were able to come. For my wife's sake. She has no acquaintance in this country, you know. And we live a very quiet life here. I am very glad,' he continued, his eyes turning upon the river bank where Lady Carrisbrook and Mary Bevan were now walking together, deep in conversation...'very glad to see her making new friends.'

There was something doubting in his voice at the last – as if he did not quite approve the friendship she was presently forming. A governess was, no doubt, an unsuitable intimate for the new Lady Carrisbrook. That was Dido's first thought; and her second was that here was an irresistible opportunity for discovery...

'You have so many friends yourself, Sir Joshua,' she began cautiously, 'that I am sure Lady Carrisbrook will soon feel herself comfortably settled here.'

'I hope it may prove so.' Sir Joshua was standing with his hands clasped behind him, gazing out into the darkening afternoon.

'Oh!...That reminds me...There is, I believe, an acquaintance of yours who is also a friend of my brother... And Charles was asking whether I had heard anything of the gentleman since my being in Richmond... A Mr Henderson? Do you know if he is still residing in Surrey?'

There was no answer; but Sir Joshua's hands began to clasp and unclasp rapidly. Dido upbraided herself for the mistake of putting the question when the gentleman's face was turned from her.

The uncomfortable silence was shattered by a roll of thunder directly over their heads. A few drops of rain hit the grass and Sir Joshua sprang forward as if anxious to escape.

'Please, excuse me, Miss Kent,' he cried and ran out to

usher his guests into the shelter of the summer house.

As they all crowded in exclaiming and laughing, the darkness thickened and the rain began in earnest: great fat drops, falling with such force that they bounced about on the lawns. Having seen them into shelter, Sir Joshua – together with Mr Lomax – set out at a run towards the house to fetch umbrellas.

Standing beneath the dripping heather thatch, Dido watched him go with regret. What might a few moments more have revealed? Would he have answered her question? She rather thought not. But why did he not wish to acknowledge the acquaintance? As she watched his soaked figure running across the lawns, it was impossible not to think that he was fleeing from her and her question. He was certainly running remarkably fast for a man of his years... Indeed, all of a sudden, he looked almost young.

Chapter Nineteen

...And so you see, Eliza, now I cannot help but suspect <u>dear</u> Mr Hewit. Which is very unpleasant indeed. I wish with all my heart that this business of solving mysteries would work out some other way and one had only to detect guilt in people one did not like. I am quite at ease suspecting the dreadful Mrs M, or even the whining Miss Neville. But Mr Hewit, who looks so very sad and talks so very gently and who is, furthermore, almost certainly in love with dear Miss Prentice, it is just too bad to have to wonder whether he is a murderer!

And then what am I to make of Sir Joshua being unwilling to talk about the mysterious Mr Henderson?

Is there, I wonder, some shame to be attached to knowing that gentleman? Shame seems the most likely cause of his evasion, does it not? And yet during the time of his residence in Richmond, Mr Henderson appears to have been entirely respectable – or else how did he associate with such people as Miss Prentice saw attending his parties?

All of which can only lead me to suppose that something has befallen him since his time here. An embarrassment over money affairs would seem the most likely misfortune to have overtaken him. Certainly his sudden removal from

Knaresborough House, together with those other proofs of his limited means, accord well with his debts having been called in.

I wish I could discover more about Mr Henderson – in particular, where he is now. And, to this end, I have taken a measure which I do not think you will approve. I have written a letter of enquiry to the agents who let the house. But do not worry! I have not exposed myself. I have only said that I was acquainted with the gentleman during his stay in Richmond, that I borrowed from him some songs to copy and I am anxious to return his property – which, by the by, I thought a remarkably clever story! And I have asked whether they can tell me where I might direct the package.

I know you will dislike this deviation from the strict path of truth. But it is only a small one – and made in a worthy cause. And there is this to be said for my little lie: it will not inflict any pain. I only wish I could say so much for the rather large truth which I must now unfold to Flora.

You see, it is only right that she should know the secret I discovered about Mr Lansdale over the game at Brooke Manor; but I do not think that she will like to hear it. For I cannot help but think that it is only her very great determination <u>not</u> to know it which has kept her blind so long…

I have just taken my scissors to some old visiting cards and made a very tolerable set of alphabets with which to show her how the trick was done…

Dido scattered her alphabets across a table in the breakfast room and Flora watched her in bewilderment.

'I do not at all see how this can be necessary! If you

would but tell me what you have to say, I daresay I would understand very well indeed.'

'I have no doubt you would. But you might not appreciate my cleverness in discovering it,' Dido answered with a smile. It would be best, she thought, to treat the whole matter as a game. She must, at any rate, not seem to think that Flora had any particular interest in the information she was about to communicate.

Flora looked out of sorts – which was not to be wondered at since her cousin was being so very mysterious – and the hood of the barouche-landau had leaked rain upon them in their return from Brooke – and this morning the rain continued to fall.

Beyond the windows, rain dripped disconsolately off roses and formed muddy little pools in the new flower garden. Within the pretty room the open netting box, the two discarded novels and the bound volume of Dr Johnson's *The Rambler* which were scattered on Flora's sofa spoke of her efforts to fill the dull, confined morning. The blank look on her face bore witness of her failure to do so.

She was in a mood to be diverted.

'You say that you have discovered what it is that Mr Lansdale is uneasy about?' she asked Dido.

'Yes. It is a secret – something which, I fear, may well make the world suspect him of harming his aunt?'

Flora looked concerned, but, for all that, she said anxiously, 'You did not ask him any horrid questions did you?'

'No,' said Dido virtuously, 'I can set your mind at rest on that point. I do not believe I addressed a single question to Mr Lansdale yesterday. I did not need to. I only had to watch the things that he said and did, in order to discover…'

'To discover what? Tell me! I declare I hate mystery more than anything in the world!'

Dido looked down at her alphabets and began to move them around the table with one finger. 'To discover,' she said quietly, 'that he is secretly engaged to Mary Bevan.'

There was silence in the room. From outside came the sound of rain splashing on the glass and running freely down the gutters. Dido pretended to be intent upon her letters: forming them into little lines, breaking them up, rearranging them.

'Engaged?' said Flora at last in a tolerably steady voice. 'How can you think so? No, he cannot be! I always know about these things.'

'Ah, but they have been most anxious to keep it hidden and I do not think…I am sure you did not wish to suspect them…' Dido continued to look at her alphabets. 'You are his friend, of course you would not wish to suspect him of double-dealing.'

'But it is just too shocking! Why ever should you think of it?'

'Well,' Dido ran on, keeping her eyes upon the table and allowing her cousin time in which to recover. 'I have suspected it these last few days. There were hints. Miss Bevan's receiving letters which she wished no one to know about was one – and then there was her choice of books. It is, in my experience, very unusual for an unmarried lady to read books upon household management, unless she is engaged and expecting soon to have a home to manage for herself. And then her reading about the lake country pointed out a possible connection with Mr Lansdale. Once that possibility had arisen, of course, I looked about for an opportunity for the engagement being formed – and I recalled that they had both been at Ramsgate last autumn.'

Dido paused and looked up quickly at Flora. To her relief, she seemed to be more wondering than distressed.

'Of course,' she continued cautiously, turning her attention back to the letters, 'his devoting himself to such a good friend as yourself was another clue. He knew that there was no danger in paying attentions to you – for such a sensible and very happily married woman would not be misled by them.'

'No. No, of course not,' said Flora with at least an air of calm.

'With you he was safe. And while he played that game, he hoped no one would suspect him of any attachment to Miss Bevan. Under cover of flattering you, he could pay attentions to Mary which she might understand, but which would pass unnoticed by everyone else. It was very cleverly done.'

'Admirably! If indeed it was done.'

'Oh, it certainly was.'

Dido judged that Flora might now be looked at again. There was a little heightening of colour in her cheeks but nothing else to suggest suffering. It was to be hoped that she really did care nothing for the young man beyond friendship. And Dido was very pleased to see that, if she did care, she was determined not to show it.

'Well! I am sure it is the strangest thing I ever heard!'

'I have been reluctant to believe it myself. But then, yesterday, all my suspicions were confirmed.'

'How? Did you overhear them talking together?'

'In a way, yes I did,' said Dido with a smile. 'I shall explain it all to you. Do you remember,' she began, 'the conversation at luncheon yesterday?'

'Very little – except it was the dullest talk in the world! I do not think Mr Lansdale said anything at all.'

'He certainly did not say a word during the last half of the meal. And do you recall the point from which his silence originated?'

'No.'

'It began after Mrs Midgely informed the company that she had procured a situation for Miss Bevan.'

'Did it?'

'Yes, I am sure that it did. And you see that news presented him with a terrible dilemma. Ever since it was decided Miss Bevan must go out as a governess I am sure he has been wondering whether or not he should make public the engagement. Publicity is much to be desired for Miss Bevan's sake and yet...'

'And yet he dared not tell his aunt of it!' cried Flora.

'Exactly so. I daresay he feared she would cut him off. And then, after she died...'

'Why! Revealing the engagement would make the gossips say that he wished his poor aunt out of the way. Oh dear, how perfectly dreadful!' Flora was sitting very straight upon her sofa now. Her hands held to her face. Whatever else the news of Mr Lansdale's attachment had meant to her, it had certainly proved a cure for ennui. 'Why, Dido! After Mrs Lansdale died, he had to keep the engagement hidden. He dared not let it be known.'

'Quite so. Though I do not think silence suited his gallantry at all. I do not doubt that he was longing to make the announcement which would save Miss Bevan from her guardian's officious schemes. And I rather fancy that it is only her opposition which has prevented him.'

'Oh yes, for I am sure he is the most gallant man that ever lived!'

'Well, I confess that I too am rather inclined to think well of Mr Lansdale after what I observed yesterday. You see news of this situation in Yorkshire burst upon him at luncheon. Clearly Miss Bevan had found no opportunity to tell him of it herself. At Brooke he discovered that Miss Bevan was to be sent away almost immediately. He could not allow it to happen and he was quite determined to prevent it. He wanted only her permission to announce the engagement to the world.'

'But how do you know this?'

'Because, my dear Flora, he asked for her permission while we were all in the drawing room.'

'But he cannot! It is impossible! How could he ask her before all those people?'

'I will show you how it was done.' She carefully assembled her alphabets into three words: relative, license, solver. 'These,' she explained, 'were the words that were made in our game yesterday. And there is a great deal of meaning hidden in them. This first one was the anagram which Mr Lansdale made and which Miss Bevan discovered.'

Flora stared at it. 'Relative? What did he mean by it? Was he referring to his aunt? Or to Mrs Midgely perhaps…but no, he cannot have been, for Mrs Midgely is not a relative of Miss Bevan's… My dear Dido why would he wish to say anything about a relative to Miss Bevan?'

'He did not. Remember, the letters were not in this order when he put them on the table. Relative is only the word Miss Bevan chose to make, in order to hide his meaning from the others. This is the message which she really saw in the letters…'

With a few quick movements Dido rearranged the letters: reveal it.

'Oh! Oh, Dido, how very clever you are!'

'Thank you,' she said feeling more gratified than she would have liked to admit – and perhaps rather better pleased with herself than the occasion merited.

'But how can you know that she understood his meaning?'

'Because she replied to him. This is the message which she passed back to him.' She took the second word – license – and rearranged the letters: silence.

'Oh! And the third word?'

'That was my message to Mr Lansdale.'

'Solver? You meant to tell him that you hoped to solve the mystery of his aunt's death?'

'Not quite – although that is what he pretended to see in my message. In fact he saw my meaning and knew that I had discovered his secret.'

She moved the letters of the last word: lovers.

Chapter Twenty

...Well, Eliza, I rather think that Flora has had enough to distress her for a while, so I have very kindly allowed her to go away to dress for dinner without saying any more about the danger which I foresee in this engagement: that it might be thought to supply a powerful motive for Mr Lansdale to wish his aunt dead. For it is undoubtedly true that Mrs Lansdale was a proud woman and would not have looked favourably upon such a connection. It is very doubtful that he could have married Miss Bevan while his aunt was alive, without losing her favour – and her fortune. In short, the publication of the attachment would provide exactly that kind of damning evidence against the young man of which Mr Lomax spoke.

All this, I am sure, is clear enough to Flora, though I think it pains her to talk of it. I hope, for her sake, that this engagement can remain secret a little longer – and for his own sake too...

Dido laid down her pen and turned to the looking glass on the toilette table beside her, frowning at the little round face which peered out so anxiously from its dark surface. She had, from the beginning, prided herself upon being disinterested. She had set out neither to blame nor

179

exonerate, only to ensure that justice was done by coming at the truth. Yet now she had to confess that she would much rather that truth was not Mr Lansdale's guilt. And she did wish most heartily that his engagement might be concealed a little longer, for its publication would certainly bring a world of trouble upon his head.

'But you have no proof at all that that trouble would be unmerited.' That is what Mr Lomax had said when she talked to him about the matter yesterday.

They had contrived to have a few minutes conversation in the hall at Brooke while they were all waiting for the carriages. They were standing by the window watching rain slant across the terrace and the rest of the party were occupied with saying their farewells.

'I think,' he had urged her, 'that you had better leave well alone. After all, my dear Miss Kent, what proof do you have of his innocence, beyond a pleasing person and very plausible manners?' He stepped closer and spoke with gentle urgency. 'Have you considered that Mrs Midgely might know of this engagement between Mr Lansdale and her ward; that it may have been the reason for her visit to Mrs Lansdale – she went to inform her of it.'

'Yes,' Dido replied quickly, 'I have considered it. And I have also considered the next point which you are about to make.'

'And what is that?'

'That Mr Lansdale might well have wished his aunt dead before Mrs Midgely could call again and expose him.'

He smiled. 'I doubt there is any need for me to argue against you when you can argue with yourself so well!'

'I have certainly argued myself out of *that* explanation, Mr Lomax. For it will not do. Why should Mrs Midgely wish to put an end to the engagement? Is she not the very woman to be delighted by a connection with the powerful family of Lansdale? Would you not expect her to enjoy visiting the great house in Westmorland? And to enjoy talking about the visit afterwards even more? No, I am convinced she knows nothing of the engagement. She would think again about maligning Mr Lansdale if she knew that such a connection was at stake.'

He sighed. 'It seems to me that you are not willing to countenance the possibility that the young man *might* be guilty!'

'I am not so unreasonable! No, I will accept that he might be guilty...' She hesitated, shook her head. 'But, if he is, what of the lap-dog?'

'Why do you believe the dog to be significant?'

'Because its death proves that there were forces at work in Knaresborough House that night which were quite unconnected with Henry Lansdale. Indeed I am convinced that the killing of the dog proves that there were *strangers* in the house that night – for I can see no other reason for its needing to be silenced.'

He sighed. 'You are very determined.'

'And,' she continued, 'there are a great many things which Mr Lansdale's guilt cannot explain – the burglary, and Jenny White and Mrs Midgely's malice.'

'Well, well, you may be right. But none of this makes Henry Lansdale an innocent man.'

'Perhaps it does not, but it proves that his trial – that his conviction – would leave a great many mysteries unexplained. And that is why I think it would be better avoided – or at least delayed.'

'And I think,' he said rather forcefully, 'that you had better not put yourself in danger by being seen to interfere. You would be well advised, Miss Kent, to allow justice to take its course.'

Unfortunately they had been interrupted before she could reply. The carriages were announced and everyone was on the move.

Now, loitering over the toilette table in her chamber, she regretted that they had not been able to talk longer, but did not think that he would have been able to convince her. She sighed and took up her pen again.

Poor Miss Bevan! My heart goes out to her, Eliza, and I find it so very difficult myself to contemplate her fate, I find myself so disgusted by the idea of her going to this terrible place which has been chosen for her, that I cannot help but doubt Mr Lansdale will allow her to go. When it comes to the point I am almost sure that he will stop it in the only way possible to him – by announcing their engagement to the world.

And then what will become of him? Oh dear, Eliza, he is a great deal too handsome to be hanged!

There is I am sure another story to be told about events at Knaresborough House upon that fateful Tuesday evening – a tale very different from the one Mr Lomax suggests. And I am quite determined to find it out.

Firstly, I must find out more about the visitors who came there. Were they Mr Henderson and Mr Hewit? Was there a lady with them to play upon the instrument? Well, there is one person who can answer these questions if he chooses – the butler, Fraser. Though I am not sure how I shall find the courage to approach so dignified a servant, nor do I have any great hopes of his telling the truth. For whatever secrets his late mistress had would not have lasted so long without his collusion. But I shall attempt it.

And, second, I intend to find out more about the burglary: in particular what part Miss Neville and her acquaintance, Jenny White, may have played in it. I find I cannot trust Miss Clara Neville. I am sure she is hiding something from me; all the time that I was talking with her at Brooke I felt that there was something <u>wrong</u> about the things she was telling me. Why should she blush and look uncomfortable while only talking about such an unexceptionable errand as visiting her mother? What was the 'bad business' which she wished Mr Vane not to talk about?

<u>And why does she associate with a woman of bad character like Jenny White?</u>

The next morning saw Flora and Dido driving along a narrow street in a rather shabby part of Richmond, in search of Mrs Neville's home.

There had been some reluctance on Flora's part; she had not wanted to pay the call. Her acquaintance with the lady was 'very slight'; and she had been intending to drive to town this morning to call upon a particular friend in Harley Street; and, from all she could remember, Mrs Neville was quite the dullest woman in the world. And that had been when she was in her right senses, you know. Now, by her daughter's account, they must expect to find her confused as well as dull. It would be perfectly dreadful!

But Dido had persevered, assuring her that it was all done for Mr Lansdale's sake, and had given an account of everything Miss Neville had told her at Brooke.

'Oh, and so you do not believe her?' Flora asked when the tale was finished. 'You do not believe that it was in order to visit her mother that she left Knaresborough House that evening?'

'I am still not sure,' confessed Dido. 'A call upon her mother would be of great use to us. At the very least we can discover whether it is true – whether Miss Neville did go there that evening.'

'Oh well, I daresay I can go to Harley Street tomorrow instead. We shall go to your Mrs Neville today; though I confess, I did not know that helping poor Mr Lansdale must involve so many visits to tedious old women.'

So here they were, in a street of small, unprosperous looking houses and shops; and it seemed that nearly everything that Dido had heard of Mrs Neville's circumstances was true. She did indeed live in a very small way. The house which she occupied was small and the portion allotted to her use was even smaller, for the house belonged to people in business and Mrs Neville had only two tiny apartments on the drawing room floor.

There was however one circumstance for which Dido was quite unprepared. Flora had told her that Mrs Neville employed no servant; but when they arrived at the house a woman appeared to show them up the stairs – and that woman was none other than Jenny White.

They exchanged very wondering looks as they climbed the narrow stairs; but there was little opportunity for talking.

'I assure you I have never seen her here before in my life!' was all that Flora could whisper as they waited on the dark landing to be announced. Then the door was thrown open, Jenny had given them a look which suggested she suspected them quite as much as they suspected her, and they were walking into the parlour.

It was a poor, threadbare, little room; low ceiled, very dark from the smallness of the windows and the extreme narrowness of the street outside, and so very noisy that the pewter candlesticks rattled on the chimney-piece whenever a carriage passed over the cobbles below. But the old lady in her chair was straight-backed and bright-eyed under her white cap. She was smaller than her daughter, with more regular features. She certainly had an air of more intelligence. She was knitting; but she set down her pins and threw a look of some keenness at them – and at her servant – as they were shown into the room.

She expressed gratitude for their visit and fell easily into conversation. The first subject, after being seated, was her work.

'Well, my dears, you find me very busy,' said she. 'I have not the eyesight for the fine work that I used to do. Which is not at all to be wondered at, at my age, is it? But I have lately learnt to knit and I find it suits me very well. And I can make all manner of little things that are of use to myself and to the poor people hereabouts.'

Her voice was as calm and rational as her appearance, and Dido was surprised. She had expected the confusion which the daughter had spoken of to be more apparent. They talked a little more of how she passed her days. And everything she said, marking as it did either her gentility, her sense, or her gentleness, was adding to Dido's surprise.

'I daresay you miss the society of your daughter a great deal,' she asked at the first opportunity.

'Well, yes, I daresay I do, my dear,' was the quiet reply. 'But I was very glad for her to go to the Lansdales, you know. She has had so little opportunity for change and variety.'

'Of course. And no doubt she has been able to visit you tolerably often?'

'Oh yes,' said Mrs Neville, 'Clara is very good. She comes to me without fail every week – on a Tuesday evening.' Quite suddenly she dropped her voice to such a whisper as they could barely hear. 'I rather fancy...' she said, setting aside her knitting and leaning very close, '...I rather fancy that she conditioned with Mrs Lansdale for coming on Tuesdays from the very beginning.'

Dido wondered at this sudden bid for secrecy; but then she followed the direction which Mrs Neville's eyes had taken and saw Jenny White, not gone away to the kitchen as she had supposed, but standing still beside the door, her stout, red, laundress's arms folded across her breast. 'Jenny,' whispered Mrs Neville, 'takes her evening off on Tuesday, you see, and Clara does not like me to be left alone.'

'Oh!' Dido looked from the eager, elderly face before her, to the broad, red, expressionless one beside the door, which had something of a prison warder's watchfulness. 'That is very thoughtful of her, I am sure.'

Mrs Neville pursed her lips, picked up her knitting and studied it for a moment. 'Yes,' she repeated, still speaking in a whisper. 'Yes, Clara fears that if I am left, I may go out on my own and there will be trouble. That is why she insisted that Jenny should come here while she is at the Lansdales. Either she or Jenny must be with me all the time.'

'I see.' Dido was whispering now too. 'I am sure it is very kind of your daughter to take such great care of you.'

'Well, yes.' She sighed. 'But you know sometimes it is very hard. It is a very dull life. Sometimes I quite long to walk out as I used to do. I do so love to walk out – and take a little look at the shops, perhaps.'

'Of course...'

'And I am quite sure,' she ran on in an eager whisper, 'that I could accomplish it safely – if I only had a companion to go with me. I say often to Clara "I do not doubt one of my neighbours when they come to call, would be so kind as to lend me their arm and walk with me as far as the green, or to Mrs Clark's shop. I am quite sure one of my visitors would oblige me..."' And she looked very significantly from Flora to Dido.

'Well...' began Dido uncertainly. But there was a loud cough behind her and she turned to see that Jenny had taken a step nearer and was frowning darkly at her mistress.

Poor Mrs Neville sighed, seemed to shrink a little, and pretended to be engrossed in her knitting again. 'It is so very dull, to never go out at all,' she said a little more loudly.

'Why, I am sure it is,' said Flora with gentle sympathy. 'I am sure it is very dull indeed.'

'You must look forward to your daughter's visits very much,' said Dido.

'I do,' she said with another sigh. 'For you know, my eyesight is not good enough to even allow me much pleasure in books – except when Clara is here to read to me.'

'And you say that she always comes on Tuesdays. She came to you on that Tuesday on which Mrs Lansdale died?'

Flora's casting up her eyes told Dido that her questions were becoming too particular. But Mrs Neville did not seem to be at all offended. 'Oh yes,' she said, more loudly, 'Clara certainly came here the night Mrs Lansdale died.'

…And you see, Eliza, I have been wondering ever since just what she meant us to understand by that. Did she mean in fact to assure us that her daughter had come. Or by speaking so loudly, did she mean to remind us that we were being overheard – and so quite deliberately make us doubt the truth of her words?

I have been puzzling over Mrs Neville ever since we returned. And, though I fear my account may be insufficient to convince you of the strangeness of the encounter, I assure you that, if you had been present, even your trusting heart would have been suspicious. If you had seen the way that woman stood in the room all the while the poor lady was talking: the look upon her face – and her manner entirely!

Flora has suggested that there may be fears for Mrs Neville's safety: that she might be subject to sudden attacks of some kind – which would explain her being constantly attended. But there was nothing about the lady to hint at such a danger – any more than there were signs of the confusion her daughter talked of. She seemed to be not only as healthy but also as sensible as you or me, Eliza.

And there is this too to consider: why should Miss Neville employ such a woman as Jenny White – with such a reputation – to care for an invalid? It is highly unsuitable and I still do not know what to make of this confederacy between Miss Neville and a woman of bad character. I have seen her myself making payment far beyond what ought to be expected in a servant waiting upon a sick old woman. And it cannot be a coincidence that Knaresborough House was robbed after Jenny White had visited it!

Is it possible that Clara Neville has employed thieves to search the house for something that is hidden there – something she very particularly wishes to obtain…something such as a will…?

Oh Eliza! I see now how you will shake your head over this letter and smile that particular smile – all affection, disbelief and exasperation. But I am not ashamed of my suspicions, nor can I consider them to be so very unreasonable. After all, we know that the window of the drawing room was broken open from the inside.

And, if Mrs Lansdale had upon that last evening carried out her threat to her nephew and drawn up some rough and ready will – might that document not have bestowed upon Miss Neville some of the wealth which was lost to him?

Miss Neville would have as powerful a motive for wishing to find such a will as Mr Lansdale would have for 'keeping it safe'.

And such an account would also explain the extraordinary situation of Mrs Neville – who seems to be imprisoned in her own home. Why is she never to be left on her own when she is as rational as you or me? Why can she not talk freely to her visitors without fearing that that woman will overhear? I can think of only one reason. _There is something she knows which she must not tell._

Well, I doubt I have convinced you, Eliza, but I am quite determined to find out more about the burglary and, to that end, I would particularly like to speak with the butler Fraser who discovered the villains in the drawing room. However, Flora tells me that that will not be possible, as the fellow has been dismissed for stealing Mr Lansdale's cigars. Which is very vexing indeed, for I would have been very interested in hearing his account.

So instead I shall go to town with Flora tomorrow when she makes her call in Harley Street. I shall go to Bond Street to see what I may discover about the emerald necklace.

Chapter Twenty-One

It had rained again in the night and Bond Street was wet and crowded: the gutters awash with water and dirt, the paving stones shining and steaming in the sun. The noise of carriage wheels and horses' hooves, and of voices raised so as to be heard above the din, was almost unbearable to Dido's country-bred ears and she was very near regretting that she had asked Flora to set her down there.

In the cool and quiet of the breakfast room it had seemed rather a good idea. Since the carriage was coming into this part of town to convey Flora to Harley Street, why should she not take the opportunity of pursuing some enquiries relative to the burglary at Knaresborough House – and the necklace which had been dropped? She would, she had decided, visit as many fashionable jewellers as she had time for and attempt to discover the one which had supplied the necklace. If she was very fortunate she might even learn who had purchased it.

So now Flora was gone on to pay her visit and Dido was in Bond Street – but not quite alone because Flora had insisted upon leaving her servant to protect her cousin from the indignity of solitude.

'Will you wait here at the door, Robert,' she said as she

turned into the first shop. 'I shall not be long.'

She was not long – not in that shop individually. But there were a great many jewellers' establishments in Bond Street and the streets surrounding it. By the time she approached Gray's in Sackville Street her ankles were weary and her head was aching – and Robert had begun the look-out for the carriage.

She climbed the stairs slowly, thinking that perhaps Mr Lansdale had been mistaken in believing the necklace newly made, or perhaps it had not been bought in London at all…

The room she entered was as bright and colourful as a jewellery case and as noisy as the room at the Exeter Exchange where the wild beasts are kept. The place was full of finely dressed people and they were all talking loudly, for when gems and gold and expense are under discussion, the talkers are seldom unwilling to have their conversations overhead.

Behind the counter there was only one person disengaged: a tall, ageing man. Smiling, Dido approached him with the tale which she seemed to have told a hundred times that morning.

She had had the misfortune to lose a jewel – an emerald – from a necklace, and was hoping to find a matching stone, and she had been advised that it would be best matched by the jeweller who had originally supplied the piece. But, you see, it had been a gift from her brother so she did not know where it had been bought. And, of course, she could not ask her brother, for she did not wish to confess that the jewel was lost. So she wondered – had the necklace been purchased at Gray's?

She described the piece of jewellery which Mr Morgan had stumbled upon in the folds of the curtain, but received in return what must surely be the morning's hundredth shake of the head.

No, he was almost sure that Gray's had not supplied the piece. But, if she would have the goodness to wait a moment, he would consult the ledgers to see if there was any record of it.

She thanked him a little absently for, while he was talking, she had noticed that the young shop-man who was next at the counter – a thin, loosely built fellow with a shock of reddish hair, who was waiting patiently while two young ladies dawdled and exclaimed over a tray of earrings – was stealing sidelong glances, as if he was attending to what she was saying. He now began to cast anxious looks at his customers. He could not address himself to someone else before their business was complete; but Dido was sure he was wanting to say something to her.

The older man returned from his ledger. 'No madam, I am afraid your necklace was certainly not bought in this shop.'

Dido thanked him and turned away. The young ladies were still consulting and laughing over the earrings.

She stepped away from the counter. She did not want to leave. She was almost certain the young man had something he wished to say. She began to find fault with the ribbons of her bonnet. She untied them, smoothed them out, retied them. She drew off her gloves and studied their buttons before pulling them back on.

Still the girls were chattering over the earrings like a pair of magpies...

Dido began to look about her as if she were waiting for someone to join her.

At last the girls were leaving the counter – without having spent sixpence between them.

'I beg your pardon, madam,' said the young man behind the counter.

'Yes?' Dido stepped back.

'I beg your pardon, madam,' he said eagerly, his wide pale eyes blinking rapidly, 'I could not help but hear you describe the emerald necklace and I wondered – has the other lady changed her mind?'

She stared at him. 'I am sorry, I do not quite understand you.'

His face blushed red, but he stumbled on. 'The other lady who came in this morning asking about just such a necklace – has she changed her mind? Does she wish us to make one for her after all?'

'There has been another lady asking about a necklace like mine?'

'Yes madam. Not two hours ago. Is she... Is she a friend of yours?'

'I do not know. What was she like?'

'Quite tall,' he said, 'and brown-haired and...' he hesitated.

'And?'

'And rather plainly dressed.'

'No.' Dido shook her head. 'I cannot think who she might be. Our asking about a similar piece of jewellery must be no more than a coincidence.'

'Oh.' He sounded disappointed. 'I hoped maybe...' He stopped and smiled shyly, his cheeks still glowing. 'The poor lady seemed so very worried about it,' he said. 'I was sorry we could not help her.'

'Did you tell her that you could not make such a necklace?'

'Oh no madam. We could make it. But unfortunately, when I told the lady the price she found that it was more than she could afford.'

...Well, Eliza, I have been at my needlework all morning – and so have had a great deal of time in which to consider matters. And, by the by, it occurs to me that there is more danger in sewing than most people suppose. Moralists, I believe, quite mistake the matter when they advise against novel reading in young women as a disturber of the mind and a creator of wild imaginings; they would do better to consider fancy-work. For I do believe that by only occupying a woman's hands and leaving her mind free to wander where it chooses, sewing is a great disturber of the imagination.

Not that I would have you believe that <u>my</u> imagination has been disturbed this morning. My musings have, naturally, been entirely rational.

To begin with – and this subject took me all around the hem of a handkerchief – there is the matter of the emeralds. It is so very strange that another woman should enquire about an identical necklace... Of course, it might really be no more than a coincidence. If you were here with me you would probably seek to assure me that it was.

But is it so very fanciful to think that someone has tried to replace the necklace? For certainly someone has lost it – and has no chance of recovering it now that Mr Lansdale has shut it away with his aunt's jewels. For that is what I understand has happened to it by the account which Mr Morgan was giving at Brooke. And if it was important to its owner, might she not seek a replacement?

I should perhaps add that Mr Lansdale is certain that the necklace had been taken by the thieves from another house and fortuitously dropped in his drawing room in the heat of the chase. He has informed the constable who has made enquiries, but as yet no one has claimed it. Nor do I think they will. For I cannot anywise approve Mr Lansdale's idea. I cannot believe thieves to be so very careless. I confess that I have no personal acquaintance within the profession, but it seems to me that they must guard more closely the plunder which they have risked their lives to obtain. Do you not think so?

There have been no other reports of burglary in Richmond; and if one of our neighbours has indeed lost the necklace, then why should she hesitate to reclaim it?

What the solution to this puzzle may be, I cannot tell. I find myself repeating again and again the description that the boy gave of the lady who spoke to him, and every time that I do it, I feel there is something missing. I feel as if he told me something else… Something which I have forgotten… Or something which I did not quite understand.

Why I should think it I cannot tell, for his account seems remarkably unenlightening – a tall, brown-haired woman, shabbily dressed. There are I am sure hundreds of such women within range of Sackville Street. Though the only one of my acquaintance who could be so described, is Miss Clara Neville…

Miss Clara Neville. I was thinking of _her_ all through the sewing of the first two flowers of my pattern! Have you noticed, Eliza, how all my enquiries seem to bring me back to Miss Clara? Do you suppose the emeralds could be hers? A gift perhaps from Mrs Lansdale? Or does she have some reserve of wealth of which we know nothing?

I am quite sure that it is Miss Neville who must be investigated if any part of this mystery is to be resolved. And so I have determined to call upon her mother again as soon as I may. I think I shall do as she wishes and accompany her upon a walk. I cannot suppose that Jenny will have the courage to oppose me: after all, her charge will be accompanied and I will undertake to ensure that no harm comes to her. It would certainly be an act of humanity to the poor woman! And, if she does indeed have something to tell, maybe she will communicate it when she is certain of not being overheard.

I shall call upon her as early as I may; but before I do so I shall pay another visit to Miss Merryweather at the circulating library.

Chapter Twenty-Two

The lady readers of Richmond were not, it seemed, particularly fond of William Shakespeare: there were very few of his plays to be found upon the library shelves. However, among those few was *Romeo and Juliet*: unhappy lovers no doubt appealing more to the literary tastes of the neighbourhood than murdered kings or Roman history.

Having secured the volume, Dido was reluctant to return home. This morning Maria Carrisbrook had come very early to the house and she and Flora were now deep in discussions over a musical party which was soon to be given at Brooke and, if Dido returned, she would, no doubt, be obliged to give her opinion upon the arranging of the dining table and the hiring of violin players.

So she walked on past the inn and the chestnut trees and came to a favourite place of hers where there was a walk deeply shaded by lime trees and a few green benches set against the wall of the royal park. Here, she had found, she could sit in tolerable retirement and yet watch over one of the busiest parts of Richmond.

She read rapidly and with mounting interest, distracted only by the sight of Mr Vane riding past importantly on his grey horse and once by three little boys whose ball had rolled under her seat. Warmed by the sun, beguiled by Shakespeare and very deep in her own thoughts, she became insensible of the scene around her and read on until she had almost finished the play…

'Here's to my love,' cried Romeo as he drank poison in Juliet's tomb. 'Oh true apothecary: thy drugs are quick. Thus with a kiss I die.'

It was at this point – and when she had a tear in her eye – that the little boys came running again to retrieve their ball and, upon consulting her watch, she discovered that it was eleven o'clock and time to make her visit. She put the book into her reticule and set off for Mrs Neville's house, very deep in thought. For the lines that had appeared in her letter were certainly there in Shakespeare's story, but they were included in such a way as to give them quite a different meaning from the one she had expected.

It was all very strange indeed…

Mrs Neville was delighted at the prospect of walking out with Miss Kent and, though Jenny White might fold her thick red arms and say, 'I reckon you'd better not go, madam. Your daughter'd not like it at all,' she could not positively forbid the airing.

'Would you like me to come with you, miss?' she asked while her mistress was putting on her things. 'In case there's trouble.'

'No, no of course not. What trouble could there possibly be?'

Jenny's face became as red as her arms. 'Well, miss you never know with old folk, do you? I think I'd better come.'

But Dido was resolute in refusing her company.

'Your maid is very careful of your safety,' she remarked gaily as they left the house and strolled out into the street. 'She guards you quite fiercely.'

'Oh yes. She is very careful indeed.' Mrs Neville clasped her gloved hands together on her capacious knitted reticule and looked happily about her like a child on a treat. 'Why I declare, how warm the sun is! I am sure it must be above a month since I took a walk.'

'Is it indeed? That is a very long time.'

'Well, Miss Kent, last time I took a walk it ended with me talking to the constable you know – and Clara was so angry about that!'

'Was she?' said Dido with great interest. 'And what was it that you talked about with the constable?'

'Oh!' Mrs Neville seemed to recollect herself and became more sober. She looked back at the shabby little house. From the parlour window a round red face was watching them. 'It is a secret. I have given my word to Clara that I will not tell it to anyone.' She turned and regarded Dido anxiously. 'I am sure you are too kind to press me.'

'Yes,' Dido consented reluctantly. 'Of course I shall not press you to tell anything you should not.'

They walked on together – Dido's mind very busy about how she might come at this secret without seeming to do so – and soon left the narrow, dirty streets behind, for broader, tree-lined thoroughfares. Mrs Neville was glad to take Dido's arm, but altogether she walked very briskly and steadily for a lady of her years.

They came to the inn and the lime-walk and sat down to rest a while upon the bench by the park wall. They had not been settled there long, and Dido had not yet hit upon an innocent seeming question which might discover more about Mrs Neville's last airing, when they spied Mrs Midgely and Miss Prentice hurrying away from the little row of fashionable shops which fronted the green. As they approached, Dido wished them both good morning and Mrs Midgely returned the greeting with a very contented smile. But there was only a nod from Miss Prentice as she hurried past.

Mrs Neville shook her head as she looked after the retreating backs: one broad and bright in puce-coloured muslin, the other narrow and grey and slightly bent. 'Dear, dear,' she said. 'Poor Miss Prentice does not look at all well, does she?'

'No,' Dido agreed, 'no, she does not.' But to herself she acknowledged that there had been more of distress than sickness in the lady's looks. Her face had been pale and there had, almost certainly, been tears sparkling on her lashes.

'What could have happened in the shops to discompose her so much?'

'Miss Kent,' said Mrs Neville tentatively when they had sat for a little while watching the passers-by, 'would you be so very kind as to accompany me into Mrs Clark's shop? I am in sore need of new gloves and I am so rarely able to make any purchases.'

Dido readily agreed and they crossed the green to the row of pretty bowed shop windows which were bright with bonnets, trinkets, handkerchiefs and parasols.

Mrs Neville was soon happily engrossed with looking at gloves on Mrs Clark's high counter and she proved to be very dilatory over her business. Dido walked off a little way along the counter and eventually found herself a seat beside two ladies who were gossiping ferociously beneath the nodding feathers of their bonnets.

'…Mr Lansdale certainly looks guilty now…' The hoarsely whispered words caught her ear as she sat down – and immediately her attention was chained.

One lady seemed to be retailing to her friend some particularly interesting information which she had just heard. 'For of course, you see, he had to keep it secret. For his aunt would never have approved. And Mrs Clark says…'

The lady's voice dropped to a particularly intriguing undertone and Dido held her breath to listen. But, unfortunately, Mrs Neville had now discovered that there were no gloves in the shop to suit her and she was forced to quit the interesting seat.

'You look distressed, my dear,' said Mrs Neville as they walked slowly into the street.

'It is nothing. Just a little…news that I have heard. But I hardly know what it was about.'

'Oh.' Mrs Neville gave her a long, considering look. 'Perhaps,' she suggested, 'if we were to visit some more shops, you might hear more.'

'Would you not find it too fatiguing?'

'No, no,' said Mrs Neville brightly. 'Not at all. I could just look at things you know – I am always happy to look at pretty things: it would be a great treat for me – and you could find out more about this news while you wait for me.'

As she spoke she hurried on to the next shop, and,

there amid its trinkets and toys, all Dido's worst fears were confirmed.

Two solemn, clerical-looking gentlemen were standing in the shop, waiting for their daughters and wives – and looking very long and black and incongruous among the bright merchandise. They were passing the time very pleasantly by exclaiming upon the ills of the modern world. 'There is such an independence of spirit abroad among the young,' declared one. 'Such wilfulness of temper and selfishness.'

'There is indeed,' agreed his companion happily. 'And here is an example of it with young Mr Lansdale. Have you heard? He formed a secret engagement with a young woman he met at a common watering place. Without any reference to the consent of the aunt who raised him!'

'Shocking!'

'Shocking indeed. It is just as I have always said, sir, young people nowadays do not like to be crossed or checked in anything. I am not at all surprised that it should end in the most dreadful of crimes…'

Dido's heart sank as she listened. And it was the same in every shop they entered. Mr Lansdale's engagement to Miss Bevan was, all of a sudden, upon everybody's lips. It seemed the news was but just got out – and was spreading very fast indeed.

And there did not seem to be one person in Richmond who could not think him guilty of murder.

'For,' as one egregious widow was declaring to the whole company in the linen-drapers, 'there is no denying that it has a very strange look. Here is Mr Lansdale engaged to a penniless girl and likely to lose all his great

204

fortune. And the next thing anyone knows, there is poor Mrs Lansdale dead and he has got everything and is free to do exactly as he likes! It is all so very convenient for him, is it not?'

By the time they entered the haberdasher's establishment, Dido had almost ceased to wonder at how the news was got out, in her very great anxiety to discover that not everyone in Richmond was condemning Mr Lansdale. In this, the last shop in the row, Mrs Neville soon became engrossed in lace – asking to see a great many samples of it – much to the disgust of the shopkeeper who clearly judged her an unlikely customer for such an article.

Leaving her by the counter, Dido made her way to the front of the shop, where the sun was shining in. Several ladies had gathered here to admire a perfect rainbow of new sewing cotton – and to chat. At first she could catch nothing of interest; but after a few moments, she discerned the name of, 'Mr Lansdale'.

She turned towards the sound.

Three smartly-dressed young women had taken seats close by the open door, from which they could watch any passing gentlemen. They seemed to have just come from the circulating library for they all held books in their hands.

'Oh yes! Poor Mr Lansdale!' was repeated several times.

Dido listened as hard as she might. And the talk had a more promising sound than her other over-hearings. Of course it was all so very shocking. But he was such a very handsome man, was he not? And charming. And he drove a very fine barouche. And to be engaged secretly! So very romantic!

Dido smiled gratefully. It was refreshing to discover that Henry Lansdale had, at least, the good opinion of some of Richmond's inhabitants. But then…

'But Julia,' murmured one of the young ladies in a lowered voice, 'do you suppose… Is it possible that he did murder his aunt?'

The three heads pressed closer together. Dido listened hard. 'Well, my dears, I hardly know. But… But you know how it is when a young man's passions are inflamed.' Julia cast a meaning look at the neat leather and gilt volume in her hand. 'I do believe, you know, there is nothing a truly passionate man would not do to gain his ends.'

'Oh!' The girls all shivered happily in the sunshine that poured through the haberdasher's window.

'It is their mothers that are at fault,' said Dido severely as she and Mrs Neville left the shop. 'They should not allow them to read Mrs Radcliffe's works.'

'Oh?' said Mrs Neville, looking a little bewildered by this outburst. 'Do you not like Mrs Radcliffe's books, my dear?'

'Well,' said Dido, fairly caught, 'I would not say I did not enjoy them myself…but for young women…at least, for thoughtless young women…' She gave up and turned the subject. 'Have you had enough of shops for today, ma'am?'

'Yes, yes I think that I have. I did not like that woman at all.' She looked back over her shoulder at the beady-eyed haberdasher. 'I did not like the way she watched me.'

They crossed the road and strolled over the green, Dido

lost in thoughts and fears of what would happen now that the engagement was known.

And how had it got out?

However, there was one question answered by her overhearing. At least she knew now why Miss Prentice had looked so very unhappy as she left the shop.

They walked on rather briskly, for Mrs Neville seemed, all at once, anxious to be at home. As they walked, Dido worried at the old problem – should she continue to look for another explanation of Mrs Lansdale's death? Perhaps the nephew was guilty after all. Unlike Flora, she was able to see beyond the handsome face and charming manner to the possibility of evil… But always she came back to those mysteries which his guilt left unexplained…

And there was this to consider too: murder would have been an extremely foolish act for a man in his situation. The suspicions of his neighbours could surely have been predicted. And, no matter what else he might be, Mr Lansdale was certainly no fool…

'I beg your pardon, madam. May I speak with you a moment?'

Dido stopped. The haberdasher was hurrying across the green towards them – and her words had a particularly grating, ungracious sound. Her narrow cheeks were tinged with red; her even narrower lips were folded into a hard line.

'If you please, madam, I would be obliged if you would both just step back into the shop with me.'

Dido looked at her in amazement. 'Thank you, Mrs Pickthorne,' she said, 'but we have completed our errands for today.'

The woman's cheeks became redder. She looked from Dido to Mrs Neville. 'No madam,' she said boldly. 'I don't think you have.'

'I beg your pardon?'

Mrs Neville said nothing, but her hold on Dido's arm tightened. By now several passers-by had stopped to eye the three women curiously.

'I think it would be better if you came back inside with me, madam,' insisted Mrs Pickthorne. 'Then we could talk things over more in private.'

'We have nothing to talk about.'

'But I think we have madam. There is the matter of what this lady,' with a nod at Mrs Neville, 'has in her bag.'

Dido opened her mouth to protest at the woman's incivility, but Mrs Neville shook her head. 'We had better go, my dear,' she said in a very small voice.

So they turned back to the shop. Mrs Pickthorne took them to the dark counter at the back and asked that Mrs Neville open her reticule. 'Or else,' she said, her face becoming redder by the minute. 'Or else I shall have to send for the constable.'

A memory stirred in Dido's mind – something about Mrs Neville's last airing – about it finishing with her talking to the constable. She looked rather fearfully at her friend who seemed all of a sudden to have become quite alarmingly small and frail. Then, turning to the shopkeeper, she demanded to know what she expected to find in the reticule.

'Something that belongs to me, madam. Something this lady had no business taking away with her.'

Scarcely able to believe that this scene was taking place, Dido looked the shopkeeper in the eye and said – with all the dignity she could command – 'Are you accusing us of stealing from you, Mrs Pickthorne?'

'Not you, Madam, no,' was the sturdy reply. 'You weren't by when she did it. You,' she said, returning Dido's level stare, 'were at the front of the shop – listening to other folk talking.' Dido blushed. 'But, if the lady'd just open up the bag, you'll see if I'm telling the truth.'

Without saying a word, Mrs Neville bent her head over her green and yellow knitted reticule and began to fumble with the bit of ribbon that held it closed. She pulled it open. And there, clear to see, even in the dark shop, was a length of the best white French lace.

'Joseph!' called the woman, leaning back into the darkness behind the counter. 'Joseph, run out and fetch the constable.'

'But,' cried Dido in dismay. 'I am sure it was a mistake. It must have been a mistake.'

'Well Madam, we shall let the constable decide about that, shall we?'

Dido gripped the counter and experienced an alarming number of visions in the time that it took for Joseph to clatter down the stairs at the back of the shop. There was a vision of Flora crying, 'A thief? You were caught in company with a thief?' – And there was one of an assize court judge pronouncing sentence – And then one of Mrs Neville, in her crisp white cap, clutching her knitted reticule as she boarded a transport ship bound for Botany Bay...

'Please,' she said weakly, 'please, there is no need to trouble the constable.'

Mrs Pickthorne made no reply. Mrs Neville only stood with her eyes upon the floor, saying nothing. And the shock seemed almost to have robbed Dido of her faculties: the only clear thought in her head being that this was an example of Mrs Neville's 'confusion'.

Chapter Twenty-Three

...Well, Eliza, it was Mr Lomax who saved Mrs Neville and me from our oppressor: coming, like the hero of a novel, at precisely the right moment. Though, naturally, the setting of Mrs Pickthorne's shop did not lend itself to the usual garb of great coat and spurs – nor was there any leaping from his horse nor challenging to duels. But, despite these deficiencies, his assistance was timely and effective.

He appeared upon the scene just as little Joseph with his black curls and his snub nose and his big, wondering eyes arrived behind the counter to stare at us. And I will not deny that I was extremely glad to see him. (I mean of course that I was glad to see Mr Lomax, not Joseph.)

He seemed to understand at once everything about the situation and his first endeavour was to persuade Mrs Pickthorne that a mistake had taken place. This she was not willing to countenance, for I truly believe that the woman has a heart of stone and in a moment would have had young Joseph running off to inform the law of Mrs Neville's crime.

However, just as I thought that all was lost, Mr Lomax said, very quiet and grave, 'Madam, it cannot possibly benefit you to pursue this matter. Your property has been recovered,' he said, 'and I promise you that the lady's family will ensure no more such mistakes are made.'

And then Mrs Pickthorne said something about property having to be protected. 'Or where would we poor shop keepers be?'

'Quite so, madam,' said he, very calm, 'quite so. But,' and at this he leant a little closer over the counter. 'But I doubt the pursuit of the law will profit you much in this case – and I fear it might do you some harm.'

'Harm sir?' says she.

'You may not be aware,' he says very quietly with a nod at Mrs Neville, 'you may not be aware madam, that this lady's daughter is a friend of the new Lady Carrisbrook.' And at this I saw her eyes widen! 'In fact,' he goes on, 'in fact, it was Lady Carrisbrook herself who sent me here on some errands this morning. My lady is a stranger in this neighbourhood and I did not hesitate to recommend your establishment to her,' he says. 'But I doubt very much whether she would wish to deal at a shop in which her friend had been…embarrassed…'

And then she changed! For though she might complain a bit more about how ill-used she was, she was not willing to forfeit such a customer and the upshot of it all was that we were allowed to leave the shop and take Mrs Neville home – where her daughter, alerted I suppose by Jenny, was waiting anxiously for her return.

I was, I confess, shaken and distressed by this adventure, Eliza. I cannot help but blame myself and I have passed an almost sleepless night…

Dido broke off as the maid announced a visitor. Mr Lomax was come and, since Flora was from home, she must receive him alone.

There was no little confusion attending the meeting, for she had not seen him since they parted yesterday at Mrs Neville's door and there had been that in his manner then which spoke, if not quite anger, then at least a very strong disapproval of her behaviour. She met him now with heartfelt, but rather nervous thanks and raised her eyes anxiously to his face.

He looked very grave as he took a seat and gazed down at the breakfast room floor.

'I hope,' he said, 'that you have recovered from the shock you sustained yesterday.'

'Oh yes, thank you. I am quite recovered.'

There was a silence and Dido longed to begin talking of something else, but somehow she could not. She knew that more ought to be said about the situation in which he had discovered her; for there had been little opportunity for discourse yesterday while Mrs Neville was with them. But she was not entirely sure what it was that must be said. She certainly did not wish to admit that she had been at fault; though she half-suspected that she *ought* to.

She tried to thank him again, but he raised a hand to stop her.

'Miss Kent,' he began, 'I perhaps presume too much upon the friendship which I hope exists between us. But I cannot help but speak. It was, if I may say so, an ill-judged undertaking to accompany Mrs Neville into a shop.'

'Yes,' she agreed quietly. 'It was.' And then discovered, rather to her dismay, that she could not stop there. She just could not. For, painful as it was to suffer his disapproval, it was even more painful to admit that she was wrong – or to accept unjust criticism. 'At least,' she said, 'if I had *known*

213

of the danger, it would have been very ill-judged indeed. But, please consider, Mr Lomax, that was not the case. I had no reason to suppose that the outing would end as it did.'

His gravity deepened. 'Pardon me,' he said, 'but I understood you to say, when we talked at Brooke, that Mrs Neville's daughter had given you a warning.'

'No,' she protested. 'No. Not quite a warning. She had only mentioned in a general way that her mother was confused and forgetful.'

Mr Lomax closed his eyes and shook his head with a pained expression. 'That should have been...' he began, but checked himself. 'It is to be regretted,' he said more calmly, 'that that general warning was not sufficient to put you upon your guard.'

'But it could not put me on my guard, Mr Lomax,' she said. She was becoming a little angry herself now. He was being unreasonable and she could not help but justify herself. 'How could it put me on my guard? For the daughter's words were entirely contradicted by the mother's demeanour. She showed no signs of confusion or forgetfulness.'

'That I believe is common among individuals who suffer from the...weakness of character which Mrs Neville has demonstrated. In all outward shows a lady or gentleman may be moral and rational, and yet have burning within this wicked desire to posses what belongs to others.'

Dido made no protest against that. She did not try to defend Mrs Neville with any claim of a 'mistake' having taken place. It would have been impossible to do so since, after she had been safely removed from the haberdasher, a search of her reticule had revealed two pairs of new kid gloves, a cameo brooch and even a toy whistle…

'I could not know,' she protested.

'But why were you so very determined to take an elderly lady upon an outing which you knew neither her maid nor her daughter would be easy about?'

Dido blushed. 'Because,' she began a little uncomfortably. 'Because it all looked so very strange. You must remember, Mr Lomax, that I did not know what the lady was capable of. I saw only a harmless…a *seemingly* harmless old lady, whose daughter prevented her from going out or talking to visitors. You must grant me, that that had a very strange…a very suspicious appearance.'

He stood up and began to walk about the hearth rug in some agitation. 'I regret, Miss Kent, that the only thing I can grant is that you have determined upon suspecting Clara Neville. You discover that she left Knaresborough House on the night that her cousin died – and immediately you suspect her. She explains to you that she left to visit her mother; but you continue to suspect her. Why? It seems to me that the concern of a dutiful daughter is explanation enough for her actions.'

'But she lied!' The words burst out before she could stop them. She forced herself to speak more calmly. 'Why should she lie about only visiting her mother?'

'For two good reasons,' he countered. 'Because of the guilt she felt on leaving her cousin alone; and because she was ashamed to admit the cause of her concern for her mother. What other reason did you have to suspect her?'

'She associates with – she employs – a woman of very doubtful character.'

215

'Consider the poor lady's dilemma. With such a secret to hide about her mother, she dare not employ a decent maid. Her only recourse would be to engage the services of such a one as Jenny White who no one else will take – and then to pay her well to hold her tongue.'

'Yes, yes I grant you, I can see that *now*. But this is not a fair argument. I did not know – I could not know – about Mrs Neville's shocking behaviour. You cannot use against me a circumstance which has only just come to light. I only saw that Clara Neville had crept away from Knaresborough House without the consent of her cousin. And that she kept her mother almost a prisoner.'

He sighed and passed a hand across his face. 'And what do you think now? Do you still harbour these suspicions against Miss Neville?'

Dido hesitated. It was a question to which a large part of her night-time musings had been devoted. 'I do not know…I cannot help but wonder what it was she was discussing with Mr Vane at church – what it was that she wished him to keep secret.'

'I think I can supply an answer to that question. I have made enquiries and I discover that Mr Vane is one of those who has suffered in the past from Mrs Neville's…weakness of character. There were, I believe, several bottles of eye tincture taken from his shop.'

'Oh!'

'Well? Have you anything else to say against the poor lady?'

'Oh well…perhaps she is innocent…But…'

'But?'

'I do not quite know why it is,' said Dido frowning,

'but there is something…I feel as if *something* she has told me is wrong…'

He cast his eyes up to the ceiling as he endeavoured to keep his temper. He had never before met with a woman so very determined to pursue her own ideas. He had always considered himself a very calm man, but here was a test even of his patience. 'But you will not trouble Miss Neville, or her mother, with more questions?' he asked at last.

'No,' she said. 'I shall try not to. But as yet I cannot decide where I ought to look next. You see, if Miss Neville is innocent, then I must admit I am no nearer discovering the truth than I ever was.'

He sat down and regarded her very earnestly. 'Miss Kent,' he began with a renewed effort at calm. 'It is very much to your credit I am sure that you should wish to spare your cousin pain by proving her friend innocent. But I cannot help but wonder whether your affection and concern are not getting the better of your considerable powers of reason in this case. After all, Mr Lansdale may well be the guilty party. He had the opportunity of committing the deed and he was the only person to benefit from the lady's death.'

'Yes, I do not deny any of this.'

'And yet you continue to defend Mr Lansdale.'

'No. I do not defend him,' she cried. 'I agree with you that he may be guilty. I only say that his being guilty cannot be a sufficient explanation for all that has happened at Knaresborough House.'

He sighed at her stubbornness. 'Well,' he said, 'since we last talked I have learnt something which I believe rather

217

supports his guilt. I asked Lady Carrisbrook about the line in your mysterious letter. And she is certain that it is taken from *Romeo and Juliet*.'

'Ah yes!' said Dido eagerly. '"The world is not their friend, nor the world's laws…" And do you believe that it is young lovers to whom the poet refers?'

'Of whom would it be more appropriate than Romeo and Juliet – or any pair of lovers suffering opposition from their families?'

'And you believe the writer of that letter meant to tell me that Mr Lansdale was guilty – but to plead that this was a special case, that the extremity of his situation excused him?'

Mr Lomax raised his brows. 'It is something which I believe you should consider,' he said.

Dido smiled. 'I have considered it, Mr Lomax,' she said. 'But, you see, there is a difficulty. I have read the play; and I find that the words are not spoken about the play's principals at all. Those lines are spoken of an *apothecary*. It is the apothecary from whom Romeo procures poison that is said to be unfriended by the world and its laws.'

He stared at her – momentarily silenced. 'I do not understand,' he said at last. 'Do you believe the writer of the letter wished to plead for Mr Vane?'

'No. Upon consideration, I do not believe that the writer meant to plead for anyone. Of course while I thought that it was a pair of lovers who were to be considered beyond the restraints of law, I believed the writer to be defending them – from some romantic notion or other. But I cannot conceive of any argument of emotion or reason which could be brought for the excuse of apothecaries. Can you?'

He shook his head.

'In short, I think the writer meant to do no more than to point me in the direction of Mr Vane.'

'But you cannot seriously suspect Vane of harming the woman. What could his motive be?'

'I did not say that I suspect Vane,' said Dido carefully. 'I only suggested that the letter might be designed to *make me suspect him*. After all, we have no reason to assume the writer of that letter is either honest, or disinterested.'

He considered a while and at last admitted, 'It is well reasoned.' She smiled, extremely well pleased to have carried her point. 'However,' he continued, 'it does not change my opinion that it is dangerous for you to interest yourself in this business. It is for a court to decide. It is their duty to determine the truth, not yours.'

Her spirit rose against that. 'No,' she said. 'No, that I cannot accept. I believe it is the duty of all rational men and women to ensure that justice is done.'

'But our duties must always be proportionate to our powers. You had better leave this matter to those better qualified to deal with it.'

She coloured. 'You rate my powers very low, Mr Lomax, but I think even you would have to agree that they extend at least to the observation of what is happening around me. You will have noticed that I am neither blind nor deaf.'

Colour rose in his face too. 'Miss Kent,' he replied. 'I do not, for one moment, doubt that you are capable of observing what is passing around you. It is an art you are very practised in. But what I would doubt – what I believe I have cause to doubt – is your power to always interpret correctly and safely the information which you gather from your observation.'

Dido could not trust herself to reply. She feared she might say something in anger which she would later regret.

Meanwhile, he had gained a little control over himself. 'I fear I am intruding upon your time,' he said rather stiffly. 'I am keeping you from your letter.' He rose from his seat. 'I hope you will forgive the freedom with which I have spoken. Nothing but my very great concern for your welfare could have induced me to do so.'

'Thank you,' she said, also rising. 'I am grateful for that concern.'

He stared down upon the floor. 'Last autumn,' he said. 'I flattered myself that there was a particular degree of understanding and regard existing between us.'

Dido also was suddenly very interested in looking at the polished wood of the floor.

'Perhaps you may feel,' he continued, 'that that very particular understanding entitles me to advise you. If that is so, my advice – my very strong advice – is that you abandon these enquiries and cease to interest yourself in the business of Mrs Lansdale's death.'

She said something – though what it was neither she nor he could tell. However, her tone was encouraging enough for him to continue.

'Of course, after due consideration, you may decide that the degree of acquaintance does not authorise me to interest myself in your well-being. If that is so, I pray you will forget entirely what I have said – and act as you please.'

Chapter Twenty-Four

He was gone, and Dido must endeavour to recover her composure before her cousin's return. But every kind of reflection served only to increase her agitation.

And, altogether, between pleasure that he should recall a 'particular understanding'; anger at the authority he supposed that understanding gave him; and confusion over how she should act next, there was no repose to be found for mind or body. She walked restlessly about the room until the walls themselves became oppressive and she was forced to fetch her bonnet and repair to the garden in the hope that fresh air and flowers might soothe her spirits and inform her decisions.

And, out among the roses, a consideration of his last speech soon produced one certainty. He would judge her upon her actions. Continuing to pursue her mystery in defiance of his advice was to be a sign that she did not value his regard. She must choose between affection and curiosity. If she was to retain his esteem, she must adopt his opinions.

She should perhaps not have taken such pleasure over identifying the Shakespearean quotation As her grandmamma had once told her long ago, 'Gentlemen most particularly dislike being contradicted. If you know that they are wrong, you had better conceal the truth rather than inform them of it.'

Now, thought Dido as she seated herself in the honeysuckle arbour, in connection with whom had she said it? Was it Mr Powel, the promising young lawyer with expectations of almost a thousand a year? No, on second thoughts, it was the reverend Mr Fawcett, with only seven hundred a year, but a *very* comfortable vicarage. She smiled at the memory. Grandmamma had been almost sure that the seven hundred and the vicarage would be hers; and Dido herself had found Mr Fawcett pleasing – until the regrettable business of the Tudor queens.

The difficulty had arisen because Mr Fawcett was sure that Mary Queen of Scots was sister to Queen Elizabeth. He had been extremely disconcerted when Dido informed him that they were but cousins. And Dido had been even more disconcerted to find that producing a history book and proving her point had not settled the matter at all – or at least had not settled it in the way that she and her grandmother had hoped. For the end of it had been that little Caroline Corner got the comfortable vicarage… And Dido had been left to rejoice in nothing but an accurate understanding of history.

Sitting now in the tranquillity of Flora's garden, watching yellow and red butterflies busy about the pansies and listening to the bubbling song of a pair of white doves that had perched on the wall behind her, she could smile easily at the memory of Mr Fawcett. But she had to acknowledge that Mr Lomax had much stronger claims, not only upon her affections but also upon the truth.

She was by no means sure that she was entirely in the right this time.

For she had blundered badly over Mrs Neville. And, though she could not believe the things she had uncovered about Mrs Lansdale's death to be of no value, she could not help but admit that she knew not what to make of them. Perhaps Mr Lomax was right and such matters were better left to the authorities appointed to deal with them.

It was, of course, intolerable that he should so doubt her powers of understanding, when, last autumn, she had proved herself to be greatly his superior in resolving mysteries... And yet it was so very kind of him to worry that she was putting herself in danger. And, since the late discovery about Mrs Neville left her at a loss to know where to turn next in the matter, perhaps she might just as well leave off...

Flora returned from her morning calls to find her cousin walking about the garden in an unusually quiet, desponding mood and she might perhaps have enquired what had happened in her absence – if only she had been able to spare time for it. But Flora was too much occupied with the information which she had to give to do more than remark upon Dido's paleness, before saying, 'I have heard such news! I declare, you will never guess it.'

'I daresay I shall,' said Dido with no great interest. 'Everyone is talking about Mr Lansdale's engagement, I make no doubt.'

'Oh yes!' said Flora. 'As to that, of course, the whole place is alive with it. And, by the by, he has behaved extremely well. He has been to Mrs Midgely, you know, and made everything open.'

'Well, I am glad to hear it,' said Dido. 'It was much to be desired for the sake of Miss Bevan's reputation. It would not do to have it only a matter of gossip. And what will the poor girl do now? She is not going to Yorkshire?'

'No. Nothing is decided upon; but she is to go to Windsor tomorrow to stay with some friends.'

'I am sure that is wise. It cannot be pleasant for her to remain here.'

'Yes, yes,' said Flora impatiently. 'But this is not my news. My news is about how the gossip was started!'

'Oh?' Flora was pleased to see that she had roused Dido from her strange lethargy. 'And how was it started?'

'By Mrs Midgely herself!' cried Flora.

'It cannot have been,' protested Dido.

'But it was! For Miss Prentice told me all about it. And very distressed she is by it, for she cannot understand why the woman should do such a thing. And no more can I!'

'Mrs Midgely let out the news of Miss Bevan's engagement?'

Flora nodded eagerly and took Dido's arm. As they walked on along the path she explained. 'Well, you see, Miss Prentice says that it happened in Mrs Clark's shop yesterday. She says that she and Mrs Midgely were gone into the village upon an errand – to the inn I believe for Miss Bevan, poor thing! was unwell with the headache, and so she had asked them to call at the inn to bespeak her a place in the coach for Yorkshire. And then, Miss Prentice says that after they had accomplished that, Mrs Midgely suddenly took it into her head to visit Mrs

Clark's. So in they went – and no sooner were they in the shop than she – I mean Mrs Midgely of course – fell to talking with Mrs Clark. Of course, Miss Prentice was not supposed to hear what was being said. But she did – for, you know, her hearing is better than you would think. She does not see so clear, but I am sure she hears as well as any creature alive. And so she heard Mrs Midgely telling the shopkeeper of the engagement. "I have long suspected them to be engaged," she heard her saying. "But now I am quite sure of it".'

Dido had been changing during this speech: looking more lively and altogether more like herself every moment. 'Is she quite sure that that is what was said?' she asked now.

'Oh yes, she is quite sure.'

'But, Mrs Midgely must have known that to let the engagement out would endanger Mr Lansdale.'

'I am sure she must.'

'But she must also…' Dido struggled to comprehend all the new ideas which were crowding into her brain. 'If she knew of the engagement… She must also have known that *Miss Bevan's* happiness was concerned in the matter.'

'Exactly so!' cried Flora. 'And that is what poor Miss Prentice cannot understand – or forgive.'

'But…' Dido sat down abruptly on a bench and stared ahead in a way which Flora found rather alarming. 'But if she has "long suspected" the engagement, then she has known – she has known all along – that Mary's well-being – her whole future and happiness – depend upon Mr Lansdale. And yet here has she been maligning him! Accusing him of murder Practically consigning him to the gallows! She has knowingly been ruining not only his prospects but Mary's too. How could she be so unfeeling to a girl who is almost a daughter to her?' She pressed both hands to her mouth: her eyes widened as the full meaning of the news bore in upon her.

'Dido, what is it? Please do not look so strange! What are you thinking of?'

She lowered her hands. 'I am thinking,' she said inexplicably, 'of a violin: a violin hanging behind a door.'

Chapter Twenty-Five

...Do you remember the violin behind the door, Eliza? We saw it on our tour into Derbyshire with Charles – at Chatsworth. I am sure you must remember it for we were all agreed that it was one of the most remarkable things that we saw in all that county of wonders. It is no more than a painting, but so very cleverly done that at first, knowing no better, you take it for a real instrument and then afterwards you walk around it and see it plainly for what it is. It is all a matter of perspective.

It is a Trump Loy – or so the housekeeper who showed it to us said – though I think her knowledge of French was a little deficient!

But I am convinced now that this hatred of Mr Lansdale which I thought I saw in Mrs Midgely was nothing but a Trump Loy. A mere deception of the eye. And all this time I have been taken in by it!

Eliza, Mrs Midgely does not hate Mr Lansdale at all. She has never borne <u>him</u> any particular ill-will. It is Miss Bevan: it is her own ward, the girl she has raised, whom she dislikes: and dislikes her so much that she will do anything to destroy her happiness!

It is as if I have walked around the picture and at last seen it plainly.

Everything Mrs Midgely has done – all this spreading of rumours and persuading the apothecary into action – has been aimed at injuring not Henry Lansdale but Miss Bevan.

As soon as it is considered from this perspective, everything becomes comprehensible.

Instead of providing for the poor girl – instead of putting her in the way of a good marriage – Mrs Midgely wished to mortify her by sending her away to earn her bread. But, at some point, she began to suspect the engagement. Marriage to such a wealthy man would ensure the girl's comfort and put her beyond Mrs Midgely's reach. So, she has turned her efforts to destroying Mr Lansdale – because that is the only sure way of preventing his marrying Miss Bevan.

First I think she tried to rob him of his inheritance by warning Mrs Lansdale of the attachment; but she was denied admittance at Knaresborough House and, of course, the lady died before she could make a second visit. So, I believe, she seized upon the suspicions of the apothecary, determined to make as much trouble as she might.

Of course, she has known all along that publication of the engagement would convince the whole world of his guilt and by hurrying on Miss Bevan's departure she hoped that he would be forced to make it public in order to save her. But Miss Bevan would not allow him to reveal the secret. She would rather go away to Yorkshire than permit him to endanger himself by acknowledging the engagement. You will notice, Eliza, that it was only after she had shown herself determined to go away – when she had actually bespoken her place in the coach – that Mrs Midgely decided to act by spreading the rumour herself.

This explains a great many little things. It explains, for example, why Miss Bevan has lately avoided her guardian's company – preferring to sit with Miss Prentice instead...

But, now that I see the picture for what it truly is, I find that there is one very important new question to be answered. Why should Mrs Midgely suddenly turn against a girl she has known for nearly twenty years?

And the dislike was certainly sudden. Flora is sure that this plan to send Miss Bevan away was never mentioned until last November. In which month, of course, according to Miss Merryweather's account, Mrs Midgely lost not only her taste for love stories but also her soul...

What can have happened last November?

It is made all the more puzzling by Flora's information that Miss Bevan <u>was not even at home</u> at this time. For in November of last year Mary was in Ramsgate – and forming her attachment to Mr Lansdale.

And this, Eliza, leads me to suppose that this hatred – and I am sorry to use so strong a word, but such I think it must be called – this hatred arose, not from anything Miss Bevan <u>did</u>, but rather something which Mrs Midgely <u>learnt about her</u>.

You will, I trust, be very distressed to hear that it is now past two o'clock in the morning and I am endangering my health by passing another sleepless night. For I cannot cease to puzzle over this conundrum. What was it that Mrs Midgely learnt during Miss Bevan's absence which rendered her soulless – and determined to be rid of her ward...

I find that there are two things which I keep remembering: there is the desk in Miss Prentice's room – and the portrait hanging above the fire in Mrs Midgely's parlour. And together these two memories point to such an answer... But I will not write it until I am certain.

Tomorrow I must visit the house and look again at these things to be sure that I am remembering correctly. And if I am… Well, then, I think I had better consult with Miss Bevan.

Of course Mr Lomax had almost persuaded me that I should leave these matters alone… But if I go about things very quietly then perhaps he need not know what I have done… And besides, now that I have come so close, I cannot leave this part of the mystery in uncertainty. I simply <u>cannot</u>. It is a great deal too much to ask of me.

Next morning Dido found Mary Bevan in the little garden at the side of Mrs Midgely's house – a dark, sunless place of severely clipped grass, grey gravel and stunted yew hedges. She was seated upon a narrow bench, looking paler than ever, with great shadows beneath her eyes; but she greeted Dido warmly and immediately said, 'I am very glad to see you, Miss Kent, for there is something I have been wanting to tell you about.'

'Oh yes? And what is that?'

'The extract in your mysterious letter – have you succeeded yet in finding its origin?'

'Oh!' said Dido with some surprise. 'Yes, I have. It comes from Romeo and Juliet.'

'Does it? I did not know.'

'Why do you ask me about it?'

'Because…' Mary stopped, looking a little confused. 'Well, it is nothing. But I happened to read it yesterday – quoted by Doctor Johnson in *The Rambler* – it is in number one hundred and seven. I thought it might be of use to you to know… But if you have already found the original…' She shrugged up her shoulders and smiled.

'Thank you,' said Dido. 'Thank you very much – that might prove very useful indeed.'

'So,' said Mary with a curious look, 'you are still pursuing your enquiries?'

'Oh yes.' She looked sidelong at her companion. 'In fact,' she said, 'I have been about them this morning.'

'Oh? And what have you been investigating?'

She hesitated again, but decided to be frank; there was something about Miss Bevan's own open manner which seemed to demand a return in the same kind. She would be honest – though she doubted very much that her companion would like what she had to say. 'I have been investigating Colonel Midgely's old desk,' she replied quietly. 'And the portrait hanging in your parlour.'

'Indeed? Have you?' cried Mary in surprise. And then they sat in silence for a little while. A blackbird sang high up on the roof of the house and, out on the street, carriage wheels rumbled by. At last Mary turned and looked her full in the face. 'And what have you learnt from the desk and the portrait?' she asked with a tolerable pretence at calm.

Dido took so deep a breath she might have been about to plunge into a cold bath. 'I believe I have learnt the cause of Mrs Midgely's…resentment against you,' she said.

A little colour rose into Mary's pale cheeks, but she showed no other sign of distress – or surprise. 'I think,' she said at last, 'that you had better explain exactly what you mean, Miss Kent.'

'Well,' began Dido, turning her eyes down upon the gravel at her feet, 'at first, you know, I could not determine why Mrs Midgely should change towards you during the short time that you were absent in Ramsgate.'

'I see.' Mary thought for a moment. 'It would, I suppose, be of no use to attempt to convince you that such a change did not take place?'

'No, I do not think you would succeed in convincing me.'

'Very well, I shall, as the saying goes, save my breath to cool my porridge.' Mary folded her hands tightly in her lap and waited calmly; it seemed she would let Dido reveal what she knew, rather than risk any disclosure of her own.

'You see,' Dido said, 'I set myself to think of what might have taken place during those two months to produce so strange a revolution in feeling.'

'Yes?'

'And the only thing I could think of was that, during that time, Colonel Midgely's book room had been emptied of its papers. You see I remembered that Mrs Midgely had told Flora that that must be accomplished before Miss Prentice could take possession of the room.'

Mary put up her hand to check a little spasm in her throat, but said nothing.

'And then you see,' continued Dido, still very intent in her study of the gravel, 'then I recalled the broken lock upon the desk. Which made me think – for I have a mind which is always seeking answers and explanations – which made me think that there must have been something locked within. Something which was only got at with violence. And then...'

'Yes? What did this remarkable mind of yours turn to next?' asked Miss Bevan, attempting to speak lightly, but with her hands all the while knotting themselves together in a way which showed her far from indifferent to what was being said.

'Well,' said Dido, 'I am afraid my mind turned next to the portrait in the parlour.'

'It is,' said Mary quickly, 'a picture of Mrs Midgely's father.'

'Yes. And a very grim old fellow he seems to have been!'

'I beg your pardon, but I cannot understand what interest he can have held for you.'

'Oh, none at all...except that he is old and ugly.'

Mary unclenched her hands and instead crossed her arms across her breast as if, all at once, she was cold. 'What were you expecting to see, Miss Kent?'

'Well, I hardly knew what to expect. You see, Flora – who has not been in the parlour since last summer – believed that it was the handsome Colonel Midgely who was hanging there; but yesterday it occurred to me that it was not a handsome man I had seen when I was in the parlour two weeks ago. I had quite a distinct memory of a scowl and a hooked nose. An impression which I confirmed this morning. And the only explanation I can think of is that there has been an exchange. An explanation which seems all the more likely from the observation I have just made of there being a narrow band of unfaded wall paper running around the frame – as if there has been, recently, a slightly larger portrait hanging in that position.'

Mary wrapped her arms tighter about herself. 'And this you believe to be of some significance?'

'Oh yes, most certainly. For why should a widow remove the portrait of her late husband from the place of honour above the parlour fire?'

Mary offered no reply.

Dido raised her eyes at last from the gravel and looked into her companion's face. 'In short, Miss Bevan. I cannot help but conclude, that something was discovered in the drawer of the desk which turned your guardian's heart not only against you but also against her husband.'

Miss Bevan said nothing, but shivered slightly and clasped her arms more tightly than ever – as if the burden of all she had had pressing upon her mind for the last months was grown almost unbearable.

Dido's conscience whispered against her, but she continued, convinced – or rather, hoping – that an end to secrecy must offer the best relief. 'I believe...' she said. 'At least, the most likely explanation would appear to be... when your history is also taken into account...' She drew a long breath. 'You are his natural daughter, are you not?' she finished quietly.

Mary avoided her eyes, but nodded. 'There were,' she whispered, 'letters in his desk...from my mother. Of course I have not seen them... But I believe they were letters of such...intimacy...as left Mrs Midgely in no doubt of the relationship subsisting between them.'

'And, until she read these letters, she had never suspected anything?'

Mary shook her head. 'Until then neither she nor I had ever thought that the colonel's actions in taking me into his family were anything but good and disinterested. It was a shock. For poor Mrs Midgely I believe it has been painful beyond measure. She has, I believe, been beside herself with the suffering of it... Miss Kent, please do not think too badly of her for what she has done. I truly believe that she scarcely knows what she is about.'

'You would defend her?' cried Dido wonderingly. 'After all she has done to injure you?'

'No,' said Mary, 'I cannot defend what I know to be wrong. But, believe me, I would gladly suffer her malice ten times over if only I could retain that affection and respect I had been used to feel for her husband: a man I have, since the age of five years old, looked up to as all that was noble and honourable.'

'It is very much to your credit that you should feel so. And I am sorry – very sorry – if anything I have said or done has added to your pain.'

Mary shook her head.

'I am sure I do not need to tell you that the information will be spread no further by my means.'

'Yes, I have no fear on that score, Miss Kent,' she replied with a small smile. 'I have observed that you are a collector rather than a disseminator of information.'

'And I would not have tormented you with this conversation if I had not thought that I could assist you in your present situation.'

'You mean then to continue with you enquiries concerning Mrs Lansdale's death?'

'Oh yes, for it will soon all be in the hands of the magistrate and his jury. And how else, but by the uncovering of the truth, is Mr Lansdale to be saved from being punished for a crime he did not commit?' As she spoke she took care to watch her companion closely. The fine brown eyes held her gaze steadily; not a muscle moved in the face to betray doubt – or any other emotion.

'He is innocent,' said Mary solemnly. 'I have no fear of you, Miss Kent. I am sure that he must…that he will, in the end, be proved entirely guiltless.' She sighed. 'I wish with all my heart the engagement had not come out. I have done everything within my means to conceal it.'

Dido eyed her keenly. 'And, may I ask – how long has the engagement existed?'

'No, I do not mind your asking at all. I have been engaged for about five months. Mr Lansdale asked me to marry him while I was at Ramsgate. I was unsure of my own feelings then; but, soon after my return, I wrote and accepted his offer. As soon as he received my answer he began to make plans to come to Richmond – so that he might be near me and so that he might work to bring about our marriage.'

'And how did he plan to do that? Considering the very great opposition he must have suffered from his aunt. Did he mean to get her consent or act without it?'

'He meant to…persuade her into acceptance. She was extremely fond of him in her own way. And he is a very determined young man. He had ways of working upon her.' She caught Dido's eye and shook her head very solemnly. 'But I know,' she said very firmly, 'that it was not his intention to harm his aunt.'

'I am very much afraid that it will appear to the jurymen that he did.'

'To my mind, Miss Kent, they would be more likely to come at the truth by attempting to find the housebreakers.

They are probably the guilty ones. For it seems to me that such fellows might have made more than one attempt upon the house. Perhaps they came on the night of Mrs Lansdale's death – carried out the murder, but failed to take anything of value – and so they returned.'

Dido looked doubtful. 'It is not easy to see how housebreakers might have poisoned the lady, but I grant you that they would have had good cause to dispose of the little dog.' She considered for a while. 'The thieves appear to have been searching for something when they entered the house,' she continued. 'Have you any notion of anything that Mrs Lansdale had which was of particular value? Something which might be the object of such a search? Something which was of greater value – at least to the thieves – than silver candlesticks?'

'No, I cannot think of anything.'

'Do you know of a particularly dangerous document which is presently in Mr Lansdale's keeping?'

For the first time since their conversation began, Mary seemed anxious to avoid her eyes. She stood up, clasping her arms about her. 'What kind of document do you mean?' she asked.

'I do not know,' said Dido, watching closely. Mary began to chafe at her arms as if she were cold, though it was such a warm day there was no chill in the air even in this shady corner. 'A will perhaps?' she suggested.

'No,' said Mary sharply. 'I know nothing about a will. However, I am quite sure that if Mr Lansdale had such a document in his possession he would not conceal it.'

'I am sorry, I did not mean to suggest anything dishonourable.'

'Of course you did not. But, I really feel that we have said enough upon this painful subject. I pray you will excuse me. I have a great deal of business to attend to, for I am to go away today.'

As she spoke, a very unexpected memory stirred in Dido's mind. She paused and took a long survey of her companion, taking in the pale face, the crossed arms, the agitated manner. She was touched by doubt – almost suspicion.

'Of course,' she said slowly as she stood up. 'I am sorry to have delayed you so long. You must have a great deal of business to attend to, Miss Bevan – I don't doubt that you have all your gowns to pack, and your travelling dress to prepare, have you not?'

'Yes,' she said, with a puzzled look, 'I have.'

Mary waited – expecting some explanation of this strange speech; but Dido merely bade her a rather distracted farewell, and walked away.

Chapter Twenty-Six

Dido walked slowly down the hill to her favourite seat by the park wall and looked about her.

It was a lively, interesting scene; two grand carriages were drawn up outside the inn to deposit a large family with all the proper busyness of footmen and trunks and band-boxes and children and nursery-maids. In the lime-walk, ladies strolled about under parasols and, close by, in the little row of shops, other ladies and gentlemen were more purposefully engaged.

But, once she was comfortably seated, her thoughts began to turn inward and she soon forgot her surroundings as she fell to considering everything which her talk with Miss Bevan had revealed.

First of all, she was quite sure that Mary believed Mr Lansdale to be innocent. There had been no doubts, no demurs; she had answered every question with candour and intelligence… At least she had done so until mention was made of a document. Then there had certainly been consciousness and a desire for evasion. Dido was sure of that – though she still held to her earlier view of Mary's character and doubted very much that she had given a direct lie. For Mary was an exceedingly bad liar. When she had lied about the letter in the post office, her red face and downcast eyes would have betrayed her to any listener more sensitive than Mrs Midgely.

But just now, in the garden, there had been no symptoms of dishonesty – though, perhaps, there had been a desire to avoid some truths…

Dido recollected her words carefully. She had said that she knew nothing of a will… Yes, it had only been a will she denied knowledge of… Did it follow then that she knew of some other document? And, if so, what could it be? And why did Mr Morgan believe that it was so dangerous to his friend…?

She shook her head helplessly and tried to come at the business in a different way entirely. She imagined how it would all look to the jurymen. Here was Mrs Lansdale dead and the apothecary saying she had died of too much opium mixture. And it would seem that there were but three people who had had opportunity to administer it. There were Mr Lansdale and Miss Neville who might have introduced the fatal dose to the evening's chocolate; and there was Mr Vane himself who might have administered it under the guise of the 'usual draught'. But Miss Neville and Mr Vane, far from having anything to gain from the terrible act, could only be made the poorer by it: she by the loss of a comfortable home and he by the loss of a wealthy patient. Only Henry Lansdale had any motive for wishing the poor lady dead.

She found herself so extremely discontent with this conclusion that she could not help but wonder whether Mr Lomax was right and she had, almost without knowing it, determined upon exonerating Mr Lansdale…

'I shall not apologise for disturbing you, Miss Kent,' said a merry voice beside her, 'for, by the look upon your face, I see that your thoughts are so unpleasant you ought to be disturbed.'

She looked up and saw Mr Lansdale himself making his bow and asking if he might sit with her a moment.

'I have,' he said as he sat down, 'been seeking you in order to ask a very great favour. I have been to Mrs Beaumont's house but found you both from home. Mrs Beaumont has, I understand, driven out to Brooke Manor, but the maid said that you had walked out and I hope you will forgive me for coming after you.'

'Of course. And I am sure that both Flora and I will be happy to help you in any way we can.'

'Thank you.' He then said nothing for a while, gazing out across the busy scene. He had begun in his usual laughing way with all his usual determination to be serious about nothing. But now he had changed and his handsome face was more solemn than she had ever seen it before. A frown had gathered on his brow. 'I am hoping,' he said at last, 'that you and Mrs Beaumont will be so kind as to perform the office of true friends to Miss Bevan.'

'In what way do you wish us to show our friendship?'

'Will you be so good as to persuade her...or, at least, to represent to her the wisdom of complying with my wishes – and marrying me immediately.'

Dido could only look the astonishment which she felt, the application had taken her so completely by surprise. He held up a hand. 'Please, Miss Kent, do not begin upon the dangers – the impolicy – of a hasty marriage. I have had it all from her.'

'I shall make no such argument, then. I shall only say that I can see no reason for such a step being taken while matters are in their present unfortunate state of uncertainty.'

Something of his usual smile returned. 'Matters,' he said, 'are perhaps not quite so uncertain as you suppose. There is at least the certainty that I am to be brought to court. I am summoned to appear at the Quarter Sessions in just five days' time. The paper was delivered to me yesterday.'

'I am extremely sorry to hear it. It grieves me beyond measure.'

'I am innocent,' he said quietly. 'And in that and in the will and justice of God, I will put my trust. However...' And, although he had been speaking with great solemnity and feeling, the irrepressible smile was returned now. 'However, when it comes to the justice of men... Well, I hope I shall not shock you when I say that I have not quite so much faith in our English laws not to suspect that they have sometimes hanged an innocent man – and may do so again.'

'I sincerely hope... It will be my most fervent prayer that, in this case, they will not.'

'Thank you. And now, as to my marriage...'

'Forgive me, but I cannot understand what possible reason there can be for hurrying it on. It had better not take place... Not until after you are released from this dreadful suspicion. For I cannot help but feel that your marriage – the apparent self-interest and heartlessness of such a measure so soon after your aunt's death – would greatly prejudice a jury against you.'

'Miss Kent,' he said, instantly solemn and fixing his eyes upon her face, 'you may not be aware – there is, of course, no reason why you should be – that a man condemned for murder forfeits his estate.'

'No,' she admitted, 'I did not know it.'

'Consider it now then. Consider that if…if the laws of England should fail me, I will lose not only my own life but also the power to provide for Miss Bevan's future comfort. I would be able to make no will. I could bequeath nothing to her.'

'I see.'

'Consider too her present poverty, her friendless state, and I am sure you will agree that a marriage – which would enable me to settle money upon her – is the best possible course of action. Jem is drawing up the settlement now. We could be married tomorrow and my mind would be at ease. Miss Kent,' he said, turning pleading eyes upon her, 'I hope I can face my own fate with fortitude; but to leave her alone and unprovided for is more than I can bear.'

Dido was so affected by this appeal that it was several minutes before she could speak; but when she was able to make a reply she could not do other than to promise her assistance in persuading the lady to an immediate marriage. 'Though I rather doubt my arguments will have any effect. She is a very…determined young woman.'

'She is indeed!' he cried, his lively air immediately restored by her promise. 'But I will be extremely grateful if you will make the attempt.'

'And are you sure that a marriage can be accomplished within four days?'

'Oh yes. It can certainly be accomplished.'

'But what about the calling of banns?'

'There need be no banns, Miss Kent.' He stood up and made his bow. 'For it just so happens that I have about me a special marriage licence!'

And, before Dido could consider all the meaning of this reply, he had made his final thanks and adieus and was walking away. She almost called him back, but then changed her mind and sat instead watching his retreating figure and thinking very hard indeed. It was one of those rare moments when human thought seems to transcend the limit of words and move with all the rapidity of a higher power.

As she watched him stride across the green – and throw a sixpence to the ragged little boy who was holding horses outside the inn – she was considering this special licence and everything that his possession of it might mean...

By the time he was hurrying past the bright bow-window of the trinket shop, she had come to an understanding of exactly what it meant...

And, before she lost sight of him in the crowd beyond the haberdasher's, she was very busily reckoning up exactly the part he had played in his aunt's death.

At last some of the tangled knots of this mystery were beginning to unravel.

Chapter Twenty-Seven

'It is all a matter of Trump Loy, Flora. It is nothing more.'

'I beg your pardon?' said Flora, though she had very little hope of understanding her cousin. When Dido was in such a mood as this, it was advisable not to attempt too much understanding – for it was liable to occasion headaches. And, just now, she would gladly forgo comprehension for the sake of only getting the french doors closed before the drawing room was quite filled with evening air. Henry Lansdale and Clara Neville were engaged to drink tea with them and she did not wish to receive them in a damp room.

But Dido was too restless to remain within doors and was gone out to pace about on the veranda while they awaited their guests. 'It is Trump Loy,' she repeated. 'Or, if you will insist upon the French being spoken correctly, "trompe l'oeil" – an appearance of reality that is entirely false. You see, Flora, for the last few weeks I have been supposing that what I saw at Knaresborough House was either murder or accident. But, the fact is, it was neither.'

Flora decided that she must, after all, expose herself to the risk of headache and her drawing room to the risk of damp. She went to stand beside the door and watched the figure of her cousin moving ceaselessly in the slanting light of the setting sun. 'Do you mean that Mr Vane is lying?' she asked hopefully. 'That it was not by taking too much medicine that Mrs Lansdale died?'

'Oh no. I am sure he is telling the truth – as far as he knows it. But he too has been deceived – deceived into seeing something which is not there.'

'Deceived by whom? Who has been lying?'

'No one has been lying. That is the remarkable thing. There have certainly been truths left unsaid, but, since Miss Neville has confessed that she left the house on the night of her cousin's death, I do not think I have detected lies in anyone. I have had before me all the details of the case – but the picture they have made has been false. False through and through! It is all a matter of perspective. A change of perspective can make those details form an entirely different picture. Do you understand?'

'No! I am sure I do not!'

Dido sighed. 'Well, I have told you about the marriage licence, have I not?'

'Yes.'

'That, you see, is what changed my perspective. Mr Lansdale made a joke of it – he laughed about just happening to have such a convenient document to hand. But I could not help but wonder why he should have it. Such a thing can only be obtained with some difficulty – and expense. He cannot have got it in a day. And only a day had passed since he was summoned to the court – and decided that he must marry Miss Bevan immediately.'

'Why then, when did he get it?'

'That is the great question! It is extremely unlikely that he would have risked getting it in the last few weeks while he has been under such suspicion. In short, I am sure that he has had it "to hand" since before his aunt's death. It was, in fact, the document which Mr Morgan wished him to destroy.'

'But why had he got it?'

'Well, when I turned to that question, I remembered something which has been puzzling me ever since I recalled it in Mrs Midgely's garden this morning. Do you remember, on the first occasion of our visiting Miss Prentice, she spoke of Mary going away to be a governess – and she said that she had had her gowns packed and her travelling dress prepared for a week.'

'Yes, yes, I do remember it! That she should be so very… resigned! I was so moved by it!'

'Yes,' said Dido, 'and so was I. But, you see, I was also moved a few days later when I heard her talking to you about going away. It was in the garden at Brooke, do you remember? "I knew that it must happen," she said, "but I have been trying not to think about it and I find that it takes me quite by surprise." And those – I think you will agree – do not sound at all like the words of a woman so resigned that she had already packed her boxes.'

'Oh, well… How very strange! I had not thought to put the two things together.'

'No, no more had I. But I have been remarkably stupid! There have been so many things which I have not put together – or simply not noticed at all.' Dido's restlessness was returned now and she must take another short turn upon the veranda before she could continue. 'There were things that you told me, Flora, which I failed to see the importance of: things about Mrs Lansdale's character. You told me that she enjoyed dramatic scenes and arguments, but that she also enjoyed forgiving her nephew; do you remember telling me that?'

'Yes, but...'

'And then there were the books she chose from the library,' Dido hurried on, too impatient, too full of her own thoughts to listen long. 'Or rather the books which her nephew chose for her. Novels and poems about love. And, do you remember what it was that he chose for her just before she died? *Romeo and Juliet*. He meant, you see, to wring her heart with that tale of unhappy lovers cruelly used by their friends.'

'But why?'

'Because, my dear cousin, at that time he was, in Mary's words "working upon her". He had a plan by which he meant to marry the woman he loved and secure his inheritance.'

'A plan? Dido, you are not, I hope, going to say that he harmed his aunt. For I give you warning: I will not listen to you if you do.'

'No, no, Henry Lansdale is not a murderer! The plan he had hit upon was entirely in keeping with his character: a merry, daring plan. Just such a plan as a man who can laugh even at his own danger might be expected to devise.'

'And what was it that he meant to do?'

Dido came to the end of the terrace and seized her cousin's hands. 'Flora, we know that Miss Bevan was not prepared to go out as a governess. And yet, about two weeks ago, she had begun to make preparations for a journey. Miss Prentice had noticed those preparations – and entirely misunderstood their purpose. So what was this journey she was preparing for? Well, can you not guess?'

Flora only stared.

'My dear cousin,' cried Dido giving their joined hands a little shake, 'she was preparing to elope!'

'Elope?' echoed Flora in bewilderment. 'But I do not understand. Mrs Lansdale would have been so angry...'

'Yes, but Mr Lansdale had decided that he must take the chance of her anger being followed by reconciliation. He had prepared her mind by reading to her the most heart-rending love story in literature. And I don't doubt that he planned to make his own marriage appear as romantic as he could, and to throw himself upon his aunt's mercy with a great many fine speeches and heroic words. He meant, in short, to make of it such a story, such an event, as she could not help but enjoy. This was his plan; and if it seems a desperate one, then we must remember that his situation was desperate too, for Mary's guardian had determined upon her humiliation and what else could he do to save her?'

Flora smiled. 'Yes,' she cried, 'I can imagine Mr Lansdale forming such a plan! And I believe it might well have succeeded. For of course he knew his aunt better than anyone else did. And so it is folly to suggest that he wished the poor lady dead, is it not? You must agree?' She paused as she saw the look on her cousin's face. 'It is folly is it not, Dido? You do agree?'

Dido thought for a moment, then looked down at her

hands which were still holding Flora's. 'Yes,' she said, 'I am quite sure that he did not wish her dead. I cannot help but have the highest regard for Mr Lansdale after our conversation of this afternoon. A man who is willing to further endanger his own life – as he must do by marrying before he faces the magistrate – a man who is prepared to run such a risk in order to provide for the woman he loves, deserves the highest respect. And such a man, I believe, may be excused for having made…an error of judgement. Even though that error has had dreadful consequences. At least he should not have to forfeit his life for it…'

'Dido?' said Flora, snatching away her hands and beginning to look uneasy. 'What are you saying? You seem to be suggesting that he is guilty after all…guilty of something.'

But, before Dido could make a reply, the door opened and the maid announced that their visitors were come.

Dido had sought this meeting with Mr Lansdale and Miss Neville – she had asked Flora to send the invitation – in order that she might explain the things which she had discovered. But, for the first half-hour of their being in the house, she had very little opportunity to speak at all. For she had done little more than prepare the guests for the discussion of serious subjects, before Flora, very full of everything she had just heard and anxious to have it all confirmed, cried out, 'Well, Mr Lansdale! Now we know everything. We have found out your secret!' and began upon her own, rambling account of the meditated elopement.

However, it suited Dido rather well to be silent a while and to give all her attention to watching the listeners. And

Miss Neville, she was soon assured, had known nothing of such a plan until now. She sat very straight and still, looking a little dark and shabby, in Flora's pale, elegant drawing room. Lacking her usual needlework, she folded her hands very neatly in her lap and listened like a child attending to an engrossing tale: her eyes widening as the matter was unfolded and the astonishment in her face increasing every moment.

But Mr Lansdale's emotions were a great deal more complicated and much less easy to read. There was concern and certainly a very quick understanding; for, no matter how Flora muddled up the account, the penetrating looks which he threw from time to time in Dido's direction assured her that he knew where the credit for these discoveries lay. There seemed to be no wish of denying the tale, but there was a great deal of rapid thought apparent in the frowning lines gathering on his handsome brow. And there was, occasionally, a lifting of the lips which hinted at amusement.

'You are right, Mrs Beaumont,' he said, when Flora was finished. 'Elopement was my plan and I truly believe that it would have succeeded. And, if it had not been entirely successful... Well, I would at least have secured that prize which I valued most.'

'And,' said Dido immediately, before Flora could speak again, 'and it was on the very evening of your aunt's death that you were to get the marriage licence was it not?'

He looked a little more wary. 'Yes,' he said slowly, 'it was. But how do you know about that?'

'Well, it had to be a matter of some importance that made you insist upon leaving the house against your aunt's wishes. And Mr Vane overheard you saying that you had business with Mr Morgan. I suspect that getting the licence was a matter of some urgency.'

'Yes,' he admitted. 'It was. For we were to be gone the very next day. I dared not delay lest Mrs Midgely return and spoil everything by telling my aunt that we were engaged. Everything was prepared. I had friends at Oxford waiting to receive us – even the priest was engaged. But I had to fetch the licence from Jem that evening. There had been a delay over procuring it, and, of course, nothing could be done without it.'

Dido leapt up restlessly, longing for the air and freedom of the veranda; but the windows were firmly closed now and all that remained of the outdoors was a trapped moth blundering against the glass. She began instead to walk about the room.

'It must,' she said, sedulously avoiding the anxious looks which Flora was throwing in her direction, 'have been very…inconvenient that evening when Mrs Lansdale began to complain of ill-usage. To have her forbid you go: to have her argue with you on the very eve of your elopement must have been quite contrary to everything which you had planned. You had hoped, no doubt, to leave her feeling as affectionate towards you as possible.'

Henry Lansdale threw back his head and regarded her with a mixture of defiance and interest. 'Yes,' he said smilingly. 'It was very inconvenient. Now, Miss Kent, do your worst. Make what accusations against me that you will!'

'No, no,' cried Flora miserably. 'I am sure she has no accusations to make. You have not, have you, Dido?'

Dido did not answer her. She stood instead behind the

sofa, her hands clasping the wood of its back. She met his gaze without flinching. 'I have heard,' she said quietly, 'that there was an argument between you and your aunt that evening, but I have not heard how the argument was resolved. And it must have been resolved somehow, Mr Lansdale. It would have been too dangerous to your plan to leave matters in such a state. I cannot believe that you went away to town while she was still railing against you.'

'No,' he said quietly. 'I did not.'

'And what did you do? What did you do to calm her?'

There was a little gasp from Miss Neville's corner of the room, but Flora only stared. In the silence the moth battered loudly at the window, desperate for escape. Mr Lansdale continued to regard her levelly for several minutes, emotion working in every feature of his face.

At last he looked down at his hands. 'It was,' he said very quietly, 'but a few drops. No more, I swear.'

There was a protest from Flora: a kind of yelp from Miss Neville. Dido held tighter to the sofa. 'Let us be sure there is no mistake here, Mr Lansdale,' she said quietly. 'It is a few drops of the opium mixture to which you refer, is it not?'

'Yes,' he replied calmly. 'She was so very distressed: shouting and sobbing to such a degree that I began to be worried for her health as much as for my own plans. I feared a nervous seizure. I did the only thing I could think of: I put a little of the medicine into her chocolate and persuaded her to drink some. But, Miss Kent, I give you my word – I swear to you upon my honour – that it was no more than enough to make her easy and to help her to sleep. No more than she was in the habit of taking.'

'I believe you,' she said. 'And I will not ask why

253

you have not admitted as much before; for, with such accusations flying about, it was not to be expected that a partial confession would fail to be exaggerated and turned into a darker admission of guilt. I quite understand that you have felt you played no part in your aunt's death: that you were unaware of how dangerous your actions were.'

'Dangerous?' he repeated. 'You say that my actions were dangerous?'

'Oh yes, they certainly were. For you see, what you did not know was that, when you introduced those drops, the chocolate was already adulterated.' She paused and then turned about abruptly. 'I am right, am I not, Miss Neville?' The attention of them all settled upon Miss Neville who was sitting now with both hands held to her mouth, her face very red and her figure trembling. 'There was already opium in the drink when you handed it to Mr Lansdale at the dressing room door, was there not?'

The poor woman tried to reply, but the sounds that she produced were so strange – so very unlike English words – that she soon pressed her hands back over her lips to prevent any more escaping.

Dido judged it kindest to speak for her. 'I have perhaps been hard upon you, Miss Neville,' she said, 'for, from the very beginning, I have suspected the things that you told me. I have felt that there was something incongruous about your statements and I sought an explanation of that incongruity in the wrong place entirely. It had, of course, nothing to do with your mother, nor with Jenny White who was no more than your mother's attendant. The contradiction which I was but half-aware of was a much simpler matter. Will you allow me to explain it to our friends?'

Miss Neville's eyes widened until they seemed to occupy almost half her face; she nodded without daring to uncover her mouth.

'You see,' said Dido, turning to the others, 'Miss Neville had talked to me very candidly about the...difficulties of performing the duties of a companion. She had told me how Mrs Lansdale had been in the habit of calling upon her at any time of the day or night if she felt herself at all unwell. And she had also told me that, sometimes, her cousin would forbid her to absent herself from the house on Tuesday evenings.' As she spoke these last words her eyes had come to rest upon Flora and there was a question in her look.

'Do you not recall, Flora, what Mrs Neville told us when we visited her? She said that her daughter always went to her on a Tuesday. And indeed, you, Miss Neville, had told me the same thing in the garden at Brooke. But I had been too stupid to understand its importance. It was not until today, when I began to consider how Mr Lansdale had got away from the house that evening, that I began to wonder how you had contrived to go.

'I had been deceived, you see, by the simple statement you made at Brooke. You told me that when Mrs Lansdale retired you had gone out. But of course, when I thought carefully about it, I saw that that would not do at all. For supposing she had awoken and felt unwell and called for you – as, by your admission, she was likely to do. Then she would have discovered your disobedience. So how was it that you contrived to absent yourself on this Tuesday and others upon which the lady had refused her permission? In short, I cannot but believe that you had fallen into the habit of ensuring that she slept soundly on Tuesday evenings.'

At last Clara Neville lowered her shaking hands from her lips. 'It was,' she said in a faltering voice, 'no more than the usual dose that I gave her that evening – enough to make her sleep soundly. Miss Kent, you know how I was placed – how I had to be with my mother when the maid was absent. I did not know...I could not know that...' She stopped and her hands flew back to her face as her eyes came to rest upon Mr Lansdale's countenance.

For the first time since he entered the room the gentleman was looking shocked. As well he might, for these two truths – these two halves of one picture – which had now been revealed, combined to form such an image of shared guilt as neither he nor his cousin had dreamt of until this moment. Each, seeing only their own story and unaware of the other's, had persuaded themselves of their entire innocence.

No one spoke. Three members of the company were beyond words, lost in the contemplation of everything that these revelations might mean. And Dido was entirely occupied in watching Henry Lansdale. His face was pale, his brow clouded with an intensity of thought which she longed to understand. For she had decided that everything was to depend upon how he conducted himself now. She was almost sure that he was an honourable man: too good a man to be delivered up to the chances of the law, if she could save him. But she was not absolutely certain. Now was the moment in which he must prove himself worthy of her assistance.

She walked slowly about the sofa and sat herself down where she might still have an uninterrupted view of his face. 'It is to be hoped,' she began very quietly, 'that the magistrates – when all the facts are laid before them – will be lenient: that they will believe a mistake only took place and that no malice was intended – by either of you.'

There was no reply. Flora was staring at nothing in particular and wringing her hands in her lap. Miss Neville was holding a shaking handkerchief to her eyes. Henry Lansdale was still deep in thought: his brow contracted into a deep frown.

Dido began to doubt him.

'I fear, Mr Lansdale, that the jurymen will be more likely to blame you,' she said a little more loudly, 'because you have gained so much from your aunt's death. But perhaps Miss Neville's confession of the part she played may do something to excuse you.'

His response to that was immediate.

He was on his feet in a moment and striding to Miss Neville's side. With one hand upon the back of her chair, he turned to face Dido, pale now, not only with shock but also with anger. 'Miss Kent, do you suppose for one moment, that I would permit a lady to stand before a public court, for no other reason than to excuse me?' He fought for control of his emotions and then continued in a calmer voice. 'It is, of course, all nonsense. Everything which we have been talking about this last half-hour is quite wrong and had better be forgotten. For the fact of the matter is that it was no hand but mine which put opium into my aunt's drink. I must have been mistaken in the measuring – no doubt my hand shook as I poured – I was unaccustomed to dispensing it. That is how it happened and I will swear it before any judge in the land.'

Dido was satisfied. He was deserving of her help.

'Mr Lansdale,' she said quietly, 'I hope that it may yet prove unnecessary for you to face any judge.'

She had the attention of the entire room. For it seemed that even the moth upon the window was still and listening. The fading light of the summer evening showed three faces turned towards her: Miss Neville's red with tears, and Flora's pale with hope – and Mr Lansdale's frowning and thoughtful – as if he feared she might suggest some other stratagem which his honour could not countenance.

'Although there can be no denying that your actions – and those of Miss Neville – played a part in the death of your aunt,' she continued, 'I cannot believe that we have uncovered the whole story. You see, Mr Lansdale, I believe that there were other events carrying on in your house that night – events about which you knew nothing. If only we could discover what those events were then we might prove that it was not your actions alone which determined poor Mrs Lansdale's fate.'

'I do not understand,' he said. 'What do you believe happened?'

Dido could only shake her head and admit, with very great reluctance, that she had, as yet, no clear idea of what might have occurred. It was still all a muddle to her of a dog that had had to be silenced, and gentlemen with hair powder; some music upon the stand of a pianoforte and red-shaded candles. 'But,' she continued, with determination, 'I will do my utmost to discover what happened. There are yet four days left before the trial and in that time I will do all that I can to come at the truth, no matter…' she hesitated, but finished firmly, 'no matter who tells me to give it up.'

Chapter Twenty-Eight

...I have but four days, Eliza, and a great deal to accomplish. I do not doubt that Mr Lomax would disapprove most heartily of the decision I have taken; but I must act while I can. Justice and humanity — as well as curiosity — revolt against inaction in this matter. Mr Lomax would say that I should leave all to the appointed authorities. But I cannot. I cannot believe that magistrates will concern themselves so much with hair powder and dead dogs and all the rest of it as to uncover the truth about what happened that evening in Knaresborough House.

For, you see, in the light of my recent discoveries, the possibility of Mr Henderson — or Mr Hewit — or anyone else — paying a visit after Mr Lansdale and Miss Neville left the house, has taken on a new significance. Eliza, if there were visitors — <u>who received them?</u> Do you see how important this question is?

If it was Mrs Lansdale — if she was alive and awake to entertain guests at eight o'clock — then she <u>cannot have drunk all the chocolate</u>, and her nephew and her companion must be innocent of her death.

This is the consideration which has made me determined to proceed, and I am to go shortly to Knaresborough House.

259

Mr Lansdale has left now to stay with Mr Morgan in town and Miss Neville is gone back to her mother. The house will soon be shut up, but the servants have been told that I am to be allowed to go where I wish – and I hope that they may also be persuaded to answer a question or two. I shall leave my letter open until I return so that I may tell you about anything I discover.

I had meant to go out as soon as we had breakfasted, but the morning is dark and threatening and I think I had better wait until the rain has fallen or else passed over. And, while I wait, I shall set down everything that I know – or suspect – about the events of that evening and hope that, by doing so, I shall begin to see it all a little more clearly.

First of all there is the dog which was alive at half after seven when Mr Lansdale left the house, but which met its death soon after. It is impossible to be certain of the reason for its death – but I would surmise that it was either killed so that its mistress might be attacked in safety, or so that it might not rouse her while some other misdemeanour was carrying on.

Secondly, there is Miss Prentice's information that a man – probably Mr Henderson – approached the house.

Thirdly, there are the marks I found in the drawing room which suggest that two elderly and unfashionable men had been there.

Fourthly, there are the red-shaded lights. And I have new information upon those: when I mentioned them to Mr Lansdale yesterday he said that he had not seen them until after his aunt's death. He says that he asked Fraser about them and Fraser said that he had had the housemaid put them on in accordance with Mrs Lansdale's instructions.

And, fifthly, there is the open pianoforte and sheet music in a household which was, professedly, unmusical.

Then, added to all these circumstances and relating to them I know not how, is the strange business of the burglary. A burglary in which everything seems to have happened backwards and quite contrary to the way it should: the window being broken from within rather than without; valuable silver not being taken, and jewels appearing in the house rather than disappearing from it.

Do you not find all these little facts intriguing, Eliza? I certainly do. But I cannot believe that a magistrate who has a whole parish to manage with all its overseers and its vagrants and its disputes – I cannot believe that such a one will find them interesting at all. It does seem most regrettable, does it not, that a woman – who is unqualified to make public such details – should be, by her leisure and habitual attention to trivial matters, best placed to observe them?

Having got so far, Dido laid down her pen and looked out of her bedchamber window at the streets of Richmond and the distant meadows, above which dark grey and purple clouds were gathering. She was now quite sure that she ought to continue with her enquiries; however, she could not help but wonder what Mr Lomax would think of her decision – and hope that he might never know about it. If she could retain his regard only by changing her character entirely and ceasing to care about justice, then she must forfeit it – or else deceive him and appear to be what she was not.

This thought made her so dissatisfied and restless, and yet so very anxious to complete her business that, despite the clouds being more threatening than ever, she determined on setting out immediately. Walking, thinking, acting – even in a shower of rain – were all much to be preferred to sitting still in her chamber regretting. She put on her spencer and hurried down the stairs. But in the hall she was delayed, first by choosing an umbrella from among several in the hall stand – and then by the housemaid bringing in the morning's post.

There were two letters for her: one thick one from Eliza which could be saved until her return and enjoyed at leisure, and another whose sender she could not guess at. It was very neatly sealed and addressed in a black, business-like hand which she did not recognise.

But, when she had broken the seal, she found that it was addressed from Messrs. Fossick and Bell, Land Agents, and was a reply to her request for Mr Henderson's new address: a request which she had all but forgotten sending. However, though she might, before receiving the note, have ceased to think about the question, her attention was immediately fixed by the extraordinary reply.

The letter was short, almost to the point of incivility.

Madam, it read, *we have to acknowledge receipt of your letter of the 12th inst. We regret that we can be of no assistance in providing a forwarding address for your acquaintance Mr Henderson as no such tenant has ever rented Knaresborough House, Richmond. We have consulted our records and can assure you that, before the present family took up residence, the dwelling had been unoccupied for almost a twelve month. You have clearly been mistaken as to the address. Frederick Bell.*

* * *

Dido's surprise was so great that she was obliged to read the message through several times before she could comprehend it. She leant upon the newel post, and closed her eyes in thought for a moment or two: then read the letter yet again.

There was no chance that she had misunderstood: no way but one of interpreting the words.

There had been no such tenant at Knaresborough House. Mr Henderson with his powdered hair and his bonneted daughters and his evening parties: the man that Miss Prentice had observed so closely did not exist.

Chapter Twenty-Nine

By the time Dido approached the gates of Knaresborough House there was a storm brewing and, although it was no more than an hour after midday, it was as dark as if it were evening. A few large drops of rain had begun to fall on the hot, thirsty dust of the street.

The house stood stark against the lowering sky, its windows blank. It had already the look of a deserted place and, hurrying up the sweep, her mind full of the letter's shocking information, Dido could not help but feel a thrill of anticipation at what she might find within: as if the storm and the letter had transformed a commonplace house, in which she had dined and visited, into the mansion of a romance. The notion that Mr Henderson had lived here – and yet had not lived here, was intriguing. It made a very strong appeal to her sense of the strange and mysterious.

The maid who answered her long ringing at the bell was the same girl who had once shown them to the wrong room. She was hot and breathless with a smudge of soot upon her cheek and certainly had nothing of romance or mystery about her. She was sorry to have kept Dido waiting and hoped she would excuse them 'all being very hard at it putting the kitchen to rights'.

Dido smiled at the girl as she walked into the entrance hall. 'You are Sarah, are you not?'

'Yes, Madam…I mean yes, miss.'

'Well, Sarah, would you be so kind as to answer a question or two before you return to your duties?'

'Yes, miss,' said the girl, pushing closed the front door and turning back, hands folded over her stained apron. Then her eyes slid anxiously towards the kitchen. 'But I must be about my work soon…'

'Oh, I shall not keep you long. I just wondered – did you serve in this house when the last tenant, Mr Henderson, lived here?'

'No miss. I come when Mrs Lansdale took the place. We all did.'

'Oh.' Dido was disappointed – and suspicious. She studied the girl's round, grimy face and her pale, rapidly blinking eyes. She seemed honest. Her cheeks were flushed, but that was no doubt caused by the heat of the kitchen. 'Are you sure? Is there no one here that was a part of Mr Henderson's household.'

'No miss…I mean, yes miss. I mean I'm sure. Because, pardon my saying it, it's what's made everything a muddle here. With everyone being new, you see and not knowing what to do. My Ma says it's always the way in a house where folk are for ever coming and going.'

Dido smiled. 'Yes, of course. It must be very trying for you. And I am sure you manage as well as anyone could. But the butler, Fraser, he was here in Mr Henderson's time, was he not?'

'Oh yes.'

'I see.' Dido lapsed into thought. It really was remarkably convenient for Mr Henderson that no one should remain here to remember his mysterious presence...

'Will that be all, miss?' asked Sarah, casting another anxious look in the direction of the kitchen and her unfinished tasks.

'There is just one other thing. On the night that Mrs Lansdale died, Miss Prentice – she lives in the house opposite the gate, you know – she believes that she saw Mr Henderson coming here to pay a visit – at about eight o'clock. Do you know if that is so, Sarah?'

The girl frowned and shook her head. 'No miss, I don't. Because I was gone home then. We all were. Only Mr Fraser was here. With the family all being out he had said we could go after dinner...'

'But did Fraser say nothing about a visit? Did he not mention it the next day?'

She thought hard. 'No, miss, I don't think he did. But everything was in an uproar next day of course, what with the poor lady being dead and everything.'

'I see.' Dido shook her head in despair.

But Sarah was thinking again. 'Perhaps,' she began slowly, 'perhaps Mr Fraser was expecting to see Mr Henderson that day.'

'Why do you say so?'

'Well, because of the letter, miss. You see, when I went to get the letters from the post office that morning – I mean the morning before Mrs Lansdale died – there was one directed to Mr Henderson and I said to Mr Fraser what should I do with it. And he said to give it to him

267

because he expected he would be seeing Mr Henderson soon and would deliver it to him.'

'Did he? Did he indeed? That is very interesting, Sarah. Do you know if there had been any other letters like that one?'

'One or two, miss, I think.'

'And Fraser always took them.'

'Yes miss.'

'So, perhaps he knew where Mr Henderson had removed to?'

'I don't know miss. Perhaps he did.'

Dido sighed. 'I wish very much that I could talk to Fraser,' she said.

But the girl just shook her head. 'No knowing where he is, miss. What with him leaving in such a hurry and being in disgrace and everything.'

'I do not suppose,' said Dido, without a great deal of hope, 'that he left anything behind him by which we might discover where he is gone. He did not leave any papers or anything of that sort?'

'Oh miss! There's papers enough left in the drawer in the butler's pantry! Cook says me and Ellen's to clear them all out and burn them as soon as we're finished cleaning the kitchen.'

Immediately Dido was alive with curiosity. 'I should dearly like to look at them.'

The maid gave her a wondering look which seemed to say it was rather an extraordinary wish. But she only said, 'Well, miss, then I suppose you had better come and see them. Mr Lansdale said you was to go anywhere you wanted.'

Though Dido would certainly have denied expecting

to find in the butler's pantry the kind of documents that so frequently resolved mysteries in novels, there was, after all, something irresistible to her imagination about the notion of papers: a great bundle of papers left behind as the writer fled. She only said that, 'perhaps she might be able to find out where the butler lived and so consult with him over Mr Henderson's visit,' but, as she followed Sarah into the offices of Knaresborough House, her mind was not untouched by thoughts of a more exciting discovery. If not the kind of obscure and thrilling narrative favoured by the writers of 'gothic' novels, then perhaps a diary kept by the butler that would describe the events of the night on which Mrs Lansdale died. Some fitting climax to the mystery she was pursuing.

But it had to be admitted that there was little of romance or mystery to be found in the kitchen passage. The place might be as dark and narrow as the corridor of a castle and the lightning was, most obligingly, flashing through the small, high windows; but the sight of drugget upon the floor, the sound of scouring coming from the kitchen and, above all, the lingering smells of lye soap and roast mutton, must temper any ideas of romance.

And the butler's pantry, which Sarah pointed out to her before hurrying away to her work, was as plain and commonplace as a room can be. She paused in its doorway and looked around, wondering about the man who had once occupied the place. There was a deal table and a small black grate; an old but comfortable chair with the horsehair stuffing coming out of the seat a little; a rag rug before the fire and a chest with a long drawer in it. There was just a hint of stale cigar smoke in the air, mixing with the smell of coal – and something else: something which Dido could not quite put a name to, but which seemed familiar and which, for some reason, brought to her mind that makeshift theatre which her brothers had created in the vicarage barn long ago...

Lightning flooded the room, showing up every scratch and stain upon the table, the spots of candle-grease on the mantelpiece. Thunder rattled at the little panes of the window. Dido stepped to the chest and opened the drawer.

It was indeed stuffed full of papers.

She drew them out eagerly, bundled them together and sat down upon the horsehair chair which was below the window and so offered the best light for reading. She drew a long breath and turned over the first sheet...

It was a washing bill.

And so was the next. And the next. She smiled to herself – aware that she had been foolish to hope for anything more and very glad that there was no one by to witness either her expectation, or her disappointment. She turned the pages over one after another – the only wonder in her mind, surprise at the amount of clean shirts, cravats and waistcoats a butler seemed to require. She had not known a manservant needed to change his cravat every day and his shirt...she checked the dates upon the bills... every two days.

She sorted out these inventories of linen and set them aside. A few papers still remained.

But her perusal of these was just as unenlightening, for they contained no more than bills for shoe string and hair powder.

She sighed, set the sheets aside on the rug, and turned back to the drawer to make quite sure that there was nothing else within. There did not appear to be any more papers; but, in order to be quite certain, she ran her hand about the drawer, reaching to the very back of it. Her fingers struck against something hard; she drew it out and discovered it to be a small brown pot.

As she held it up to the light of the window, she was aware that the smell which she had been unable to identify on entering the room had now become stronger. She unscrewed the top of the pot and sniffed at the yellowish, sticky contents.

It was gum arabic. The very stuff which her brothers had used to attach the beards and side-whiskers of the villains they had played.

Dido sat for several minutes, quite stunned, and with the little pot clutched tight in her hand. Rain battered at the window; away in the kitchen a woman was singing as she scrubbed. Another flash of lightning fell into the room, showing up the coarse characters of the papers on the hearthrug. She turned back to them. And the thought darted into her mind, with all the quickness and brilliance of the lightning itself, that here was a manuscript quite as strange and exciting as any she had fancied finding. For never had there been a manservant so remarkably well dressed!

And besides, here before her was a bill for hair powder. A bill which had been sent to a man who was completely bald…

Chapter Thirty

…It is three a.m. Eliza – or so the watchman in the street below has just called out. He has also assured me that 'all is well', but this I am less inclined to believe. I am convinced that all is far from well in Richmond. There are matters afoot here – deception and dishonesty and I know not what! I fear that respectable appearances may be covering all manner of corruption.

For it is true: Mr Henderson does not exist – he never did. My fanciful notion was not so very fanciful after all. There never was any such gentleman. There was only the fellow Fraser in a wig and false side-whiskers – and a great many more clean shirts and waistcoats than any servant ever required!

I have been puzzling a long while over how he could have imposed so upon the neighbourhood; but, upon reflection, I realise that, by Miss Prentice's account, he took care to avoid his neighbours – and the guests he entertained all came from town. It was very carefully – and very cleverly – done.

But why he should have entered upon such a strange and dangerous deception I cannot begin to understand – nor why, on the night of Mrs Lansdale's death, he should, for just a few hours, have resumed his disguise: his pretence of being the master of the house.

For that is certainly what he did. And Miss Prentice saw him on the lawn. And the things which I saw in the drawing room, the stains of hair powder upon the chairs and the music on the pianoforte, were all evidences of another of Mr Henderson's famous evening parties.

Do you see, Eliza, how, incredible though this seems, it does bring a great many other incredible things 'within the compass of belief'? For such a party to take place the dog would have had to be destroyed for he would have raised the alarm the moment strangers entered the house. I do not doubt that that was what Mr Henderson – I mean Fraser – was doing out on the lawn when Miss Prentice saw him.

And then there is the burglary… That very contrary and back to front burglary.

The company who gathered in Knaresborough House on the evening of Mrs Lansdale's death came there in secret. Now, Eliza, supposing something was left behind by mistake that evening – something of value. The only way it could be retrieved would be by stealth…

Do you understand? I mean to say that, perhaps, Fraser searched the drawing room for something that had been left by one of his visitors – and was surprised by his master as he did so – and broke open the window and started the story of 'two big rough-looking men', in order to explain the evidence of his searching, and to draw suspicion away from himself.

Perhaps you will say that I am being too fanciful once more; but, if you are inclined to doubt my genius, I would respectfully remind you that my fancies have in the past proved rather well founded; and I would also draw your attention to the fact that those big rough fellows were never seen by anyone but Fraser. They were – we are told – gone before Mr Lansdale entered the room. The watchmen cannot recollect seeing them; they seem to have vanished the moment they left Knaresborough House. Which, you must grant, is a very remarkable thing for two such large and obviously criminal-looking men to do – unless, of course, they never had any corporeal existence at all and were nothing more than useful products of the butler's invention.

But, leaving aside the thieves for a moment and returning to the night of Mrs Lansdale's death, there is another, more pressing, question which I am sure you have anticipated: what steps did Fraser take that evening to ensure that his party passed undetected by the real tenant of the house – who was upstairs in her chamber all the time that he was entertaining his guests?

Now you and I know that Mrs Lansdale presented no danger because she had been drugged by her nephew and her companion. <u>But Fraser cannot have known that</u>. And yet he had so much confidence in her insensibility that he dared to invite strangers into her drawing room!

As I have been sitting here tonight, I have remembered my meeting with Mrs Midgely in the post office. She told me then that, in Mr Vane's opinion, <u>four times</u> the usual dose of Black Drop had been drunk. So, was some part of it introduced by Fraser while the chocolate was preparing in the kitchen?

I think that it may have been, and that he may share in the guilt of the lady's death.

But how am I to prove that it was so? It pains me to admit it, even to a sister, but there are limits to my genius. I cannot yet come at a certain proof – or even a full explanation of the events of that night. And as for understanding the reasons *for Fraser's deception – I have some strange ideas – half-memories of things I have been told, and unformed suspicions. But nothing more… However, I have confidence in my own abilities and I do not despair of soon achieving a complete understanding.*

And, in all seriousness, I must attempt it, for I do not yet know enough, or understand enough to be of use to poor Mr Lansdale. I have a great deal still to accomplish if he is to be saved and I had better attempt to sleep before day begins to break and the importunate baby birds in the nests outside my window put an end to all hope of repose. I have a busy day before me.

Flora has rearranged all her engagements so that the carriage may be at my disposal all day. Do you see what a remarkable degree of consequence this business of mystery solving confers? Upon my word, it is almost as good as being married.

The last word brought her pen to a standstill, for, by a series of very natural and very painful connections, it brought her to Mr Lomax. And she had been trying all day not to think about Mr Lomax.

Her continuing activity in this matter would probably come to his attention. She hardly dared to hope that it would not. And if he discovered what she was about he would be angry and disapproving…extremely disapproving…

But it could not be helped. She certainly could not reconcile her conscience to leaving an innocent man to hang simply to save herself from an unpleasant scene. And there was nothing to be gained from worrying about the business, nor rehearsing arguments she might never be called upon to make.

She returned to her letter and did her best to think only of her plans for the next day…

I think the poor horses and coachman will be quite worn out by the time I am finished tomorrow, for I have a great many errands to perform. First of all I must send a message to Mr Lansdale asking him to perform a very particular favour. Then I must drive to Windsor and call upon Miss Bevan. I must fulfil my promise to Mr Lansdale and attempt to persuade her to an early marriage – although I am almost sure that I will fail. And I have besides several questions to put to her about Mr Henderson's daughters – and about Mrs Midgely's card parties. And then I must go to Sackville Street and ask the boy at Gray's to repeat his description of the lady who enquired about an emerald necklace – and see how much he blushes. And finally, I must visit Miss Prentice once more and ask her about the beggar who was outside Knaresborough House on the night Mrs Lansdale died: it is essential to know on which side of the gate he was standing.

It was after five o'clock when Dido returned home in the afternoon, very tired, very thoughtful and very silent – a great deal too silent for the taste of Flora who had been waiting anxiously for her return.

There was no answer to be got at all to such questions as, 'what have you discovered?' and, 'what can be done for poor Mr Lansdale?' and only the information that a small package had been delivered for her drew even a smile from Dido.

'Is the parcel of importance?' asked Flora as she handed it to her cousin.

'Yes, I hope it may be.'

'Who is it from?'

'Mr Lansdale.'

'And what is in it?'

'Something which I hope to return to its rightful owner.'

'But what is it?'

Dido did not reply; but only sat down in the cool of the drawing room and pressed her fingers to her brow. Her head ached and she did not know how she ought to proceed. All her attempts at discovering exactly what had happened on the night of Mrs Lansdale's death had led her to more puzzles and uncertainty. She wondered – she doubted – but she could be certain of nothing. What should she do? She dared not speak for fear of being wrong. And yet, how could she remain silent when Mr Lansdale's life might depend upon her?

Flora watched her for a little while, biting at her lip in impatience. 'Dido,' she burst out at last, 'this is not fair! Please! You must tell me what you know!'

'But, my dear cousin,' cried Dido helplessly, 'I cannot. For the truth is I do not *know* anything. I suspect a great deal. But there is no certainty about anything. And to tell you of suspicions would be wrong, for I might be slandering the innocent – and doubting the honesty of people we both esteem…'

'Who are you talking about?' said Flora, catching at the suggestion immediately. 'Dido if you know anything against my friends, then you must tell it.'

'I cannot. It may, after all, be nothing.'

'But you must tell! You cannot say so much – and leave me wondering.'

Dido hesitated, then decided upon disclosure – partial disclosure – in the hope of discovery. For there seemed nothing else to be done. Her heart was overburdened and she felt that she must speak – or else run mad.

'Well,' she said slowly, looking down at her own hands, 'what is your opinion of Mary Bevan? You have known her for longer than I have. Is she to be trusted?'

'Mary? Of course she is! I declare, I would trust Mary Bevan with my life! Why should you ask such a question?'

'Because,' said Dido with a heavy sigh, 'because I cannot help but think that she has behaved a little – just a little – suspiciously throughout this whole affair.'

'Suspiciously? Why, whatever can you mean?'

'Flora, do you remember when Miss Prentice first talked to us about the evening Mrs Lansdale died?'

'Yes.'

'And do you remember her saying that she did not stay beside the window long because, just after she had seen Mr Henderson approaching Knaresborough House, Miss Bevan persuaded her to go away to Mrs Midgely's party?'

'Yes, I remember it; but I am sure I cannot see why you should think ill of poor Miss Bevan for only inviting her neighbour to a card party.'

'But she did more than invite. By Miss Prentice's account, she insisted.'

'Well, and what if she did? I daresay she meant to be kind. She did not like to think of poor Miss Prentice sitting alone while there was company in the other drawing room.'

'But she did not usually do so. I asked Miss Prentice today and she informs me that she had never attended one of Mrs Midgely's parties before. She is not fond of cards. And I am sure Mrs Midgely did not desire her presence that evening.'

'Why not?'

'Because, my dear cousin, the rest of the company consisted only of Mrs Midgely herself, Mrs Barlow and Mr Vane. With Miss Bevan, the table was made up. A fifth would have been extremely unwelcome. Five people at a whist party is the most awkward number imaginable!' Dido shook her head, as if by doing so she might rearrange all the troubling thoughts that filled it. 'In short, Flora, I cannot help but suspect that Miss Bevan had another motive. I think she wished to draw Miss Prentice away from the window that evening – she did not wish her to see any more visitors arriving at Knaresborough House.'

'But why? Why should she care what Miss Prentice saw?'

'That is one of the many things I cannot yet determine,' said Dido and lapsed into silence for several minutes. 'You see,' she continued slowly at last, 'I cannot make Miss Bevan out. I see that she is very clever, but beyond that…' She shook her head again. 'Would you, for example, say that she is a well-mannered girl, Flora?'

'Most certainly! She has the nicest manners in the world! She is a great deal better bred than her guardian – which I have always attributed to the colonel sending her to the very best schools.'

'Yes,' said Dido rather regretfully, 'that is just what I would have said of her from my own observation. She has strong feeling I think, but she always behaves correctly – always keeps to the correct forms. When Mrs Midgely is coarse or makes ill-judged remarks, Miss Bevan is sure to attempt to turn the conversation. And when she herself speaks with too much violence or emotion, she apologises for her warmth. Yes, she is a very correct young woman indeed.'

'But I cannot at all see why you should make such a point of this?'

Dido could sit it out no longer. She simply had to be in motion. She jumped up from her seat and walked restlessly to the window. 'Flora,' she said, with her hand upon the latch of the french door, 'why should such a very correct young woman ignore all the rules of polite behaviour and form an acquaintance with strangers she had met in a park – without any introduction?'

She opened the door and walked out onto the veranda. Out here it was still warm, but the evening scents of honeysuckle and damp grass were beginning to fill the air and, beyond the garden, the street was busy with footsteps and carriage wheels as people hurried to dinner engagements. Dido leant upon the rail of the veranda, gazing out across the lengthening shadows on the lawn. She wished – yes, a part of her could not help but wish – that she had never set out to solve this mystery. It really was quite one of the evils of mystery solving to begin to doubt acquaintances one had been used to esteem.

Flora came and stood beside her, peering anxiously into

her face. 'Dido, you cannot truly believe that Miss Bevan has done anything wrong?'

'I am not sure... Except...' Her fingers began to beat a rhythm on the rail. 'There is something of which I am certain,' she said, avoiding Flora's eyes and looking determinedly at the roses and the lawn. 'Since I spoke to her in Mrs Midgely's garden yesterday, I have been quite certain that it was Miss Bevan who sent that unsigned letter to me – that it was she who wished to warn me about some people being unfriended by the world.'

'No!' protested Flora. 'I cannot believe it! She is the last person in the world who would... Why should she do any such thing?'

'I wish with all my heart that I knew! I cannot make it out at all. But it is certain that she sent it. For she spoke to me yesterday about the quotation in my "mysterious letter" – and asked if I had succeeded in discovering its source.'

'Well, what of it? You had told her about the letter at Brooke. I heard you ask her if she knew the lines.'

'No,' said Dido, turning to her cousin and leaning her back against the rail, 'no, I did not tell her about the letter. I only said that the lines had been "brought to my attention". So how did she know that I had received them in a letter? Unless she wrote that letter herself.'

Flora was silent. Dido took a turn along the veranda to relieve her feelings a little – and also to prevent herself from saying more. The truth was that she had taken an early opportunity of looking at the essay Miss Bevan had mentioned in Dr Johnson's works – but she certainly had no wish to discuss with Flora what she had discovered there.

Oh, this mystery was the most contrary and awkward business imaginable! She had never supposed that the quiet death of a respectable old lady could lead her into such dark and distressing matters – or uncover so many shocking secrets…

At present everything was uncertainty, apprehension and suspicion. If only she could be sure of something then, perhaps, she would know how she ought to proceed.

Flora sighed loudly and turned to walk inside. 'Well,' she said, discontentedly, 'I had hoped that all would be settled today. I hoped that if you took the carriage and spent all day upon the business you would understand everything. I said as much in my note to Lady Carrisbrook.'

'Lady Carrisbrook?' said Dido sharply. 'Why did you write to her about this?'

'Oh do not worry. I did not tell her everything. I only said that you had very important business to attend to and must have the use of the carriage – I had no choice but to tell her something, you know, for I had to explain why we should not be at her musical party this evening.'

'Her party?' Dido looked thoughtful. 'Is this the evening of the Carrisbrooks' music party?'

'Yes,' said Flora, and then she could not help but add, a little resentfully as she walked into the house, 'and very sorry I am not to be there, for she was most pressing in her invitation: so very anxious to know my opinion of all her arrangements.'

Dido remained a moment or two upon the veranda, frowning severely at the shadows on the lawn. Then she followed her cousin into the drawing room. 'Flora,' she began cautiously, 'it seems to me that Maria Carrisbrook relies a great deal upon your taste. She seems to have no confidence at all in her own opinion. That seems – odd, does it not? After all, she is a very elegant young woman.'

'Oh yes, but she has had little experience of housekeeping, you know, and I fancy Sir Joshua is hard to please. She has been particularly anxious that he should not disapprove of anything tonight.'

'Has she? Has she indeed?' Dido hesitated just inside the room, her hand still upon the french door. 'Flora do you know what it is, exactly, that she is worried about?'

'Oh, she is worried about everything! She is worried about the professional harpist she has engaged – whether he will play well enough. And she cannot determine which amateur performers should be asked to play upon the pianoforte. And then, you know, there is the supper and which room it should be set out in. And she is very worried about what she will wear herself; she thinks Sir Joshua will not approve her appearance...'

'She is worried about her own appearance?' cried Dido. 'Flora, are you quite sure of that? I think this may be very important. Can you remember what she said about it?'

'I hardly remember... She said something about a white and green silk gown – that she ought to wear it, but that Sir Joshua would think her appearance odd if she did... Dido what is it? What have I said?'

Dido had changed. Her hand was upon her mouth; she was thinking rapidly. 'Did Lady Carrisbrook reply to your note?' she said at last.

'Yes, she did. She said...'

'May I see her reply?'

Flora looked puzzled, but went to her writing desk and returned with a little sheet of hot-pressed paper. Dido seized it and looked it over so rapidly that it seemed impossible she could have understood its contents. But all at once she had become quite certain of what she should do next. Her face was alight and she moved purposefully across the room. 'Flora,' she said with great determination, 'we must go to the party at Brooke after all.'

'But, we will be late! – and it will be the rudest thing imaginable to go there now when I have said we cannot come.'

'Do not worry. I am quite sure Lady Carrisbrook will forgive us – when I return her property to her.' And she picked up Mr Lansdale's parcel and slipped it into her reticule before hurrying away to dress.

Chapter Thirty-One

They were not so very late arriving at Brooke after all, for, such was Flora's horror of incivility that she insisted upon sending to the inn for fresh horses before they started and was most urgent in her instructions to the coachman.

It was not quite nine o'clock as they approached the house and the first, faltering strains of a harp were but just beginning. Candles in paper lanterns were hung along the terrace showing up the dark yew trees and the fine black and white front of the old house. The door and all the windows were thrown open so that the guests strolling about outside might enjoy the music coming from the drawing room.

'It looks very pretty, does it not?' said Flora as they hurried up the steps. 'Maria has been at a great deal of trouble, I am sure.'

'Yes.' Dido paused, looking up at the handsome Tudor house brought to life with light and music, and judging it no bad representation of the marriage which had lately taken place here: of the bright, pretty young wife come to adorn the life of a solid, ageing widower. 'I hope,' she said, 'that her cares will not be thrown away.' Then another thought seized her. 'Flora,' she said, taking hold of her cousin's arm. 'Do you know if Mr Lansdale is to be here this evening?'

'No,' said Flora. 'I do not believe he was invited. Maria did not seem to want…'

'That is well,' cried Dido. 'I am glad he is not here. That at least is one thing she need not worry over.'

Flora demanded to know what she meant, but Dido only smiled and hurried on up the steps and into the house.

Within, everything was very brightly lighted up and the warm air was sweet with the scents of rosewater and of beeswax polish and of hot-house lilies in great arrangements covering every table. Extra chairs had been set out in the oak-panelled drawing room and it was thronged with an elegant company of maybe twenty ladies and gentlemen, all listening to the harp; others had spilt out of the open door into the hall to work away vigorously with their fans and chat while politely inclining one ear in the direction of the music; and, in the library, a little party of gentlemen, who did not even pretend to musical taste, were comfortably settled with wine and cards.

It took several minutes for Dido to discern her host through the crowd but, at last, she saw him standing by the fireplace in the drawing room. His hands were clasped behind his back and his face confirmed all her apprehensions. His eyes were fixed upon the musician as they ought to be, but his cheeks were dark red and his brows drawn up into such a scowl as showed him to be as dissatisfied with everything around him as his poor wife had feared.

Flora saw him too and she was just beginning upon a

whispered remark when their hostess came hurrying into the hall to greet them.

Lady Carrisbrook was lovelier than ever in white and green silk with emeralds glinting in her ears; and she was quite delighted that they were come – it was just exactly what she had wished for to make her own pleasure in the evening complete. Come, she would find them seats close to the musicians. No, no, they must not say another word about being late – that did not signify at all! And as for the note which had said they would not come – well, the disappointment it had caused only made her present pleasure the greater, did it not?

There was no resisting such delightful manners in so very pretty a woman. In spite of everything, Dido felt flattered and at ease with herself. And she could only wonder more at the husband who, just now catching his wife's eye, scowled at her so darkly, the poor woman's smile faltered.

'Lady Carrisbrook,' she said quietly, laying a hand upon her arm. 'I wonder if I might speak with you a moment – alone.'

Her ladyship looked troubled. 'I regret that I am rather occupied with my guests, Miss Kent...'

'I wish,' Dido whispered, 'to return something which I believe belongs to you.'

'I beg your pardon.'

'I have something which I believe you have lost.' As she spoke, Dido raised one finger and just touched her own throat.

The effect upon the lady was immediate. Her hand also flew to her own throat – which was quite bare of jewels.

'I see,' she stammered and looked about her anxiously to be sure no one had overheard. 'That is very...kind of you, Miss Kent. Will you perhaps come this way with me.' She linked arms with Dido and, with a hurried apology to Flora, was just turning away to the screen passage at the back of the hall when another figure appeared at the door of the drawing room.

Mr William Lomax was making his bow and smiling as he greeted them. Never before had he looked more kindly – or more handsome. And never before had Dido been so very sorry to see him!

'Miss Kent,' he cried, 'it is a particular pleasure to see you here. For, something Lady Carrisbrook said made me fear that you had too much business on hand to spare time for your friends! I am very glad to discover that that is not the case after all.' And he really did seem remarkably well pleased. Flora's note had, no doubt, alerted him to the fact that she was still pursuing her mystery; but now, seeing her at Brooke, he believed that she had abandoned it – that she had complied with his wishes. There was something very particular in his manner – both Flora and Maria Carrisbrook were regarding him and Dido with smiling suspicion.

'Will you allow me to show you and your cousin to your seats?' he said, bowing again with mock formality and holding out an arm to each.

Her cheeks burnt. A part of her quite longed to take his arm; to walk with him into the drawing room – and let Flora smile as much as she pleased! But Lady Carrisbrook was waiting for her; and Mr Lansdale's package was still in her reticule, and if she did not act now she might never know the whole solution of her mystery. And besides...

If she went with him now; if she allowed him to pay her such very public attentions, then what could she do but deceive him as to her behaviour of the last two days? And she did not think that she could bear to do that. It would be lying where she most wished to confide: replacing trust and honesty with dissembling and pretence...

'I am sorry, Mr Lomax,' she said, 'but it is, in part, business which has brought me to Brooke this evening. I pray you will excuse me – if you and Flora will just go on ahead – I must consult with Lady Carrisbrook for a moment or two.' She smiled sadly at him as she walked off, and she felt his eyes following her, until a turn in the passage took her beyond his reach.

She was led quickly down three steps, around another corner, up two more steps and into a cool, pretty little room where there was a wide bowl of dried rose-petals standing on a gate-legged table, and a casement window standing open upon a herb garden. Here the harp music was no more than a faint echo, like the playing of a ghost.

'Now, Miss Kent,' said Lady Carrisbrook, leading her to the deep, old-fashioned window-seat. 'Please tell me what you mean.' Her face was alive with curiosity – and hope. 'What is it that you wish to return to me?'

As she was speaking, Dido was drawing the package from her reticule. Now, taking care to watch her companion's face, she unwrapped it and revealed the emerald necklace. The little cry – the eager look of pleasure and relief as it appeared confirmed all her ideas.

'It is yours, is it not?' she said holding it out.

Maria nodded, took the jewels and fastened them about her neck. And if there had been any doubt remaining in Dido's mind it must have been done away in that moment, for there could be no doubting that the necklace had been chosen to match the green and white silk gown – and the emerald earrings. It was as if, until that moment, the toilette had been incomplete.

'Now, I think your husband will be more inclined to smile!'

Maria bent her head. 'Miss Kent,' she said very seriously. 'How did you know that the jewels were mine?'

Dido turned away from her: gazed out into the darkening herb garden and listened a moment to the faint, rippling of the music. 'It was not so very difficult to discover,' she said, 'though I confess that at first I was rather stupid about it.'

'Please, you must tell me everything.'

'Well, you see, I made enquiries at Gray's about an emerald necklace and I discovered that someone – another lady – had applied to them to have a replacement made for just such a piece as this. A rather tall, brown-haired, poorly dressed lady.'

Maria was not altogether pleased by the description. 'And you guessed that it was me?' she said.

'No, not at first, for I was blinded by the "poorly dressed" and was foolish enough to suppose that it might be Miss Neville.' She shook her head. 'So very stupid of me! For, if one does not wish to be recognised, it is easy enough to put on a shabby gown, is it not? But beauty and charm, they are not so easily put on and off.' She smiled. 'I do not think that even when she was one and twenty poor Miss Neville had the power to throw a tradesman into such confusion – to make him blush and stammer – or to make him so very anxious about her welfare. You see, all the time the shop-boy was talking to me I had felt there was something he was telling me which I was not understanding. Today when I spoke to him he confirmed my suspicion – the one thing that he had not previously put into words, but which his whole manner had declared, was that his mysterious customer was extremely beautiful!'

Maria seemed better pleased. 'I see,' she said. 'And… And you guessed that the necklace was a gift from my husband?'

'Yes. You have been very anxious about this evening as the date approached. I guessed that there was some particular difficulty facing you. And of course, this was the first occasion since your marriage when he would most certainly expect you to wear the necklace. And the fact that you had not come forward – with some kind of story – to claim it, made it certain that Sir Joshua did not know that it was lost.'

Maria was watching her keenly. 'With some kind of story?' she repeated, raising her brows.

'Oh yes. You would have had to manufacture some tale. You could not, of course, have told Mr Lansdale the truth about how your emeralds came to be in his drawing room.'

'No,' she admitted quietly. 'I could not.' She hesitated for a moment, and then seemed to make up her mind: to determine to know the worst. 'Miss Kent,' she said firmly. 'How much do you know? How much do you know about me – about my life before I was married?'

Dido did not answer for several minutes. She rested her warm cheek against the cool stone of the old window embrasure and gazed into the darkening herb garden where the dark shapes of bats were beginning to skitter out from under the eaves of the roof. The harp had ceased and, after a moment or two, it was replaced by the notes of the pianoforte.

'I know,' Dido began cautiously, 'that you were Miss Henderson before you were married.' She kept her eyes upon the garden, not turning to look at her companion. 'And I know that your…family occupied Knaresborough House for several months, without the permission – or knowledge – of the agents responsible for its letting.'

'I see. And do you know why…I mean, do you know what our purpose was in occupying that house?'

Dido leant out into the dusk and took a long breath, as if intent upon enjoying the scents of mint and thyme. 'Such a house,' she said carefully, 'such a very respectable, solid house, would make a very advantageous setting for three beautiful, unmarried girls. It would do a great deal to disguise their poverty – and desperation.' She stopped and turned her eyes slowly upon the woman beside her. For a moment neither of them spoke. But the memory of her guilt coloured Maria's cheeks. Far away in the drawing room the sweet voices of glee singers were joined to the music of the pianoforte. 'For you, Lady Carrisbrook, I believe the undertaking answered rather well. Sir Joshua's visits to that house ended in him making you an offer of marriage.'

'Yes, they did.'

'But,' said Dido with a smile, 'there was something rather strange about that offer. By my reckoning, it cannot have been made until after the Lansdale's came to Knaresborough House. For when, at Flora's picnic, Sir Joshua told us – so happily – of his engagement, he spoke of it as having just been formed – within the last week. But by then, of course, Mrs Lansdale and her nephew had been resident at Knaresborough for a month.'

Maria smiled briefly. 'He had,' she said, 'very nearly come to the point when we were obliged to leave the house. I was sure – absolutely sure – that one more visit would settle the matter.'

'And so you decided that for one evening, your household must be reformed? Sir Joshua must be deceived into paying one more call upon the charming Miss Henderson – deceived into entering another man's home without his knowledge.'

'But how do you know this?' cried Maria. 'How can you possibly know so much. We were so very careful.'

'I am sure you were, Lady Carrisbrook. But I have a strange habit of noticing small things which when added together... Well, you see what is achieved when they are added together.'

'But what kind of small things did you notice?'

'Oh, things like the music that you had left behind on the pianoforte. Your handwriting, you know is singular – particularly your Ss and Ws. I recognised the hand immediately when I saw the note which you had sent to my cousin.'

Maria's eyes widened.

'And I noticed that Sir Joshua wears hair powder – like

the man who was entertained in Mr Lansdale's drawing room that evening.' She hesitated: dissatisfied with herself. 'I was rather foolish about that,' she admitted. 'I had not paid enough attention to Sir Joshua's hair. After all, one rather expects a man of his age to have greying hair. It was not until his hair powder was washed away in the thunderstorm that I realised the natural colour of his hair is black.'

Maria shook her head wonderingly. 'And was there anything else?' she said.

'Well, there was your anxiety to keep Mr Lansdale away from Brooke. It must have been a great worry to you to discover that he was acquainted with your husband. For of course you did not wish Sir Joshua to discover that his friend occupied the very house he had visited. And then of course,' she continued, 'there was the beggar.'

'The beggar?' cried Maria, 'Do you even know about the beggar, Miss Kent?'

'Oh yes! He stood by the gate all evening – I imagine that he was paid to do so. To be exact – for I consulted with Miss Prentice most particularly over this – he stood upon the left hand side of the gate. With him standing just there, of course, it would be impossible for anyone arriving at the house to read the name-plate which young Sam fixed there a few weeks ago. It would not have done to have Sir Joshua knowing the name of the house at which he was being entertained!'

Maria was beginning to look fearfully at Dido. 'It seems,' she said anxiously, 'impossible to keep a secret from you, Miss Kent.'

Dido looked down and said nothing. Maria reached

out a shaking hand and laid it upon her arm. 'Please,' she whispered. 'I am quite at your mercy. I beg you will say nothing of this to Sir Joshua. He does not know the truth about that evening. He must never know. He would be so angry, so very, very angry if he knew that he had himself been exposed to discovery and embarrassment. You will not tell, will you?'

Dido looked from the clutching hand to the lovely, anxious face and hesitated. Should she make such a promise? Could it be right to conceal self-interest and shameless deception?

'It was – if I might say so, My Lady – a very bold, indeed a desperate plan. A great many things might have gone wrong.'

'But my dear Miss Kent, you must consider how much I had to gain from the scheme – how very much I had to lose by never seeing Sir Joshua again!'

'I beg your pardon,' said Dido quietly. 'I had not realised that you were so excessively attached to your husband.'

Maria blushed and lowered her eyes.

'Ah! I see that is was this that you feared to lose.' Dido made a scornful gesture which encompassed not only the pleasant house in which they sat, but also the estate around it – and all Sir Joshua's possessions beyond. 'It was wealth and consequence that you were prepared to risk all for – not the man himself.'

'No!' Maria jumped up from her seat. 'No, you are wrong, Miss Kent. It was for an establishment that I took that risk: for security and an end to poverty and friendlessness. You may think my actions reprehensible, but I have not yet grown so used to comfort and prosperity as to condemn my own behaviour. And, no matter what my past has been, no matter what I may have been guilty of in getting a husband, I would defy even you to discover any fault in my behaviour as a wife. Sir Joshua will never, never have any cause to regret his choice.'

Dido shook her head helplessly: moved in spite of herself. 'Lady Carrisbrook,' she said, 'you do not know what you are asking when you wish me to be silent on this matter. For the truth is that the charade you enacted that night was the cause – the partial cause – of Mrs Lansdale's death. And in just two days time her nephew must answer for that death before the court. What am I to do? Am I to stand by and see him hanged for a killing of which he is no more guilty than you and your friends?'

Maria turned pale. She sat down beside Dido again. 'You are mistaken,' she said earnestly. 'Completely mistaken. We played no part in that lady's death – I swear to you that we did not.'

'Did you not?' said Dido looking steadily into the beautiful hazel eyes. 'Tell me, My Lady, how could you be certain that she would sleep through the whole of the evening?'

She looked away, traced out the shape of one of the little leaded panes of the window with her finger. 'We gave her a little of the laudanum mixture she was in the habit of using,' she said quietly. 'It was put into her chocolate while it was in the kitchen. But I promise you – upon my life, I swear – that it was only a few drops. Enough to make her sleep a few hours: no more. It cannot, it certainly cannot have brought about her death.'

'It was poor Mrs Lansdale's misfortune,' said Dido with a sigh, 'to be very much in the way that evening. She seems to have been an inconvenience to everyone around her. Everyone wished her to sleep!'

'I do not understand.'

'Would it be brought more within your comprehension if I were to tell you that I have spoken to two other people who also put a sleeping draught into that very same jug of chocolate?'

Maria's hand went to her lips and Dido watched dawn upon her face an understanding of shared guilt such as she had seen in Mr Lansdale and Miss Neville. For several minutes she was too aghast to speak. Then she said, in a trembling voice, 'Do you mean to expose me?'

Dido would dearly have loved to protest against the question – to abdicate such a heavy responsibility. But it could not be done. She may have entered too lightly upon this business of investigation; but she recognised that it would not be so lightly got out of. For there is no unknowing truths once they are discovered.

To expose Maria: to publish all the events of that night; to destroy all her happiness – and Sir Joshua's too – was more, a great deal more, than she felt herself capable of. And yet not to do so would leave Henry Lansdale in as much danger as ever...

'I do not know,' she said. 'I do not know what I ought to do – except... Except that I cannot permit Mr Lansdale to bear all the blame for what happened that night. It would not be right or just.'

Tears gathered in Maria Carrisbrook's eyes; but she did not attempt to argue against this. Dido took a long draught of the cool, thyme-scented air from the window. There was no escaping it…'But…' she said quietly, 'there may be…I think, perhaps, there may be another way of saving Mr Lansdale.'

The hope was so frail – so fraught with difficulties – that she had hoped she need never try it. And she shrank from voicing it. But what other chance was there?

'Yes?' Maria's voice was small and hopeful. 'What is it?'

She leant back in the window embrasure and closed her eyes. With a great effort she drew together the thoughts and suspicions which had been on the very edges of her mind for the last hours.

'There was a fourth dose,' she said very slowly.

'A fourth dose?'

'Yes. If Mr Vane was correct in his description then there were four usual doses of opium. But – as yet – we know of only three. In short, there was yet one more person who wished Mrs Lansdale to sleep that night. If we could but find out that fourth person…'

Maria looked troubled. 'And you would force that person to bear the guilt of all?'

'No – not quite.' Dido jumped up. Now that her mind was pressed into action her body could not remain still. 'No,' she said, pacing restlessly across the room. 'I hope – that is if this last portion of blame falls where I believe it does – I hope that all those who played a part in Mrs Lansdale's death might be…' she hesitated, looking at Maria's lovely, tearful face. 'I will not say excused entirely, My Lady…but rather left to bear only that punishment which I am sure their own consciences will inflict.'

Maria Carrisbrook had the gift – rare even among beautiful women – of crying prettily. Tears were now pouring freely down her cheeks and her lip trembled a little; but there was no sobbing or snuffling, no blowing of the nose. Dido found the performance strangely disquieting and wondered inconsequentially whether Maria had been born with the talent or whether it was an accomplishment she had acquired. She very much wished that it would stop; but the tears flowed on as Maria applied a dainty handkerchief to her eyes and looked hopefully over the top of it.

'Do you really think you could arrange things so very... satisfactorily, Miss Kent?'

'I think it must be attempted.'

'But what will you do? Will you challenge this person? Tell him what you suspect?'

'Ah! There – as someone says in one of Shakespeare's plays – is the rub. I cannot. It would not be right. You see, if my plan is to work, then the facts must be put rather... forcefully. A kind of threat will need to be made...' She walked around the table; stirred up the rose-petals in their bowl and breathed in their sweet, dusty scent. 'It is not something to which I feel I am equal – I do not think any woman of ordinary delicacy would feel equal to it. It would need a man. A gentleman would have to play the part for us.'

'Perhaps,' said Maria eagerly, tucking away her handkerchief, 'perhaps Mr Lansdale...'

But Dido shook her head immediately. 'No,' she said. 'That would not do at all. He must not be seen to interest himself in the business. If the magistrates were to hear of it, it would appear very bad indeed.'

'Then who can we ask to act for us?'

Dido was silent for some moments – not from not knowing the answer to the question, but rather from being reluctant to speak it. However, there was no avoiding it…

'I think,' she said, 'that Mr William Lomax would be the most proper person for the task. He knows a great deal about the business already, and understands the workings of the law.'

Maria looked a little sly. 'I am sure he would be very willing to carry out any commission of yours.'

Dido only scowled at the compliment. 'I am sure there is no man living who I would less like to ask,' she said. 'For, though I cannot think his humanity will allow him to refuse the errand; I know he will blame me for devising it. However, I shall go and consult with him now.' She dusted fragments of rose petal from her hands and turned towards the door with determination. 'It cannot be helped. It seems that there is no choice: either I must sink even lower in his esteem – or else Mr Lansdale must be hanged!'

Maria watched her, very puzzled; but, just as she reached the door, she called her back. 'Miss Kent, I have not yet thanked you.'

Dido turned back reluctantly. The thought of the interview ahead of her was unpleasant, but it was not in her nature to delay a task on which she had determined and she was very eager to have everything settled.

'There is nothing to thank me for, Lady Carrisbrook. I have only returned to you what was your own.'

'But you are being so very kind in trying to save me

302

from exposure and… And you have shown great… delicacy in the questions you have asked me. And, most particularly,' she added with a nervous smile, 'in those questions you have not asked me.'

Dido said nothing, but only stood holding the open door in her hand.

'Forgive me, I cannot help but ask – are you not curious about my life before my marriage? The things you have discovered about my residence at Knaresborough House are such as might make the dullest of women curious. And you are certainly not the dullest of women.'

'Thank you.'

'And yet you ask no questions at all about me…or about my family.'

Dido gazed down upon the floor and looked exceedingly awkward. 'A married woman,' she said, 'belongs to her husband's family. She takes his name – his title. Who, or what, she was before ceases to be of any consequence. I see no reason to trouble you with impertinent questions, Lady Carrisbrook.'

And with that, she turned and walked away in search of Mr Lomax.

Chapter Thirty-Two

It was the supper hour when Dido returned into the hall. The glees were over and some of the guests were already gone into the dining room; while some were still chattering in the drawing room; and others had escaped entirely from the excessive heat of the house to walk about on the candle-lit terrace.

And it was among this last group that she discovered Mr Lomax. He was standing a little apart, beside one of the great yew bushes that flanked the steps to the lawn. The light from a paper lantern showed his eyes downcast and his jaw thrust out in just such a way as, had he been but a child, everyone would have called a sulk. Dido smiled to herself, rather taken with the notion of sending him away to a corner of the nursery until he had 'learnt how to conduct himself'. But, unluckily, dealing with a grown man in an ill temper could not be so simple.

He must, somehow, be persuaded into performing her errand: that was the point of first importance. That he might also be persuaded into approving her conduct was, she acknowledged, all but impossible. Yet her spirit rose at the prospect of his disapproval. She had done nothing wrong: her own conscience acquitted her entirely. And besides, it really was rather gratifying to discover that at five and thirty she could still arouse such strong emotion in a gentleman's breast – even if the emotion was, as it had always tended to be, exasperation rather than any softer feeling.

She held up her head and stepped forward to meet him with a defiant smile. But his greeting was not propitious. He bowed and hoped, rather stiffly, that 'her business was now settled to her satisfaction.'

'It is very kind of you to ask, Mr Lomax,' she said, continuing to smile graciously. 'My business is…going on fairly promisingly.'

'Do you mean that it is not yet finished?' he demanded. 'You are still engaged upon this dangerous course of investigation into Mrs Lansdale's death?' He began to search her face with a very satisfactory anxiety. It pleased her greatly to think that some part at least of his anger was born of concern for her welfare.

'You need not trouble yourself,' she said. 'There is no danger at all. For I find that, after all, there was no murder. There was not even any house-breaking. So, you see, there cannot be any villain waiting in the dark to exact some terrible revenge upon me for my temerity in investigating his affairs.'

He frowned: he put his fingers together and rested his chin upon them – as was his habit whenever he was endeavouring to understand something. 'Do I understand you correctly, Miss Kent? Are you saying that Mrs Lansdale's death was entirely natural?'

'No. I only said that she was not murdered.' She smiled invitingly. 'Would you like me to explain it all to you?'

He hesitated and she was amused to see that curiosity was now contending with annoyance upon his face. Behind them the voices of their fellow guests were beginning to fade as they made their way towards the supper table. In the quiet of the terrace a moth beat against a paper lantern.

It ended with him making no concession; he only held out his arm to her and suggested that they take a turn along the terrace. But, judging that this was all the invitation his pride would allow him to give, Dido launched into her account of Mrs Lansdale's three doses of Black Drop. And he listened to it all without a protest.

As they walked, passing from shadows to pools of light along the terrace, she tried to study his profile which, though it was as handsome as ever, was inscrutable. The only change that she detected as she spoke was a little more jutting of the jaw – which certainly did not bode well. And the arm, upon which her hand rested, was held stiffly away from his body.

They walked slowly and reached the end of the terrace and the end of her narrative at about the same time.

'And so you see,' she finished, 'I find I must now ask for your help.'

He stopped and stared down wonderingly at her. 'You would ask me to help you?' he said. 'When you are aware of what my opinion has always been. You know that I consider you…mistaken in pursuing this matter.'

She withdrew her hand from his arm. 'But, Mr Lomax,' she said, 'I cannot believe you to still hold that opinion. When you have heard all that I have discovered! Things which would still remain hidden if I had followed your

307

advice. Come, admit it, you must have changed your mind.'

He drew himself up stiffly. 'I do indeed still hold that opinion Miss Kent and I will repeat it. You should not have meddled in this business.'

She was annoyed. She had not expected him to be so very unbending. 'Forgive me for saying so,' she replied, her cheeks blazing, 'but I cannot believe your position to be reasonable. When I have proved to you how very much there was to discover, it is not reasonable to say that I should have been content with ignorance!'

'Your appeal to reason in this case is faulty on two counts,' he replied, coldly. 'Firstly, you are, I believe, basing the defence of your actions upon the good which you think they have achieved. But can you be sure that any real benefit will result from them? You have certainly discovered a great deal; but you admit yourself that the enormity of uncovering Lady Carrisbrook's deceptions is beyond your powers. And if she is not to be exposed, then how can Mr Lansdale benefit from all your busyness?'

'But if...'

He held up his hand. 'And secondly. Even if your investigations were to have the most beneficial results imaginable, I should still maintain that you had erred in undertaking them. For when you embarked upon your course of action the outcome was unknown and it would be very poor morality indeed if our actions were to be deemed good or bad only by hindsight. I will not – I cannot in all conscience – change my opinion of your behaviour simply because it has proved more beneficial – and less dangerous – than either of us could have predicted.'

'And so you believe that it would have been more virtuous in me to wring my hands and do nothing while poor Mr Lansdale was taken away to the hangman? Upon my word, Mr Lomax, this is much worse morality – to permit our friends to be endangered for the sake of preserving ourselves from a little exertion and danger! I am very glad that your creed is not more general in this kingdom. For what would become of our commonwealth if our brave soldiers and sailors were to imbibe a little of your morality?'

'Miss Kent!' he cried, 'you are, I believe, taking pleasure in misunderstanding me. You are neither a soldier nor a sailor: you are an unprotected woman. Morality must, of course, depend upon situation. What is right for one, may not be right for another.'

'Then you will not help me?'

'I cannot. It would be wrong – it would be entirely inconsistent of me to assist you in an undertaking I cannot condone.'

She fought to overcome her anger. He really was insufferable! But, perhaps she should not have argued so strongly, or contradicted him so forcefully. Perhaps then he might have consented to help her. She might apologise and plead her cause more meekly... But she could not bring herself to form the words.

She walked to the stone balustrade which marked the end of the terrace, leant against it and peered over into the little wilderness below. The light of the lanterns showed thick foliage and a patch of ghostly white elder blossom. Above the dark shapes of the trees a crescent moon was rising and an owl hooted long and low. All was beauty and tranquillity in nature – but within her mind there was turmoil such as she had scarcely ever known before.

She looked back at him. He was standing beside the last lantern on the terrace, his hands clasped behind his back and his expression everything that was stubborn and unyielding. What was she to do? She must have his consent – he must be made to help her or everything would have been in vain: all her reasoning, all her discovering of secrets, and above all, the loss of his esteem, would all have been for nothing and poor Mr Lansdale would be condemned.

But try as she might, the soft, conciliatory words would not form in her mouth.

And suddenly it flashed into her mind that maybe there was another way. If his disapproval could not be overcome, then maybe that same disapproval could be made to operate in quite a different direction.

'Very well, then,' she said quietly. 'If you will not help me, I suppose I must act on my own.'

'Miss Kent,' he said anxiously and came to stand beside her. 'What is it, precisely, that you believe should be done?'

She turned her face from him and stared out into the trees. 'There was a fourth dose of opium,' she said calmly.

'I beg your pardon.'

'Mr Vane has said that Mrs Lansdale was given four times the usual dose of sleeping draught. I have so far accounted for only three. So, who gave her the other one?'

There was a silence. Clearly he was hoping that she would continue without prompting from him. But at last he was forced to speak. 'There is that in your voice,' he said, 'which convinces me that you know – or suppose that you know – the answer to your own question.'

'Yes,' she said, 'I believe I do.' She turned and smiled at him. 'Poor Mrs Lansdale,' she said, 'she really was a very great encumbrance to everyone around her that evening. Her nephew wished to go to town; her companion had to attend to her mother – and even her physician would not do as she wished and remain in the house with her.' She could see that she had his complete attention. 'That is what she wished him to do, you know. She considered herself to be very unwell: she wished Mr Vane to stay with her. But he declined. He said that he would be at home all evening and that she must send for him if she felt herself at all worse.'

Mr Lomax frowned – a great deal more interested than he would have liked to confess. 'And this you believe to have been of some consequence?'

'Oh yes, for you see, Mr Vane was not at home all that evening. He went to play cards at Mrs Midgely's house.'

His chin was once more upon his fingertips – which must be considered a very good sign. 'Are you suggesting that Vane himself drugged Mrs Lansdale?'

'I think it is…possible. By doing so, you see, he could ingratiate himself with two wealthy widows at once – he could attend upon Mrs Midgely without Mrs Lansdale suspecting that he was neglecting her. Indeed I cannot help but think his behaviour otherwise was very strange indeed. Mrs Lansdale was his wealthiest, most important patient: was he likely to risk her waking and sending for him – and discovering that he had not done what he had

311

promised to do. And of course, we cannot know that the dose he administered that evening was no more than her usual cordial.'

'But it is he who has started the story of an unnatural death.'

'Yes, because, like everyone else who wished the poor lady to sleep that night, he cannot conceive that he is guilty of doing anything wrong.'

Lomax stood for several moments, watching her closely as he thought. 'And you believe that the magistrates should be informed of these suspicions?'

'Oh! No. Not quite. For then, you know, the whole story would have to come out, and there is no telling what the upshot of it all might be. No, Mr Lomax, what I am proposing is that Mr Vane should be informed of these suspicions.'

'To what end?'

'Why, so that he might be persuaded into withdrawing his accusations, of course. He should be made to understand that if he insists upon taking the matter to court there might be very unpleasant consequences for himself as well as Mr Lansdale. It should be pointed out that, if everything was brought to light, he would look as guilty as Mr Lansdale. His habit of ingratiating himself with wealthy women is, I am sure, well known…the jurymen might suspect that he had hopes of a legacy from Mrs Lansdale…'

'In plain language, you mean that Mr Vane should be threatened.'

'Ah…Yes, I believe that I do.'

'I see.' He continued to watch her; but unluckily the

light was behind him and she could not see the expression of his face. 'And this,' he said at last, 'is what you mean to do? You mean to approach Mr Vane and threaten him into silence?'

It had certainly not needed the incredulity in his voice to make her modesty shrink from the prospect. She very much doubted whether all her sense of justice and indignation could make her capable of it. But she must stake everything upon the pretence.

'It is not,' she said, lowering her eyes demurely, 'it is certainly not an errand which I – or any woman – would wish to undertake, Mr Lomax. But, as you have pointed out, I am alone, unprotected. I have no gentleman to act for me.'

'This,' he cried stepping back from her and bringing his hand down upon the balustrade with considerable force. 'This is intolerable! Now you are threatening me!'

'I am very sorry that you should think so, Mr Lomax. That was certainly not my intention.'

'Pardon me for contradicting a lady, but I rather think that it was.'

She made no reply.

He had half-turned as he stepped back and now the light of a lantern was shining upon one side of his face. His warring emotions were visible in every feature. The muscles moved in his throat as he forced back furious words. She guessed that anger and humanity were fighting it out inside him; but did not suspect the rest of his torment. For she did not see how pleasantly the shaded light played across her own face, nor how the heat of argument had brightened her eyes and brought

313

back the bloom of youth to her cheeks.

At last he let out a kind of groan. 'If,' he said slowly. 'If I consent to act for you in this matter, Miss Kent. If I take it upon myself to approach Vane and to…bring all these matters to his attention, it will be purely in order to protect you from further…unpleasantness. You must understand that it does not, in any way, mean that I condone your past behaviour.'

'No, of course not,' she said quietly. 'I understand that entirely, Mr Lomax.'

Chapter Thirty-Three

'It is a great pity,' observed Flora at breakfast two days later, 'a very great pity that you should have been at so much trouble over this affair of Mr Lansdale's. For after all, you know, there was nothing to be done and it has all worked out quite harmlessly in the end.'

'Oh! Oh yes,' said Dido looking up from the note which she was reading. 'It was very fortunate indeed that Mr Vane should have failed to appear in the court and that the magistrate should have discharged Mr Lansdale.'

'Well, perhaps,' said Flora with a sly smile, 'perhaps you might now agree with dear Mr Lomax that such matters are best left to the authorities appointed to deal with them.'

Dido laid down her letter with a frown. 'Has he expressed that opinion to you?'

'Oh yes, he told me all about it at Brooke – while you were talking with Maria, you know. But,' she added, 'he also gave me to understand that it is the only point upon which you and he disagree. Oh yes! We had the most delightful conversation about you! And he assures me that in all else you and he are in perfect accord. And as for your person,' she finished, 'you are quite the loveliest and cleverest woman in the world!'

'Well,' said Dido ungraciously, 'when you and Mr Lomax next discuss me, you may tell him that I am not at all sure that I have changed my opinion of the appointed authorities, for they have shown themselves to be neither diligent nor clear-sighted in the performance of their duty.'

'You may tell him whatever you wish yourself – he is to call here this morning. It is to be a farewell visit, for he returns to Belsfield tomorrow,' said Flora – still smiling. 'And so, since I am sure the two of you must have a great deal to talk about, I shall take care to leave you alone together.'

'Oh no!' Dido rose hastily from the table. 'You will not do anything of the kind, my dear cousin, for I shall not be here to see Mr Lomax. I have another engagement.' She picked up her letter. 'It so happens that Mary Bevan has written and asked me to meet with her this morning.'

'But you cannot go!' cried Flora. 'I am sure he wishes most particularly to see you.'

'On the contrary,' said Dido as she walked out of the room, 'I think Mr Lomax will be very happy to find that he has missed me!'

This morning the weather was rather cooler than it had been of late. Small white clouds were drifting across the sky and a pleasant breeze pulled at the ribbons of Dido's bonnet as she walked down the hill towards the green and the inn.

As she approached Mrs Midgely's house she discerned Miss Prentice's white cap at its usual station beside the

316

window. She raised her hand to wave, but then, as she drew nearer, she saw that, for once, the lady was not looking outward at all – nor was she alone. Mr Hewit was there – sitting so close and talking so earnestly that his companion had no attention to spare even for the window and the activities of the neighbourhood.

Dido smiled. She could not but suppose that the gentleman must be saying something very interesting indeed to hold her attention, for there was actually a coroneted coach driving past; furthermore, just across the road at Knaresborough House, a wagon was drawn up on the sweep and men were carrying the trunks and boxes of new tenants up the steps.

Suppressing a desire to stop and watch the couple, Dido passed on, pausing instead by the big stone gateposts of Knaresborough and gazing up at the solid, peaceful bulk of the house. The breeze was rustling through the ivy on its walls and one thin column of smoke was rising from a back chimney. She recalled how she had stood here on that first day – and thought how very respectable the place looked. She had then had no notion of everything these red-brick walls might contain. She could not have predicted hidden passion, nor thieving, nor elopement, nor the daring charade which ambition had played out here… And she certainly could not have had any suspicion of that other, more terrible sin which she believed to have taken place here…

Of course, she thought as she turned and continued on her way down the hill, she might be mistaken – only Mary Bevan could confirm, or dispel this final suspicion. And very glad she was that Mary had agreed to meet with her and satisfy her curiosity. This last detail of her mystery might be something which she could never speak about to anyone else – she had certainly lacked the courage to enter into the subject with Lady Carrisbrook – but it was, nevertheless, a matter which she could not bear to remain in ignorance of.

As she came within sight of the inn she saw that the London coach was stopped on the green, attended with all its usual bustle of boxes and parcels being lifted up into the basket and horses being led out of the shafts and passengers hurrying into the parlour to eat and drink as fast as they might. Miss Bevan was sitting upon a bench nearby – which was what her letter had led Dido to expect. But what she was not entirely prepared for was the travelling cloak lying on the bench – and the corded trunk beside it. She frowned rather thoughtfully as she made her way across the grass, through the little throng of gossiping friends, dawdling lovers and darting children.

'Are you going upon a journey, Miss Bevan?' she asked as they shook hands.

'Yes, I am just now taking the coach to London and there I get into another – for Yorkshire.'

Dido sat down and took a long look at her companion. Her face was white and every strand of hair had been scraped back into the dark, severe bonnet. Her wide brown eyes looked larger than ever – there was a suggestion of fear in them, but also great determination.

'You go to the house of Mr Grimbauld?'

A smile darted across Mary's face. 'I do indeed, and it is to be hoped that his nature is pleasanter than the sound of his name!'

'I sincerely hope that it is.'

Dido was now the one being scrutinised. 'I think,' said Mary, 'that you are not entirely surprised by my decision.'

'I was not quite prepared for Mr Grimbauld,' admitted Dido. 'I had not expected you to go away today – to Yorkshire.'

'When once we have determined upon a right course of action, I believe it is best to embark upon it straight away – otherwise it is all too easy to begin to argue against ourselves.'

'I am sure you are right.'

'So, Miss Kent, you, at least, did not expect me to stay here and marry Mr Lansdale?'

'No, I do not think that I did.'

'May I ask why?'

Dido only shrugged and repeated Mary's own words back to her, 'It is better to be a governess – better even to be a teacher in a school – than to marry a man one does not care for.'

'Oh!' Mary turned aside with a look of great consciousness and, one of the guards just then appearing, began to busy herself over getting her box tied onto the coach. When that was all settled and the man had warned her, with a broken-toothed smile, that they were to, 'be off in just ten minutes, miss,' she resumed her seat and folded her arms tightly about herself. 'You know then that I do not...? You understand my feelings?'

'Yes,' said Dido gently. 'Though when you first spoke those words to me, I did not quite understand that you were speaking about yourself. It was only afterwards...'

'Afterwards?'

'Yes, after I realised that it was you who had sent the mysterious letter to me. Then, you see, I began to wonder about your behaviour and your motives. And, of course, I recollected that at Ramsgate you had been unwilling to accept Mr Lansdale's offer – that it was only after the discovery of your parentage – when your need for a home was pressing – it was only then that you accepted him.'

Mary bowed her head. 'I should not have consented. But I persuaded myself that there was nothing wrong in what I was doing. After all, there was no shame in marrying prudently: it was no more than what other women were doing every day. And he seemed to be so very much in love…' She stopped and shook her head. 'This will not do. I cannot excuse myself. The truth is that I was desperate. When Mrs Midgely said that I must leave her house, I did not know what I would do. It is very hard, Miss Kent, to be entirely friendless.'

'Yes, I am sure that it is. I do not wonder at what you did. I only wonder at what you have failed to do.'

'And what is that?'

'Why, you have failed to fall in love with Mr Lansdale! Which, considering he is young, handsome, rich, lively and good-natured, besides being excessively in love with you, is, I think, rather remarkable.'

'You are right to wonder at it! There was a time when I wondered at it myself. At Ramsgate, when he first made his offer, I was unsure. Though I did not doubt my present feelings, I thought that they might change. I thought that I might learn to love him. That is why I did not give him an outright refusal – but only asked for time in which to consider.'

'But now you are sure you can never love him?'

Mary hunched up her shoulders and folded her arms tightly across her breast. 'Since the discovery in the book room...' she began, but her voice faltered – that subject could not be talked of with safety. 'Miss Kent,' she said simply, 'I do not think that I could ever confide in a man again. And if I were to marry Mr Lansdale I should despise myself forever. I should hate myself because I would know that I had been mercenary; and I would know that I had nothing to give in return for everything I had received from him – nothing but a pretence of affection.' She stopped, pressed her hand to her mouth as if to prevent any more words escaping it, and sat a while in silence before asking, 'How did you know? It must have been more than just the timing of my acceptance. What made you suspect that I was indifferent to him?'

'Well, when I came to consider carefully I saw that your behaviour over these last weeks has been...wrong. You see, although you have been uneasy, even distressed, you have not behaved like a woman who sees the life of the man she loves under threat. Not at all. If you had really loved Mr Lansdale you would not have been able to hide your concern for him. Nothing else would have mattered to you but his safety.' She stopped, half-expecting Mary to protest; but she only shrugged up her shoulders and gave a little nod of understanding.

'Well, that is not how you have behaved. You have been reserved – quiet. You have not come forward with the information which you had about the night his aunt died – though from the beginning you have known things which must – at the very least – have shifted blame and attention from him. And then, when you did act – when you sent that note to me – it was not to protect Mr Lansdale – it was to protect Maria Carrisbrook, was it not?'

There was a very slight nod from Mary.

'It was for the destitute, the desperate and friendless that you pleaded: you pleaded for women like Maria Henderson – women like yourself. You wished to protect her because you felt such a strong affinity with her. You were the same. Two women who must both sell their accomplishments in order to make their way in the world. "The world is not their friend, nor the world's laws." You meant that Maria should be excused for thinking only of herself – just as you should be.'

Mary had been watching anxiously through this last speech: her face becoming more shocked as Dido progressed. 'You know!' she cried when it was finished. 'You know the truth about Maria!'

'Yes, I believe I do.'

'But how? How can you know?'

Dido hesitated awkwardly, for once unsure about explaining herself. But fresh horses were now, with much shuffling of hooves and shaking of heads, being backed into the shafts of the coach and two farmers were already climbing up to take their seats on the roof. There would not be much more time for talking.

'Well,' she began cautiously, 'first of all there was your interest in her – which I traced to the time of your returning from Ramsgate. I knew that – after the discovery in the book room – you were uncomfortable in Mrs Midgely's company and fell into the habit of sitting in the back parlour with Miss Prentice. And, as I have discovered myself, to sit with Miss Prentice is to sit beside the window – and to begin to watch out of that window as she does.'

Mary smiled. 'It seems impossible to avoid it.'

'It does indeed! But your eyesight is rather better than Miss Prentice's I think – and your mind perhaps a little quicker. Though you might not have watched Knaresborough House so long, I think you saw a great deal more than she did!' She paused, but Mary said nothing. 'You were not taken in by the unbecoming clothes and bonnets in which the Misses Henderson walked abroad – you saw that they were very pretty women. More than pretty – quite beautiful. And, though I am only guessing at it, I think you saw other little things which made you suspect that this was a rather…unusual household.'

'What kind of little things, Miss Kent?' asked Mary with interest.

'Oh well… Perhaps you saw that Mr Henderson bore a likeness to the butler Fraser. And perhaps – while Miss Prentice saw only that family carriages arrived in the evenings – you were able to discern more. You were able to see, perhaps, that it was not families who descended from those carriages – but only gentlemen. Certainly you saw enough to make you so interested in the inhabitants of Knaresborough House that you were prepared to set aside propriety and introduce yourself to the young ladies in the park.'

'You are right, of course. And you are right too in supposing that my interest was heightened by the similarity I saw in our situations. I was, you must understand, very unhappy at that time – my consent was given to Mr Lansdale and he was beginning to plan our elopement, but already I was blaming myself for agreeing – and yet, independent of him, my future was so very unpromising that I had not the courage to withdraw my consent.'

'Of course, I quite understand.'

Mary looked curiously at her. 'You seem to understand me very well, Miss Kent, and I daresay I am more transparent than I had hoped! But how do you come to understand Maria Carrisbrook? That is beyond my comprehension.'

'Oh well, it was her accomplishments that I first wondered at,' said Dido.

'Her accomplishments?'

'Yes. You see I watched her very carefully during our day at Brooke and I concluded that hers had been a very strange education indeed! Maria Carrisbrook plays and sings; she knows French; she knows how to charm and put people at their ease; she is able to enter into pleasant conversation upon any subject. In all these things she is remarkably accomplished. But there are odd deficiencies. Why, I wondered should she be so very anxious about a cold collation? And why did she not know what entertainments were usual at a summer garden party? Why had she never been instructed in these little matters – or observed how they were done by others?'

Mary was now watching her talk with unabashed wonder. Dido smiled and shook her head. 'In short, Miss Bevan, I concluded that, although she had been taught how to captivate and delight a man, she had not been taught the business of being a wife.' Colour rose in Dido's cheeks. She looked down. 'Marriage,' she finished quietly, 'was not the purpose of her education.'

'No,' said Mary. 'It was not.'

Now the coach passengers were beginning to come out of the inn parlour and the guard with the broken tooth was reminding Mary that they would 'be off in just two minutes, miss.'

'And then, of course,' Dido hurried on, 'there was the way in which Sir Joshua behaved when I asked him about Mr Henderson. He became very uncomfortable indeed at the sound of the name. As he ought to be! For he knew his own guilt! He knew very well that the establishment the butler had had the audacity to form in Knaresborough House was…a disreputable one.'

'So,' said Mary, taking up her cloak, 'you did not need me to point out the meaning of my letter in Dr Johnson's essay?'

'Ah yes! That is what confirmed everything! The use to which the good doctor puts those lines explains everything!' They stood up. For now the other passengers had all taken their seats and the coachman was picking up his whip, the outriders mounting their horses. The bustle around them helped to overcome the awkwardness of finishing her story. 'Of course,' she said, 'it is not lovers, nor apothecaries, to whom he claims the world and its laws are no friend. It is prostitutes.'

As she spoke the word, they both stopped and for a moment looked one another in the eye. Two very respectable young women in their plain morning gowns and simple bonnets, standing amid all the loud busyness of the coach's departure. Dido held out her hand in farewell; Mary took it and held it fast a moment. 'You will not expose her, will you?' she said.

Dido shook her head.

Mary smiled gratefully and turned towards the coach. But, just as she was about to step into it, Dido took her arm. They might never meet again. She must ask the question. 'Do you really believe,' she said urgently, 'that you and Maria Carrisbrook are so very alike?'

Mary pulled the travelling cloak about her; she looked up at the coach and seemed to see in it everything that lay before her: the journey; Yorkshire; her future of laborious duty and mortification. 'No,' she said quietly. 'After all, Maria and I are not so very alike – we have made different choices.'

'But if you had chosen differently? If you had married Mr Lansdale?'

Mary said nothing. She turned away and climbed up into the coach. Dido pressed forward to the window, hoping still for an answer. But now the door was being closed, the horn was blowing, the harness creaking as the horses strained against it. Mary's pale face at the window only smiled; she raised her hand in farewell and Dido was forced to step back as the great vehicle lumbered into motion.

Chapter Thirty-Four

When the coach had rumbled and clattered out of Richmond, Dido walked slowly to her seat beside the lime-walk. And there she was soon engrossed so deep in contemplation of all that had happened in the last few weeks as to leave her insensible of time and of everything passing around her.

The true cause of Mrs Lansdale's death must create a deep impression upon any thinking mind. For though no one was guilty of her murder, here were four people to be blamed with neglecting her and wishing her out of the way – four people who had each gone a little way towards that terrible extremity of selfishness which is murder. And, besides all this, was that other shameful crime which had been carrying on in the very heart of respectable society.

Here was more than enough to occupy her thoughts! But, as she sat there in the breezy sunshine, her mind was less occupied with such moralising than with the extraordinary behaviour of Miss Bevan – and with the belief which had prompted that behaviour: the belief that there was an affinity, a fellowship, even, subsisting between herself and the Misses Henderson. Her silence at the final moment of parting – what had it signified?

Did Mary Bevan truly believe that if she had married Mr Lansdale she would have been as guilty as those women…? And guilty of the same crime? Was this not principle run mad? Dido remembered how, when they had talked in Mrs Midgely's parlour, she had been troubled by the extreme delicacy of Miss Bevan's feelings. She had worried then that such refinement would not make the girl happy. And so it had proved…

But… But she found she could not dismiss the matter so easily. For phrases that Mary had spoken would recur. 'I do not believe I could ever confide in a man again,' and, 'I would have nothing to give but a pretence of affection.'

…And there was truth in her words. If one could not confide in one's partner in life – if there was no trust, no honesty, how could there be genuine attachment? What could there be but a pretence of affection?

And what was it but a pretence of affection which the young ladies had offered to the gentlemen who visited the establishment in Knaresborough House?

When her thoughts had reached such a point as this it was not to be wondered at that Dido's cheeks should first become red and then turn pale, nor that she should hurriedly put her hand to her brow in an effort to still the raging of her brain.

But to the man who was now standing beside her, knowing nothing of the ideas passing in her head, her appearance was that of a woman upon the point of swooning.

'Good God! Miss Kent, are you unwell?'

She looked up to see William Lomax bending over her: his expression all tenderness and concern.

'Yes, yes, I thank you. I am quite well. Just...' One did not, after all, like to dispel such pleasing concern entirely, 'just a little faint.'

He sat down beside her and spoke with considerably more gentleness than might have been expected from their parting upon the terrace at Brooke. 'I came in search of you,' he said. 'I did not like to leave Surrey without first bidding you farewell.'

'That is very kind of you.' She lowered her eyes, unable to meet his solemn gaze from an apprehension that her recent shocking thoughts might somehow be discernable in her face. 'And I am very glad to have this opportunity of saying goodbye – and, of course, of thanking you for the service you did me in talking with Mr Vane.'

He assumed his gravest, most dignified look. 'Well,' he said, 'it was a distasteful business; but it had the desired outcome. It would certainly seem that you were right in suspecting him.'

Dido said nothing.

He studied her face a while. 'Miss Kent,' he began gently, 'two nights ago – at Brooke – I believe I may have spoken...with more force than perhaps I should. I have been considering the matter and, upon reflection, I recognise that your behaviour...had I seen it in someone else...well, I would still have thought it wrong, but I doubt I would have condemned it so violently. It would not have roused such anger. I beg you to understand that it was only because I was so very concerned for your safety, your well-being...'

'Please,' she cried. 'There is no need to continue. I do not doubt the benevolence of your motives in trying to prevent my investigations; as, I hope, you do not doubt mine in making them. As far as good intentions go, we have both been in the right. And, since I do not believe that we will ever agree upon more than that – that no amount of disputation would prove to either of us that we have been in error – I feel that there is no more to be said upon the subject.'

'No. No, of course not. You are quite right; the whole business had better be forgotten,' he said a little doubtingly and looked at her as if he knew not whether to rejoice in her words – or to regret them. 'I wonder,' he began falteringly after a moment, 'if you are sufficiently recovered from your faintness to do me the honour of taking a turn along the avenue with me. There is something further I wish to say.'

Dido consented with some reluctance. She suspected that, despite his assurance, he would be wanting to revive the subject and she was in no mood this morning to argue with him. The parting with Mary had left her too discomposed and distressed for disagreement – particularly disagreement with him. He offered his arm as she stood up; but she felt it best to decline. Being close to him seemed only to distress her more. Thank you, but she was fully recovered now: could walk quite well on her own.

So he clasped his hands behind his back, fell into step beside her, and did not speak until they had entered the lime-walk, which was particularly pleasant this morning. The breeze, delicately scented with blossom, shifted the leaves about so that they walked in a dancing pattern of sunlight and shade with sun sparkling and winking through the foliage overhead. Once they were fairly begun upon their promenade, he said, very seriously, 'I had another reason for coming after you this morning: a very particular reason…'

Something in his voice made her suspect – she raised her eyes and saw, with a shock, such a look upon his face as could leave her in no doubt as to what his particular reason had been. There was a tenderness in his eyes; an unusual hint of colour on his cheeks; a hesitancy, an uncertainty, in his expression that was particularly becoming upon a face which was usually all gravity and self-possession.

She looked away in confusion and he began to speak rapidly as if he feared he might lose his courage. His circumstances were improved of late. He was still not a wealthy man; but the recent death of his old employer and the succession of the heir at Belsfield had rather improved his situation. And he had, furthermore, had some moderate success in business matters of his own. He was still burdened with heavy debts of his son's making; but he had now greater hopes of paying them within a reasonable length of time and trusted that he might, with a little luck and a great deal of economy, clear himself of them in three – perhaps even two years… He quite understood that it was neither fair nor reasonable to ask any lady to enter into an engagement which could not be fulfilled within such a length of time as two – perhaps three – years; but the strength of his feelings, the ardency of his admiration was such as must make him try to secure her hand…

For several moments Dido could not speak, so great was her surprise. That his affection, instead of being done away by her behaviour of the last weeks was instead augmented – one might even say inflamed – was incomprehensible! But there seemed to be no escaping the conviction that while quiet decorum had failed to wrest from him a positive declaration, defiance and argument had succeeded.

'Mr Lomax, you do me a great deal of honour. I cannot help but be gratified that you should esteem me so highly. But...'

'But?' He caught anxiously at the word. He reached out as if he might attempt to take her hand, then checked himself in time. 'But?'

'But I confess that I am surprised – amazed – at your declaration. That you should feel such tender emotions, when we have so lately been in violent disagreement with one another – and when we cannot even now be at peace together without avoiding discussion of some very important subjects. It is quite beyond my comprehension.'

He swallowed. The colour deepened on his cheeks. 'My dear Miss Kent, I doubt it is possible that any two people in the world will always agree upon every subject.'

Dido stopped walking and turned up her face, letting the sunshine move across her cheeks and dazzle her eyes. Oh, it would be so easy to agree with him! To let him take her hand. To consent. And just a few days ago she would have done so. But now... Truths once discovered cannot be unknown – even when the discoveries are only truths about our own heart.

'May I ask you,' she said gravely, 'what brought you to this decision – I mean why did you decide that you must declare yourself before going away?'

He looked offended. 'Why...I hardly know.'

'Do you not?' she pressed on, hardening her heart against his looks of pain. 'I think I do. I am quite sure that it was upon the terrace at Brooke that you first decided I was essential to your happiness. Come, admit it, was it not the case? It was only in arguing with you that I became irresistible.' She watched his face eagerly as she spoke, quite dreading his response.

But, to her amazement, he remained calm. Instead of protesting, he pressed his fingertips together and rested his chin upon them. Incredible though it seemed, there was no escaping the conviction that he was considering her suggestion as rationally as he did everything else. Really, the man was the most exasperating mixture of reason and unreason!

'This point of when exactly I decided to try for your hand seems to be of very great importance to you.'

'Yes it is.'

'Why?'

'Because you cannot marry upon the strength of an argument, Mr Lomax!' she cried. 'For however delightful you might find defiance in the period of courtship, I assure you that you would find it no such thing in marriage!'

He frowned and continued to ponder. 'I think,' he said at last, 'that your argument is weak on two points. First – though I will not deny that the moment you speak of was rather decisive to my feelings – we need not necessarily conclude that it was the argument per se which had that effect. Might it not have been that your contrariness in that moment made me fear that you would cease to respect me – that, in short, you might be lost to me forever. Such an apprehension would do a great deal to make me understand my own heart and strengthen my resolution of trying to win you. And, secondly…'

She could not help but laugh outright at his gravity. He smiled. 'And secondly,' he proceeded eagerly, 'why should you suppose that our life together would be one of continual dispute? The circumstances which occasioned our late disagreement were, you must grant, exceptional. I daresay we could go through fifty years of happy matrimony without there ever again occurring this situation of one of our acquaintance being accused of murdering his aunt!'

'Oh!' said Dido resuming her walk, 'I daresay I should find enough to argue with you about!'

'Well then,' he suggested, falling into step beside her, 'you might learn not to argue. Where there is real, solid affection, I am sure it is possible to learn control of the temper. When I was your husband you might find it easier to heed my advice.'

His smile broadened; but she was quite determined not to be diverted by the pleasure of conversing with him. She merely shook her head sadly and walked on.

Then, as they reached the end of the avenue and turned back, she sighed heavily and said, 'I do not think that it would be wise for us to marry in the hope of such a material change in my character. Such a course would involve too much…struggling against my feelings. Too much dishonesty. Mr Lomax I am persuaded that without honesty – without being able to confide entirely in her husband – a wife would find herself quite unable to feel all that she ought – that she would, in fact, be able to offer him only the pretence of affection in return for all the material advantages which he bestowed upon her.'

He stared at her. Puzzled, offended, but, above all, extremely unhappy. She could stay with him no longer. It was too dangerous. With a few more hasty words of gratitude for his offer, she shook her head, begged him to excuse her and began to hurry away along the avenue.

For a moment he stood and watched her, his face betraying all the agony that he felt. But, at last, the sight of her determined little figure retreating through the shifting sunlight was more than he could bear. Without knowing that he was doing it, he pressed the tips of his fingers together. 'There is of course a third possibility,' he said quietly to himself. 'You could simply continue to argue with me.'

He smiled at the prospect and, although he feared he was going to regret what he was doing, he called out, 'Miss Kent!'

She did not falter in her walking.

'Miss Kent! Please! Please wait a moment!' And he began to run so that he might catch up with her before she reached the end of the lime-walk.

THE DIDO KENT SERIES